PENGUIN BOOKS

MAURICE

Edward Morgan Forster was born in London in 1879, attended Tonbridge School as a day boy, and went on to King's College, Cambridge, in 1897. With King's he had a lifelong connection and was elected to an Honorary Fellowship in 1946. He declared that his life as a whole had not been dramatic, and he was unfailingly modest about his achievements. Interviewed by the B.B.C. on his eightieth birthday, he said: 'I have not written as much as I'd like to . . . I write for two reasons: partly to make money and partly to win the respect of people whom I respect . . . I had better add that I am sure that I am not a great novelist.' Eminent critics and the general public have judged otherwise and in his obituary *The Times* called him 'one of the most esteemed English novelists of his time'.

He wrote six novels, four of which appeared before the First World War, *Where Angels Fear to Tread* (1905), *The Longest Journey* (1907), *A Room with a View* (1908), and *Howards End* (1910). An interval of fourteen years elapsed before his most famous, and perhaps his greatest work, *A Passage to India*, was published. It won both the Prix Femina Vie Heureuse and the James Tait Black Memorial Prize. *Maurice*, completed in 1914, was published posthumously in 1971. He also published two volumes of short stories; two collections of essays; a critical work, *Aspects of the Novel*; *The Hill of Devi*, a fascinating record of two visits Forster made to the Indian State of Dewas Senior; two biographies; two books about Alexandria (where he worked for the Red Cross in the First World War), and, with Eric Crozier, the libretto for Britten's opera *Billy Budd*. He died in June 1970.

E. M. FORSTER

MAURICE

INTRODUCTION BY
P. N. FURBANK

Penguin Books

PENGUIN BOOKS

Published by the Penguin Group
27 Wrights Lane, London W8 5TZ, England
Viking Penguin Inc., 40 West 23rd Street, New York, New York 10010, USA
Penguin Books Australia Ltd, Ringwood, Victoria, Australia
Penguin Books Canada Ltd, 2801 John Street, Markham, Ontario, Canada L3R 1B4
Penguin Books (NZ) Ltd, 182–190 Wairau Road, Auckland 10, New Zealand

Penguin Books Ltd, Registered Offices: Harmondsworth, Middlesex, England

First published by Edward Arnold 1971
Published in Penguin Books 1972
19 20

Printed and bound in Great Britain by
Cox & Wyman Ltd, Reading
Set in Monotype Bembo

Begun 1913
Finished 1914

Dedicated to a Happier Year

Introduction

by P. N. Furbank

THE success of *Howards End*, published in 1910, had a disturbing effect on Forster's life. It filled him with superstitious forebodings, among them the fear of becoming sterile as a writer. He was restless for the whole of the succeeding year, fretted against his home life and was unable to settle to anything. He began a new novel, *Arctic Summer*, but got into a muddle with it and went to India in the winter of 1912–13 wondering if he would ever produce fiction again. India made a profound impression on him; it gave him a new viewpoint and – as he thought – shook him for ever out of his insular and suburban pre-occupations. All the same, it was no cure. He began an Indian novel on his return but soon got into difficulties and could not see his way through it. Privately, he accused himself of feebleness, and began to wonder if anyone so idle had the right to pass judgement on those who worked for their living. He would grow 'queer and unpopular', he feared, if he went on as he was doing now.

Then, in September 1913, he went on a visit to Edward Carpenter, the prophet of the simple life and high-minded homosexuality, and he experienced a revelation. He has described what took place in his own Terminal Note (see page 217): Carpenter's friend George Merrill touched him on the backside, and the sensation, as he put it, travelled straight through the small of his back into his ideas. On the instant, an entire new novel shaped itself in his mind: it was to deal with homosexuality, would feature three main characters, and would have a happy ending.

At last he knew what had been wrong. For years *Maurice*, or something like *Maurice*, had been demanding to be born. Already, he had been seeking relief by writing facetious stories on a homosexual theme; but this had not been enough, though he was not ashamed of them, just as discipline and self-repression had not been enough, though he didn't mean to give these up. The time had come for him to commit himself, in imagination if it could not be in life, to the belief that homosexual love was good. He needed to affirm, without

7

possibility of retreat, that love of this kind could be an ennobling and not a degrading thing and that if there were any 'perversion' in the matter it was the perversity of a society which insanely denied an essential part of the human inheritance.

His depression vanished. He sat down to work immediately, in a state of exaltation, and within three months had finished a first draft of Maurice's boyhood and Cambridge experiences. Then his enthusiasm suffered a check: Lowes Dickinson read one of his facetious stories and was shocked and disgusted by it. This seriously upset him, but he persevered in spite of it; and then in the following April he received a more serious shock. In the Cambridge section of the novel he had drawn heavily on his friendship with H. O. Meredith;[1] but Meredith, when shown the manuscript, seemed completely bored with it – not only that, he didn't even seem to feel his indifference mattered. The blow caused Forster to consider abandoning the novel; but the mood did not last, and by July 1914 *Maurice* was completed.

There was no question in his mind of publishing it: such a thing could not happen, he thought, 'until my death and England's'. In fact, his original idea was that he was writing for himself alone. However, he soon began showing it to selected friends. The first to see it was Dickinson, who – to his vast relief – admired it and found it moving, though he thought the happy ending too contrived. Forster knew himself that this was the weak part of the book, and he set to work (for the first of many times) to improve it. He could see where the trouble lay; it had to do with his whole motive in writing the book. 'I might have been wiser to let that also [the Alec Scudder part] resolve into dust or mist,' he wrote to Dickinson (13 December 1914),

but the temptation's overwhelming to grant to one's creations a happiness actual life does not supply. 'Why not?' I kept thinking. 'A little rearrangement, rather better luck – but no doubt the rearrangement's fundamental. It's the yearning for permanence that leads a novelist into theories towards the end of each book. The only permanence that is not

1. This is what he told me. But his reference in his Terminal Note to a 'slight academic acquaintance' does not fit Meredith, who for many years was his closest friend, nor do some of the other details. However, Meredith was still living when he wrote the Terminal Note, so it is possible he was slightly doctoring the facts.

a theory but a fact is death. And perhaps I surfeited myself with that in *The Longest Journey*. At all events the disinclination to kill increases.

A month or two later, with some nervousness, he showed the novel to Forrest Reid, a more recent friend. Reid was not shocked, as Forster feared he might be, but the novel didn't really suit him, and his objections stimulated Forster to a lengthy defence.

I do want to raise these subjects out of the mists of theology: Male and Female created He not them. Ruling out undeveloped people like Clive . . . one is left with 'perverts' (an absurd word, because it assumes they were given a choice, but let's use it). Are these 'perverts' good or bad like normal men, their disproportionate tendency to badness (which I admit) being due to the criminal blindness of Society? Or are they inherently bad? You answer, as I do, that they are the former, but you answer with reluctance. I want you to answer *vehemently*! The man in my book is, roughly speaking, good, but Society nearly destroys him, he nearly slinks through his life furtive and afraid, and burdened with a sense of sin. You say, 'If he had not met another man like him, what then?' What indeed? But blame Society not Maurice, and be thankful even in a novel when a man is left to lead the best life he is capable of leading!

This brings me to another point. . . Is it ever right that such a relation should include the physical? Yes – sometimes. If both people want it and both are old enough to know what they want – yes. I used not to think this, but now do. Maurice and Clive would have been wrong, Maurice and Dicky more so, M. and A. are all right, some people might never be right . . .

My defence at any Last Judgement would be 'I was trying to connect up and use all the fragments I was born with' – well you had it exhaustingly in *Howards End*, and Maurice, though his fragments are more scanty and more bizarre than Margaret's, is working at the same job . . .

Over the years, and in reaction to different friends' reactions, his opinion of the novel went up and down. There were times when he was sure he had done 'something absolutely new, even to the Greeks'. At others he had doubts – mostly about the latter part of the novel, where Maurice finds physical happiness. 'Nothing is more obdurate to artistic treatment than the carnal,' he wrote to Siegfried Sassoon in 1920, 'but it has to be got in, I'm sure: everything has to be got in.' He did more work on this difficult last section in 1919 and again in

9

1932, and he revised it once more, fairly drastically, in 1959–60. A reader had raised a query about the *dénouement*, in which Maurice watches Alec's boat sail for the Argentine and then turns his face towards England, in a brave blur of exalted emotion. It was stirring and impressive; but how was Maurice actually going to *find* Alec? The point worried Forster, and he added a passage in which Maurice was safely brought to Alec's arms.

By the 1960s, his mother and most of his near relations being dead and attitudes to sexual questions having changed so greatly, he could, if he wished, have published the novel. Friends actually suggested it, but he firmly refused. He knew the endless fuss and brouhaha it would lead to. Also, the book had become rather remote to him. He said he was less interested now in the theme of salvation, the rescuer from 'otherwhere'; he thought it was a 'fake'. People could help each other, but they were not decisive for each other in that way. Moreover, one or two friends to whom he had shown it recently had thought it 'dated'. He made careful preparations for posthumous publication, but his final comment (inscribed on the cover of the 1960 typescript) was 'Publishable – but worth it?' Few readers of this masterly and touching novel will feel any doubt about the answer.

A note on the text

WITH a small number of exceptions, the 1960 typescript has been faithfully followed, even where it reads a trifle oddly – as when Alec Scudder, batting in a cricket match, is made to 'resign' (i.e. retire), or 'Whitmannic' is used in place of 'Whitmanesque', or some sentences in the Terminal Note need revising in the light of the Sexual Offences Act of 1967. The exceptions are as follows.

1. The surname of one of the characters has, on the author's written instructions, been altered throughout, and one or two contingent changes made.

2. Spelling, punctuation and capitalization have, where no nuance is involved, been regularized in accordance with normal practice today.

3. A number of obvious typing errors (or in some cases possibly slips of the pen) have been corrected.

4. A number of suspected errors have been confirmed as such by reference to earlier typescripts, and have been corrected accordingly.

5. Rather more diffidently, the following readings have been adopted with the aim of correcting what appear to be either typing errors or slips on Forster's part:

Page	Line	Reading Adopted	Typescript
38	20	but he held . . . Durham	but held . . . he
40	15	watching for Durham	watching Durham
43	24	was	is
94	15	coasting	hoosting or boosting
147	19	evidently he had	had evidently
160	2	that he should telephone next week	for next week

6. Finally, on page 104, a famous phrase from Sophocles ('Not to be born is best' – *Oedipus Coloneus*, 1224–5) has been inserted where the 1960 typescript has a blank space, and an earlier typescript supplies a slightly inaccurate version of the quotation.

Part One

I

ONCE a term the whole school went for a walk – that is to say the three masters took part as well as all the boys. It was usually a pleasant outing, and everyone looked forward to it, forgot old scores, and behaved with freedom. Lest discipline should suffer, it took place just before the holidays, when leniency does no harm, and indeed it seemed more like a treat at home than school, for Mrs Abrahams, the Principal's wife, would meet them at the tea place with some lady friends, and be hospitable and motherly.

Mr Abrahams was a preparatory schoolmaster of the old-fashioned sort. He cared neither for work nor games, but fed his boys well and saw that they did not misbehave. The rest he left to the parents, and did not speculate how much the parents were leaving to him. Amid mutual compliments the boys passed out into a public school, healthy but backward, to receive upon undefended flesh the first blows of the world. There is much to be said for apathy in education, and Mr Abrahams's pupils did not do badly in the long run, became parents in their turn and in some cases sent him their sons. Mr Read, the junior assistant, was a master of the same type, only stupider, while Mr Ducie, the senior, acted as a stimulant, and prevented the whole concern from going to sleep. They did not like him much, but knew that he was necessary. Mr Ducie was an able man, orthodox, but not out of touch with the world, nor incapable of seeing both sides of a question. He was unsuitable for parents and the denser boys, but good for the first form, and had even coached pupils into a scholarship. Nor was he a bad organizer. While affecting to hold the reins and to prefer Mr Read, Mr Abrahams really allowed Mr Ducie a free hand and ended by taking him into partnership.

Mr Ducie always had something on his mind. On this occasion it was Hall, one of the older boys, who was leaving them to go to a public school. He wanted to have a 'good talk' with Hall, during the outing. His colleagues objected, since it would leave them more to do, and the Principal remarked that he had already talked to Hall, and that the boy would prefer to take his last walk with his school-fellows. This was probable, but Mr Ducie was never deterred from doing what is right. He smiled and was silent. Mr Read knew what the 'good talk' would be, for early in their acquaintance they had touched on a certain theme professionally. Mr Read had disapproved. 'Thin ice,' he had said. The Principal neither knew nor would have wished to know. Parting from his pupils when they were fourteen, he forgot they had developed into men. They seemed to him a race small but complete, like the New Guinea pygmies, 'my boys'. And they were even easier to understand than pygmies, because they never married and seldom died. Celibate and immortal, the long procession passed before him, its thickness varying from twenty-five to forty at a time. 'I see no use in books on education. Boys began before education was thought of.' Mr Ducie would smile, for he was soaked in evolution.

From this to the boys.

'Sir, may I hold your hand ... Sir, you promised me ... Both Mr Abrahams' hands were bagged and all Mr Read's ... Oh sir, did you hear that? He thinks Mr Read has three hands! ... I didn't, I said "fingers". Green eye! Green eye!'

'When you have quite finished –!'

'Sir!'

'I'm going to walk with Hall alone.'

There were cries of disappointment. The other masters, seeing that it was no good, called the pack off, and marshalled them along the cliff towards the downs. Hall, triumphant, sprang to Mr Ducie's side, and felt too old to take his hand. He was a plump, pretty lad, not in any way remarkable. In this he resembled his father, who had passed in the procession twenty-five years before, vanished into a public school, married, begotten a son and two daughters, and recently died of pneumonia. Mr Hall had been a good citizen, but lethargic. Mr Ducie had informed himself about him before they began the walk.

'Well, Hall, expecting a pi-jaw, eh?'

'I don't know, sir – Mr Abrahams's given me one with "Those Holy Fields". Mrs Abrahams's given me sleeve links. The fellows have given me a set of Guatemalas up to two dollars. Look, sir! The ones with the parrot on the pillar on.'

'Splendid, splendid! What did Mr Abrahams say? Told you you were a miserable sinner, I hope.'

The boy laughed. He did not understand Mr Ducie, but knew that he was meaning to be funny. He felt at ease because it was his last day at school, and even if he did wrong he would not get into a row. Besides, Mr Abrahams had declared him a success. 'We are proud of him; he will do us honour at Sunnington': he had seen the beginning of the letter to his mother. And the boys had showered presents on him, declaring he was brave. A great mistake – he wasn't brave: he was afraid of the dark. But no one knew this.

'Well, what did Mr Abrahams say?' repeated Mr Ducie, when they reached the sands. A long talk threatened, and the boy wished he was up on the cliff with his friends, but he knew that wishing is useless when boy meets man.

'Mr Abrahams told me to copy my father, sir.'

'Anything else?'

'I am never to do anything I should be ashamed to have mother see me do. No one can go wrong then, and the public school will be very different from this.'

'Did Mr Abrahams say how?'

'All kinds of difficulties – more like the world.'

'Did he tell you what the world is like?'

'No.'

'Did you ask him?'

'No, sir.'

'That wasn't very sensible of you, Hall. Clear things up. Mr Abrahams and I are here to answer your questions. What do you suppose the world – the world of grown-up people – is like?'

'I can't tell. I'm a boy,' he said, very sincerely. 'Are they very treacherous, sir?'

Mr Ducie was amused and asked him what examples of treachery he had seen. He replied that grown-up people would not be unkind to boys, but were they not always cheating one another? Losing his schoolboy manner, he began to talk like a child, and became fanciful and amusing. Mr Ducie lay down on the sand to listen to him, lit his pipe and looked up to the sky. The little watering-place where they lived was now far behind, the rest of the school away in front. The

17

day was grey and windless, with little distinction between clouds and sun.

'You live with your mother, don't you?' he interrupted, seeing that the boy had gained confidence.

'Yes, sir.'

'Have you any elder brothers?'

'No, sir – only Ada and Kitty.'

'Any uncles?'

'No.'

'So you don't know many men?'

'Mother keeps a coachman and George in the garden, but of course you mean gentlemen. Mother has three maid-servants to look after the house, but they are so idle that they will not mend Ada's stockings. Ada is my eldest little sister.'

'How old are you?'

'Fourteen and three quarters.'

'Well, you're an ignorant little beggar.' They laughed. After a pause he said, 'When I was your age, my father told me something that proved very useful and helped a good deal.' This was untrue: his father had never told him anything. But he needed a prelude to what he was going to say.

'Did he, sir?'

'Shall I tell you what it was?'

'Please, sir.'

'I am going to talk to you for a few moments as if I were your father, Maurice! I shall call you by your real name.' Then, very simply and kindly, he approached the mystery of sex. He spoke of male and female, created by God in the beginning in order that the earth might be peopled, and of the period when the male and female receive their powers. 'You are just becoming a man now, Maurice; that is why I am telling you about this. It is not a thing that your mother can tell you, and you should not mention it to her nor to any lady, and if at your next school boys mention it to you, just shut them up; tell them you know. Have you heard about it before?'

'No, sir.'

'Not a word?'

'No, sir.'

Still smoking his pipe, Mr Ducie got up, and choosing a smooth piece of sand drew diagrams upon it with his walking-stick. 'This will make it easier,' he said to the boy, who watched dully: it bore no relation to his experiences. He was attentive, as was natural when he was the only one in the class, and he knew that the subject was serious and related to his own body. But he could not himself relate it; it fell to pieces as soon as Mr Ducie put it together, like an impossible sum. In vain he tried. His torpid brain would not awake. Puberty was there, but not intelligence, and manhood was stealing on him, as it always must, in a trance. Useless to break in upon that trance. Useless to describe it, however scientifically and sympathetically. The boy assents and is dragged back into sleep, not to be enticed there before his hour.

Mr Ducie, whatever his science, was sympathetic. Indeed he was too sympathetic; he attributed cultivated feelings to Maurice, and did not realize that he must either understand nothing or be overwhelmed. 'All this is rather a bother,' he said, 'but one must get it over, one mustn't make a mystery of it. Then come the great things – Love, Life.' He was fluent, having talked to boys in this way before, and he knew the kind of question they would ask. Maurice would not ask: he only said, 'I see, I see, I see,' and at first Mr Ducie feared he did not see. He examined him. The replies were satisfactory. The boy's memory was good and – so curious a fabric is the human – he even developed a spurious intelligence, a surface flicker to respond to the beaconing glow of the man's. In the end he did ask one or two questions about sex, and they were to the point. Mr Ducie was much pleased. 'That's right,' he said. 'You need never be puzzled or bothered now.'

Love and life still remained, and he touched on them as they strolled forward by the colourless sea. He spoke of the ideal man – chaste with asceticism. He sketched the glory of Woman. Engaged to be married himself, he grew more human, and his eyes coloured up behind the strong spectacles; his cheek flushed. To love a noble woman, to protect and serve her – this, he told the little boy, was the crown of life. 'You can't understand now, you will some day, and when you do understand it, remember the poor old pedagogue who put you on the track. It all hangs together – all – and God's in his heaven, All's right with the world. Male and female! Ah wonderful!'

'I think I shall not marry,' remarked Maurice.

'This day ten years hence – I invite you and your wife to dinner with my wife and me. Will you accept?'

'Oh sir!' He smiled with pleasure.

'It's a bargain, then!' It was at all events a good joke to end with. Maurice was flattered and began to contemplate marriage. But while they were easing off Mr Ducie stopped, and held his cheek as though every tooth ached. He turned and looked at the long expanse of sand behind.

'I never scratched out those infernal diagrams,' he said slowly.

At the further end of the bay some people were following them, also by the edge of the sea. Their course would take them by the very spot where Mr Ducie had illustrated sex, and one of them was a lady. He ran back sweating with fear.

'Sir, won't it be all right?' Maurice cried. 'The tide'll have covered them by now.'

'Good Heavens . . . thank God . . . the tide's rising.'

And suddenly, for an instant of time, the boy despised him. 'Liar,' he thought. 'Liar, coward, he's told me nothing.' . . . Then darkness rolled up again, the darkness that is primeval but not eternal, and yields to its own painful dawn.

2

MAURICE's mother lived near London, in a comfortable villa among some pines. There he and his sisters had been born, and thence his father had gone up to business every day, thither returning. They nearly left when the church was built, but they became accustomed to it, as to everything, and even found it a convenience. Church was the only place Mrs Hall had to go to – the shops delivered. The station was not far either, nor was a tolerable day school for the girls. It was a land of facilities, where nothing had to be striven for, and success was indistinguishable from failure.

Maurice liked his home, and recognized his mother as its presiding genius. Without her there would be no soft chairs or food or easy games, and he was grateful to her for providing so much, and loved her. He liked his sisters also. When he arrived they ran out with cries of joy, took off his greatcoat and dropped it for the servants on the floor of the hall. It was nice to be the centre of attraction and show off about school. His Guatemala stamps were admired – so were 'Those Holy Fields' and a Holbein photograph that Mr Ducie had given him. After tea the weather cleared, and Mrs Hall put on her goloshes and walked with him round the grounds. They went kissing one another and conversing aimlessly.

'Morrie . . .'

'Mummie . . .'

'Now I must give my Morrie a lovely time.'

'Where's George?'

'Such a splendid report from Mr Abrahams. He says you remind him of your poor father . . . Now what shall we do these holidays?'

'I like here best.'

'Darling boy . . .' She embraced him, more affectionately than ever.

'There is nothing like home, as everyone finds. Yes, tomatoes –' she liked reciting the names of vegetables. 'Tomatoes, radishes, broccoli, onions –'

'Tomatoes, broccoli, onions, purple potatoes, white potatoes,' droned the little boy.

'Turnip tops –'

'Mother, where's George?'

'He left last week.'

'Why did George leave?' he asked.

'He was getting too old. Howell always changes the boy every two years.'

'Oh.'

'Turnip-tops,' she continued, 'potatoes again, beetroot – Morrie, how would you like to pay a little visit to grandpapa and Aunt Ida if they ask us? I want you to have a very nice time this holiday, dear – you have been so good, but then Mr Abrahams is such a good man; you see, your father was at his school too, and we are sending you to your father's old public school too – Sunnington – in order that you may grow up like your dear father in every way.'

A sob interrupted her.

'Morrie, *darling* –'

The little boy was in tears.

'My pet, what is it?'

'I don't know . . . I don't know . . .'

'Why, Maurice . . .'

He shook his head. She was grieved at her failure to make him happy, and began to cry too. The girls ran out, exclaiming, 'Mother, what's wrong with Maurice?'

'Oh, don't,' he wailed. 'Kitty, get out –'

'He's overtired,' said Mrs Hall – her explanation for everything.

'I'm overtired.'

'Come to your room, Morrie – Oh my sweet, this is really too dreadful.'

'No – I'm all right.' He clenched his teeth, and a great mass of sorrow that had overwhelmed him by rising to the surface began to sink. He could feel it going down into his heart until he was conscious of it no longer. 'I'm all right.' He looked around him fiercely and dried his eyes. 'I'll play Halma, I think.' Before the pieces were set, he was talking as before; the childish collapse was over.

He beat Ada, who worshipped him, and Kitty, who did not, and then ran into the garden again to see the coachman. 'How d'ye do,

Howell. How's Mrs Howell? How d'ye do, Mrs Howell,' and so on, speaking in a patronizing voice, different from that he used to gentlefolks. Then, altering back, 'Isn't it a new garden boy?'

'Yes, Master Maurice.'

'Was George too old?'

'No, Master Maurice. He wanted to better himself.'

'Oh, you mean he gave notice.'

'That's right.'

'Mother said he was too old and you gave him notice.'

'No, Master Maurice.'

'My poor woodstacks'll be glad,' said Mrs Howell. Maurice and the late garden boy had been used to play about in them.

'They are Mother's woodstacks, not yours,' said Maurice and went indoors. The Howells were not offended, though they pretended to be so to one another. They had been servants all their lives, and liked a gentleman to be a snob. 'He has quite a way with him already,' they told the cook. 'More like his father.'

The Barrys, who came to dinner, were of the same opinion. Dr Barry was an old friend, or rather neighbour, of the family, and took a moderate interest in them. No one could be deeply interested in the Halls. Kitty he liked – she had hints of grit in her – but the girls were in bed, and he told his wife afterwards that Maurice ought to have been there too. 'And stop there all his life. As he will. Like his father. What is the use of such people?'

When Maurice did go to bed, it was reluctantly. That room always frightened him. He had been such a man all the evening, but the old feeling came over him as soon as his mother had kissed him good night. The trouble was the looking-glass. He did not mind seeing his face in it, nor casting a shadow on the ceiling, but he did mind seeing his shadow on the ceiling reflected in the glass. He would arrange the candle so as to avoid the combination, and then dare himself to put it back and be gripped with fear. He knew what it was, it reminded him of nothing horrible. But he was afraid. In the end he would dash out the candle and leap into bed. Total darkness he could bear, but this room had the further defect of being opposite a street lamp. On good nights the light would penetrate the curtains unalarmingly, but sometimes blots like skulls fell over the furniture. His heart beat violently, and he lay in terror, with all his household close at hand.

23

As he opened his eyes to look whether the blots had grown smaller, he remembered George. Something stirred in the unfathomable depths of his heart. He whispered, 'George, George.' Who was George? Nobody – just a common servant. Mother and Ada and Kitty were far more important. But he was too little to argue thus. He did not even know that when he yielded to this sorrow he overcame the spectral and fell asleep.

3

SUNNINGTON was the next stage in Maurice's career. He traversed it without attracting attention. He was not good at work, though better than he pretended, nor colossally good at games. If people noticed him they liked him, for he had a bright friendly face and responded to attention; but there were so many boys of his type – they formed the backbone of the school and we cannot notice each vertebra. He did the usual things – was kept in, once caned, rose from form to form on the classical side till he clung precariously to the sixth, and he became a house prefect, and later a school prefect and member of the first fifteen. Though clumsy, he had strength and physical pluck: at cricket he did not do so well. Having been bullied as a new boy, he bullied others when they seemed unhappy or weak, not because he was cruel but because it was the proper thing to do. In a word, he was a mediocre member of a mediocre school, and left a faint and favourable impression behind. 'Hall? Wait a minute, which was Hall? Oh yes, I remember; clean run enough.'

Beneath it all, he was bewildered. He had lost the precocious clearness of the child which transfigures and explains the universe, offering answers of miraculous insight and beauty. 'Out of the mouths of babes and sucklings . . .' But not out of the mouth of the boy of sixteen. Maurice forgot he had ever been sexless, and only realized in maturity how just and clear the sensation of his earliest days must have been. He sank far below them now, for he was descending the Valley of the Shadow of Life. It lies between the lesser mountains and the greater, and without breathing its fogs no one can come through. He groped about in it longer than most boys.

Where all is obscure and unrealized the best similitude is a dream. Maurice had two dreams at school; they will interpret him.

In the first dream he felt very cross. He was playing football against a nondescript whose existence he resented. He made an effort and the nondescript turned into George, that garden boy. But he had to be careful or it would reappear. George headed down the field towards him, naked and jumping over the woodstacks. 'I shall go mad if he turns wrong now,' said Maurice, and just as they collared this happened, and a brutal disappointment woke him up. He did not connect it with Mr Ducie's homily, still less with his second dream, but he thought he was going to be ill, and afterwards that it was somehow a punishment for something.

The second dream is more difficult to convey. Nothing happened. He scarcely saw a face, scarcely heard a voice say, 'That is your friend,' and then it was over, having filled him with beauty and taught him tenderness. He could die for such a friend, he would allow such a friend to die for him; they would make any sacrifice for each other, and count the world nothing, neither death nor distance nor crossness could part them, because 'this is my friend.' Soon afterwards he was confirmed and tried to persuade himself that the friend must be Christ. But Christ has a mangy beard. Was he a Greek god, such as illustrates the classical dictionary? More probable, but most probably he was just a man. Maurice forbore to define his dream further. He had dragged it as far into life as it would come. He would never meet that man nor hear that voice again, yet they became more real than anything he knew, and would actually –

'Hall! Dreaming again! A hundred lines!'

'Sir – oh! Dative absolute.'

'Dreaming again. Too late.'

– would actually pull him back to them in broad daylight and drop a curtain. Then he would reimbibe the face and the four words, and would emerge yearning with tenderness and longing to be kind to everyone, because his friend wished it, and to be good that his friend might become more fond of him. Misery was somehow mixed up with all this happiness. It seemed as certain that he hadn't a friend as that he had one, and he would find a lonely place for tears, attributing them to the hundred lines.

Maurice's secret life can be understood now; it was part brutal, part ideal, like his dreams.

As soon as his body developed he became obscene. He supposed some special curse had descended on him, but he could not help it, for even when receiving the Holy Communion filthy thoughts would arise in his mind. The tone of the school was pure – that is to say, just before his arrival there had been a terrific scandal. The black sheep had been expelled, the remainder were drilled hard all day and policed at night, so it was his fortune or misfortune to have little opportunity of exchanging experiences with his school-fellows. He longed for smut, but heard little and contributed less, and his chief indecencies were solitary. Books: the school library was immaculate, but while at his grandfather's he came across an unexpurgated Martial, and stumbled about in it with burning ears. Thoughts: he had a dirty little collection. Acts: he desisted from these after the novelty was over, finding that they brought him more fatigue than pleasure.

All which, if it can be understood, took place in a trance. Maurice had fallen asleep in the Valley of the Shadow, far beneath the peaks of either range, and knew neither this nor that his school-fellows were sleeping likewise.

The other half of his life seemed infinitely remote from obscenity. As he rose in the school he began to make a religion of some other boy. When this boy, whether older or younger than himself, was present, he would laugh loudly, talk absurdly and be unable to work. He dared not be kind – it was not the thing – still less to express his admiration in words. And the adored one would shake him off before long, and reduce him to sulks. However, he had his revenges. Other boys sometimes worshipped him, and when he realized this he would shake off them. The adoration was mutual on one occasion, both yearning for they knew not what, but the result was the same. They quarrelled in a few days. All that came out of the chaos were the two feelings of beauty and tenderness that he had first felt in a dream. They grew yearly, flourishing like plants that are all leaves and show no sign of flower. Towards the close of his education at Sunnington the growth stopped. A check, a silence, fell upon the complex processes, and very timidly the youth began to look around him.

4

HE was nearly nineteen.

He stood on the platform on Prize Day, reciting a Greek Oration of his own composition. The Hall was full of schoolboys and their parents, but Maurice affected to be addressing the Hague Conference, and to be pointing out to it the folly of its ways. 'What stupidity is this, O andres Europenaici, to talk of abolishing war? What? Is not Ares the son of Zeus himself? Moreover, war renders you robust by exercising your limbs, not forsooth like those of my opponent.' The Greek was vile: Maurice had got the prize on account of the Thought, and barely thus. The examining master had stretched a point in his favour since he was leaving and a respectable chap, and moreover leaving for Cambridge, where prize books on his shelves would help to advertise the school. So he received Grote's *History of Greece* amid tremendous applause. As he returned to his seat, which was next to his mother, he realized that he had again become popular, and wondered how. The clapping continued – it grew to an ovation; Ada and Kitty were pounding away with scarlet faces on the further side. Some of his friends, also leaving, cried 'speech'. This was irregular and quelled by the authorities, but the Headmaster himself rose and said a few words. Hall was one of them, and they would never cease to feel him so. The words were just. The school clapped not because Maurice was eminent but because he was average. It could celebrate itself in his image. People ran up to him afterwards saying 'Jolly good, old man', quite sentimentally, and even 'It will be bilge in this hole without you.' His relations shared in the triumph. On previous visits he had been hateful to them. 'Sorry, mater, but you and the kids will have to walk alone' had been his remark after a football match when they had tried to join on to him in his mud and glory: Ada had cried. Now Ada was chatting quite ably to the Captain of the School, and Kitty was being handed cakes, and his mother was listening to his housemaster's wife, on the disappointments of installing hot air.

Everyone and everything had suddenly harmonized. Was this the world?

A few yards off he saw Dr Barry, their neighbour from home, who caught his eye and called out in his alarming way, 'Congratulations, Maurice, on your triumph. Overwhelming! I drink to it in this cup' – he drained it – 'of extremely nasty tea.'

Maurice laughed and went up to him, rather guiltily; for his conscience was bad. Dr Barry had asked him to befriend a little nephew, who had entered the school that term, but he had done nothing\– it was not the thing. He wished that he had had more courage now that it was too late and he felt a man.

'And what's the next stage in your triumphal career? Cambridge?'

'So they say.'

'So they say, do they? And what do you say?'

'I don't know,' said the hero good-temperedly.

'And after Cambridge, what? Stock Exchange?'

'I suppose so – my father's old partner talks of letting me in if all goes well.'

'And after you're let in by your father's old partner, what? A pretty wife?'

Maurice laughed again.

'Who will present the expectant world with a Maurice the third? After which old age, grandchildren and finally the daisies. So that's your notion of a career. Well, it isn't mine.'

'What's your notion, Doctor?' called Kitty.

'To help the weak and right the wrong, my dear,' he replied, looking across at her.

'I'm sure it is all our notions,' said the housemaster's wife, and Mrs Hall agreed.

'Oh no, it's not. It isn't consistently mine, or I should be looking after my Dickie instead of lingering on this scene of splendour.'

'Do bring dear Dickie to say how d'ye do to me,' asked Mrs Hall. 'Is his father down here too?'

'Mother!' Kitty whispered.

'Yes. My brother died last year,' said Dr Barry. 'The incident slipped your memory. War did not render him robust by exercising his limbs, as Maurice supposes. He got a shell in the stomach.'

He left them.

'I think Dr Barry gets cynical,' remarked Ada. 'I think he's jealous.' She was right: Dr Barry, who had been a lady killer in his time, did resent the continuance of young men. Poor Maurice encountered him again. He had been saying good-bye to his housemaster's wife, who was a handsome woman, very civil to the older boys. They shook hands warmly. On turning away he heard Dr Barry's 'Well, Maurice; a youth irresistible in love as in war,' and caught his cynical glance.

'I don't know what you mean, Dr Barry.'

'Oh, you young fellows! Butter wouldn't melt in your mouth these days. Don't know what I mean! Prudish of a petticoat! Be frank, man, be frank. You don't take anyone in. The frank mind's the pure mind. I'm a medical man and an old man and I tell you that. Man that is born of woman must go with woman if the human race is to continue.'

Maurice stared after the housemaster's wife, underwent a violent repulsion from her and blushed crimson: he had remembered Mr Ducie's diagrams. A trouble – nothing as beautiful as a sorrow – rose to the surface of his mind, displayed its ungainliness and sank. Its precise nature he did not ask himself, for his hour was not yet, but the hint was appalling, and, hero though he was, he longed to be a little boy again, and to stroll half awake for ever by the colourless sea. Dr Barry went on lecturing him, and under the cover of a friendly manner said much that gave pain.

5

HE chose a college patronized by his chief school friend Chapman and by other old Sunningtonians, and during his first year managed to experience little in university life that was unfamiliar. He belonged to an Old Boys' Club, and they played games together, tea'd and lunched together, kept up their provincialisms and slang, sat elbow to elbow in hall and walked arm in arm about the streets. Now and then they got drunk and boasted mysteriously about women, but their outlook remained that of the upper fifth, and some of them kept it through life. There was no feud between them and the other undergraduates, but they were too compact to be popular, too mediocre to lead and they did not care to risk knowing men who had come from other public schools. All this suited Maurice. He was constitutionally lazy. Though none of his difficulties had been solved, none were added, which is something. The hush continued. He was less troubled by carnal thoughts. He stood still in the darkness instead of groping about in it, as if this was the end for which body and soul had been so painfully prepared.

During his second year he underwent a change. He had moved into college and it began to digest him. His days he might spend as before, but when the gates closed on him at night a new process began. Even as a freshman he made the important discovery that grown-up men behave politely to one another unless there is a reason for the contrary. Some third-year people had called on him in his digs. He had expected them to break his plates and insult the photograph of his mother, and when they did not he ceased planning how some day he should break theirs, thus saving time. And the manners of the dons were even more remarkable. Maurice was only waiting for such an atmosphere himself to soften. He did not enjoy being cruel and rude. It was against his nature. But it was necessary at school, or he might have gone under, and he had supposed it would have been even more necessary on the larger battlefield of the university.

Once inside college, his discoveries multiplied. People turned out to be alive. Hitherto he had supposed that they *were* what he *pretended* to be – flat pieces of cardboard stamped with a conventional design – but as he strolled about the courts at night and saw through the windows some men singing and others arguing and others at their books, there came by no process of reason a conviction that they were human beings with feelings akin to his own. He had never lived frankly since Mr Abrahams's school, and despite Dr Barry did not mean to begin; but he saw that while deceiving others he had been deceived, and mistaken them for the empty creatures he wanted them to think he was. No, they too had insides. 'But, O Lord, not such an inside as mine.' As soon as he thought about other people as real, Maurice became modest and conscious of sin: in all creation there could be no one as vile as himself. No wonder he pretended to be a piece of cardboard; if known as he was, he would be hounded out of the world. God, being altogether too large an order, did not worry him: he could not conceive of any censure being more terrific than, say, Joey Fetherstonhaugh's, who kept in the rooms below, or of any Hell as bitter as Coventry.

Shortly after this discovery he went to lunch with Mr Cornwallis, the Dean.

There were two other guests, Chapman and a B.A. from Trinity, a relative of the Dean's, by name Risley. Risley was dark, tall and affected. He made an exaggerated gesture when introduced, and when he spoke, which was continually, he used strong yet unmanly superlatives. Chapman caught Maurice's eye and distended his nostrils, inviting him to side against the newcomer. Maurice thought he would wait a bit first. His disinclination to give pain was increasing, and besides he was not sure that he loathed Risley, though no doubt he ought to, and in a minute should. So Chapman ventured alone. Finding Risley adored music, he began to run it down, saying, 'I don't go in for being superior,' and so on.

'I do!'

'Oh, do you! In that case I beg your pardon.'

'Come along, Chapman, you are in need of food,' called Mr Cornwallis, and promised himself some amusement at lunch.

''Spect Mr Risley isn't. I've put him off with my low talk.'

They sat down, and Risley turned with a titter to Maurice and said, 'I simply *can't* think of any reply to that'; in each of his sentences he accented one word violently. 'It is so humiliating. "No" won't do. "Yes" won't do. What *is* to be done?'

'What about saying nothing?' said the Dean.

'To say nothing? Horrible. You must be mad.'

'Are you always talking, may one ask?' inquired Chapman.

Risley said he was.

'Never get tired of it?'

'*Never.*'

'Ever tire other people?'

'*Never.*'

'Odd that.'

'Do not suggest I've tired you. Untrue, untrue, you're beaming.'

'It's not at you if I am,' said Chapman, who was hot-tempered.

Maurice and the Dean laughed.

'I come to a standstill again. How amazing are the difficulties of conversation.'

'You seem to carry on better than most of us can,' remarked Maurice. He had not spoken before, and his voice, which was low but very gruff, made Risley shiver.

'Naturally. It is my forte. It is the only thing I care about, conversation.'

'Is that serious?'

'Everything I say is serious.' And somehow Maurice knew this was true. It had struck him at once that Risley was serious. 'And are you serious?'

'Don't ask me.'

'Then talk until you become so.'

'Rubbish,' growled the Dean.

Chapman laughed tempestuously.

'Rubbish?' He questioned Maurice, who, when he grasped the point, was understood to reply that deeds are more important than words.

'What is the difference? Words *are* deeds. Do you mean to say that these five minutes in Cornwallis's rooms have done nothing for you? Will you *ever* forget you have met me, for instance?'

33

Chapman grunted.

'But he will not, nor will you. And then I am told we ought to be doing something.'

The Dean came to the rescue of the two Sunningtonians. He said to his young cousin, 'You're unsound about memory. You confuse what's important with what's impressive. No doubt Chapman and Hall always will remember they've met you –'

'And forget this is a cutlet. Quite so.'

'But the cutlet does some good to them, and you none.'

'Obscurantist!'

'This is just like a book,' said Chapman. 'Eh, Hall?'

'I mean,' said Risley, 'oh how clearly I mean that the cutlet influences your subconscious lives, and I your conscious, and so I am not only more impressive than the cutlet but more important. Your Dean here, who dwells in Medieval Darkness and wishes you to do the same, pretends that only the subconscious, only the part of you that can be touched without your knowledge is important, and daily he drops soporific –'

'Oh, shut up,' said the Dean.

'But I am a child of light –'

'Oh, shut up.' And he turned the conversation onto normal lines. Risley was not egotistic, though he always talked about himself. He did not interrupt. Nor did he feign indifference. Gambolling like a dolphin, he accompanied them whithersoever they went, without hindering their course. He was at play, but seriously. It was as important to him to go to and fro as to them to go forward, and he loved keeping near them. A few months earlier Maurice would have agreed with Chapman, but now he was sure the man had an inside, and he wondered whether he should see more of him. He was pleased when, after lunch was over, Risley waited for him at the bottom of the stairs and said,

'You didn't see. My cousin wasn't being human.'

'He's good enough for us; that's all I know,' exploded Chapman. 'He's absolutely delightful.'

'Exactly. Eunuchs are.' And he was gone.

'Well, I'm –' exclaimed the other, but with British self-control suppressed the verb. He was deeply shocked. He didn't mind hot stuff in moderation, he told Maurice, but this was too much, it was bad

34

form, ungentlemanly, the fellow could not have been through a public school. Maurice agreed. You could call your cousin a shit if you liked, but not a eunuch. Rotten style! All the same he was amused, and whenever he was hauled in in the future, mischievous and incongruous thoughts would occur to him about the Dean.

6

ALL that day and the next Maurice was planning how he could see this queer fish again. The chances were bad. He did not like to call on a senior-year man, and they were at different colleges. Risley, he gathered, was well known at the Union, and he went to the Tuesday debate in the hope of hearing him: perhaps he would be easier to understand in public. He was not attracted to the man in the sense that he wanted him for a friend, but he did feel he might help him – how, he didn't formulate. It was all very obscure, for the mountains still overshadowed Maurice. Risley, surely capering on the summit, might stretch him a helping hand.

Having failed at the Union, he had a reaction. He didn't want anyone's help; he was all right. Besides, none of his friends would stand Risley, and he must stick to his friends. But the reaction soon passed, and he longed to see him more than ever. Since Risley was so odd, might he not be odd too, and break all the undergraduate conventions by calling? One 'ought to be human', and it was a human sort of thing to call. Much struck by the discovery, Maurice decided to be Bohemian also, and to enter the room making a witty speech in Risley's own style. 'You've bargained for more than you've gained' occurred to him. It didn't sound very good, but Risley had been clever at not letting him feel a fool, so he would fire it off if inspired to nothing better, and leave the rest to luck.

For it had become an adventure. This man who said one ought to 'talk, talk' had stirred Maurice incomprehensibly. One night, just before ten o'clock, he slipped into Trinity and waited in the Great Court until the gates were shut behind him. Looking up, he noticed the night. He was indifferent to beauty as a rule, but 'what a show of stars!' he thought. And how the fountain splashed when the chimes died away, and the gates and doors all over Cambridge had been fastened up. Trinity men were around him – all of enormous intellect and culture. Maurice's set had laughed at Trinity, but they could not ignore its disdainful radiance, or deny the superiority it scarcely troubles to affirm. He had come to it without their knowledge, humbly, to ask its help. His witty speech faded in its atmosphere; and his heart beat violently. He was ashamed and afraid.

Risley's rooms were at the end of a short passage, which since it contained no obstacle was unlighted, and visitors slid along the wall until they hit the door. Maurice hit it sooner than he expected – a most awful whack – and exclaimed 'Oh damnation' loudly, while the panels quivered.

'Come in,' said a voice. Disappointment awaited him. The speaker was a man of his own college, by name Durham. Risley was out.

'Do you want Mr Risley? Hullo, Hall!'

'Hullo! Where's Risley?'

'I don't know.'

'Oh, it's nothing. I'll go.'

'Are you going back into college?' asked Durham without looking up: he was kneeling over a castle of pianola records on the floor.

'I suppose so, as he isn't here. It wasn't anything particular.'

'Wait a sec, and I'll come too. I'm sorting out the Pathetic Symphony.'

Maurice examined Risley's room and wondered what would have been said in it, and then sat on the table and looked at Durham. He was a small man – very small – with simple manners and a fair face, which had flushed when Maurice blundered in. In the college he had a reputation for brains and also for exclusiveness. Almost the only thing Maurice had heard about him was that he 'went out too much', and this meeting in Trinity confirmed it.

'I can't find the March,' he said. 'Sorry.'

'All right.'

'I'm borrowing them to play on Fetherstonhaugh's pianola.'

'Under me.'

'Have you come into college, Hall?'

'Yes, I'm beginning my second year.'

'Oh yes, of course, I'm third.'

He spoke without arrogance, and Maurice, forgetting due honour to seniority, said, 'You look more like a fresher than a third-year man, I must say.'

'I may do, but I feel like an M.A.'

Maurice regarded him attentively.

'Risley's an amazing chap,' he continued.

Maurice did not reply.

'But all the same a little of him goes a long way.'

'Still you don't mind borrowing his things.'

He looked up again. 'Oughtn't I to?' he asked.

'I'm only ragging, of course,' said Maurice, slipping off the table. 'Have you found that music yet?'

'No.'

'Because I must be going;' he was in no hurry, but his heart, which had never stopped beating quickly, impelled him to say this.

'Oh. All right.'

This was not what Maurice had intended. 'What is it you want?' he asked, advancing.

'The March out of the Pathétique –'

'That means nothing to me. So you like this style of music.'

'I do.'

'A good waltz is more my style.'

'Mine too,' said Durham, meeting his eye. As a rule Maurice shifted, but he held firm on this occasion. Then Durham said, 'The other movement may be in that pile over by the window. I must look. I shan't be long.' Maurice said resolutely, 'I must go now.'

'All right, I'll stop.'

Beaten and lonely, Maurice went. The stars blurred, the night had turned towards rain. But while the porter was getting the keys at the gate he heard quick footsteps behind him.

'Got your March?'

'No, I thought I'd come along with you instead.'

Maurice walked a few steps in silence, then said, 'Here, give me some of those things to carry.'

'I've got them safe.'

'Give,' he said roughly, and jerked the records from under Durham's arm. No other conversation passed. On reaching their own college they went straight to Fetherstonhaugh's room, for there was time to try a little music over before eleven o'clock. Durham sat down at the pianola. Maurice knelt beside him.

'Didn't know you were in the aesthetic push, Hall,' said the host.

'I'm not – I want to hear what they're up to.'

Durham began, then desisted, saying he would start with the 5/4 instead.

'Why?'

'It's nearer waltzes.'

'Oh, never mind that. Play what you like. Don't go shifting – it wastes time.'

But he could not get his way this time. When he put his hand on the roller Durham said, 'You'll tear it, let go,' and fixed the 5/4 instead.

Maurice listened carefully to the music. He rather liked it.

'You ought to be this end,' said Fetherstonhaugh, who was working by the fire. 'You should get away from the machine as far as you can.'

'I think so – Would you mind playing it again if Fetherstonhaugh doesn't mind?'

'Yes, do, Durham. It is a jolly thing.'

Durham refused. Maurice saw that he was not pliable. He said, 'A movement isn't like a separate piece – you can't repeat it' – an unintelligible excuse, but apparently valid. He played the Largo, which was far from jolly, and then eleven struck and Fetherstonhaugh made them tea. He and Durham were in for the same Tripos, and talked shop, while Maurice listened. His excitement had never ceased. He saw that Durham was not only clever, but had a tranquil and orderly brain. He knew what he wanted to read, where he was weak and how far the officials could help him. He had neither the blind faith in tutors and lectures that was held by Maurice and his set nor the contempt professed by Fetherstonhaugh. 'You can always learn something from an older man, even if he hasn't read the latest Germans.' They argued a little about Sophocles, then in low water Durham said it was a pose in 'us undergraduates' to ignore him and advised Fetherstonhaugh to re-read the *Ajax* with his eye on the characters rather than the author; he would learn more that way, both about Greek grammar and life.

Maurice regretted all this. He had somehow hoped to find the man unbalanced. Fetherstonhaugh was a great person, both in brain and brawn, and had a trenchant and copious manner. But Durham listened unmoved, shook out the falsities and approved the rest. What hope for Maurice who was nothing but falsities? A stab of anger went through him. Jumping up, he said good night, to regret his haste as soon as he was outside the door. He settled to wait, not on the staircase itself, for this struck him as absurd, but somewhere between its foot and Durham's own room. Going out into the court, he located the latter, even knocking at the door, though he knew the owner was absent, and looking in he studied furniture and pictures in the fire-light. Then he took his stand on a sort of bridge in the courtyard. Unfortunately it was not a real bridge: it only spanned a slight depression in the ground, which the architect had tried to utilize in his effect. To stand on it was to feel in a photographic studio, and the parapet was too low to lean upon. Still, with a pipe in his mouth, Maurice looked fairly natural, and hoped it wouldn't rain.

The lights were out, except in Fetherstonhaugh's room. Twelve struck, then a quarter past. For a whole hour he might have been watching for Durham. Presently there was a noise on the staircase and the neat little figure ran out with a gown round its throat and books in its hand. It was the moment for which he had waited, but he found himself strolling away. Durham went to his rooms behind him. The opportunity was passing.

'Good night,' he screamed; his voice was going out of gear, and startling them both.

'Who's that? Good night, Hall. Taking a stroll before bed?'

'I generally do. You don't want any more tea, I suppose?'

'Do I? No, perhaps it's a bit late for tea.' Rather tepidly he added, 'Like some whisky though?'

'Have you a drop?' leaped from Maurice.

'Yes – come in. Here I keep: ground floor.'

'Oh, here!' Durham turned on the light. The fire was nearly out now. He told Maurice to sit down and brought up a table with glasses.

'Say when?'

'Thanks – most awfully, most awfully.'

'Soda or plain?' he asked, yawning.

'Soda,' said Maurice. But it was impossible to stop, for the man was tired and had only invited him out of civility. He drank and returned to his own room, where he provided himself with plenty of tobacco and went into the court again.

It was absolutely quiet now, and absolutely dark. Maurice walked to and fro on the hallowed grass, himself noiseless, his heart glowing. The rest of him fell asleep, bit by bit, and first of all his brain, his weakest organ. His body followed, then his feet carried him upstairs to escape the dawn. But his heart had lit never to be quenched again, and one thing in him at last was real.

Next morning he was calmer. He had a cold for one thing, the rain having soaked him unnoticed, and for another he had overslept to the extent of missing a chapel and two lectures. It was impossible to get his life straight. After lunch he changed for football, and being in good time flung himself on his sofa to sleep till tea. But he was not hungry. Refusing an invitation, he strolled out into the town and, meeting a Turkish bath, had one. It cured his cold, but made him late for another lecture. When Hall came, he felt he could not face the mass of Old Sunningtonians, and, though he had not signed off, absented himself, and dined alone at the Union. He saw Risley there, but with indifference. Then the evening began again, and he found to his surprise that he was very clear-headed, and could do six hours' work in three. He went to bed at his usual time, and woke up healthy and very happy. Some instinct, deep below his consciousness, had advised him to let Durham and his thoughts about Durham have a twenty-four hours' rest.

They began to see a little of one another. Durham asked him to lunch, and Maurice asked him back, but not too soon. A caution alien to his nature was at work. He had always been cautious pettily, but this was on a large scale. He became alert, and all his actions that October term might be described in the language of battle. He would not venture onto difficult ground. He spied out Durham's weaknesses as well as his strength. And above all he exercised and cleaned his powers.

If obliged to ask himself, 'What's all this?' he would have replied, 'Durham is another of those boys in whom I was interested at school,' but he was obliged to ask nothing, and merely went ahead with his mouth and his mind shut. Each day with its contradictions slipped into the abyss, and he knew that he was gaining ground. Nothing else mattered. If he worked well and was nice socially, it was only a by-product, to which he had devoted no care. To ascend, to stretch a hand up the mountainside until a hand catches it, was the end for which he had been born. He forgot the hysteria of his first night and his stranger recovery. They were steps which he kicked behind him. He never even thought of tenderness and emotion; his considerations about Durham remained cold. Durham didn't dislike him, he was sure. That was all he wanted. One thing at a time. He didn't so much as have hopes, for hope distracts, and he had a great deal to see to.

7

NEXT term they were intimate at once.

'Hall, I nearly wrote a letter to you in the vac,' said Durham, plunging into a conversation.

'That so?'

'But an awful screed. I'd been having a rotten time.'

His voice was not very serious, and Maurice said, 'What went wrong? Couldn't you keep down the Christmas pudding?'

It presently appeared that the pudding was allegorical; there had been a big family row.

'I don't know what you'll say – I'd rather like your opinion on what happened if it doesn't bore you.'

'Not a bit,' said Maurice.

'We've had a bust up on the religious question.'

At that moment they were interrupted by Chapman.

'I'm sorry, we're fixing something,' Maurice told him.

Chapman withdrew.

'You needn't have done that, any time would do for my rot,' Durham protested. He went on more earnestly.

'Hall, I don't want to worry you with my beliefs, or rather with their absence, but to explain the situation I must just tell you that I'm unorthodox. I'm not a Christian.'

Maurice held unorthodoxy to be bad form and had remarked last term in a college debate that if a man had doubts he might have the grace to keep them to himself. But he only said to Durham that it was a difficult question and a wide one.

'I know – it isn't about that. Leave it aside.' He looked for a little into the fire. 'It is about the way my mother took it. I told her six months ago – in the summer – and she didn't mind. She made some foolish joke, as she does, but that was all. It just passed over. I was thankful, for it had been on my mind for years. I had never believed since I found something that did me better, quite as a kid, and when I came to know Risley and his crew it seemed imperative to speak out.

43

You know what a point they make of that – it's really their main point So I spoke out. She said, "Oh yes, you'll be wiser when you are as old as me": the mildest form of the thing conceivable, and I went away rejoicing. Now it's all come up again.'

'Why?'

'Why? On account of Christmas. I didn't want to communicate. You're supposed to receive it three times a year –'

'Yes, I know. Holy Communion.'

'– and at Christmas it came round. I said I wouldn't: Mother wheedled me in a way quite unlike her, asked me to do it this once to please her – then got cross, said I would damage her reputation as well as my own – we're the local squires and the neighbourhood's uncivilized. But what I couldn't stand was the end. She said I was wicked. I could have honoured her if she had said that six months before, but now! now to drag in holy words like wickedness and goodness in order to make me do what I disbelieved. I told her I have my own communions. "If I went to them as you and the girls are doing to yours my gods would kill me!" I suppose that was too strong.'

Maurice, not well understanding, said, 'So did you go?'

'Where?'

'To the church.'

Durham sprang up. His face was disgusted. Then he bit his lip and began to smile.

'No, I didn't go to church, Hall. I thought that was plain.'

'I'm sorry – I wish you'd sit down. I didn't mean to offend you. I'm rather slow at catching.'

Durham squatted on the rug close to Maurice's chair. 'Have you known Chapman long?' he asked after a pause.

'Here and at school, five years.'

'Oh.' He seemed to reflect. 'Give me a cigarette. Put it in my mouth. Thanks.' Maurice supposed the talk was over, but after the swirl he went on. 'You see – you mentioned you had a mother and two sisters, which is exactly my own allowance, and all through the row I was wondering what you would have done in my position.'

'Your mother must be very different to mine.'

'What is yours like?'

'She never makes a row about anything.'

44

'Because you've never yet done anything she wouldn't approve, I expect – and never will.'

'Oh no, she wouldn't fag herself.'

'You can't tell, Hall, especially with women. I'm sick with her. That's my real trouble that I want your help about.'

'She'll come round.'

'Exactly, my dear chap, but shall I? I must have been pretending to like her. This row has shattered my lie. I did think I had stopped building lies. I despise her character, I am disgusted with her. There, I have told you what no one else in the world knows.'

Maurice clenched his fist and hit Durham lightly on the head with it. 'Hard luck,' he breathed.

'Tell me about your home life.'

'There's nothing to tell. We just go on.'

'Lucky devils.'

'Oh, I don't know. Are you ragging, or was your vac really beastly, Durham?'

'Absolute Hell, misery and Hell.'

Maurice's fist unclenched to reform with a handful of hair in its grasp.

'Waou, that hurts!' cried the other joyously.

'What did your sisters say about Holy Communion?'

'One's married a clerg – No, that hurts.'

'Absolute Hell, eh?'

'Hall, I never knew you were a fool –' he possessed himself of Maurice's hand – 'and the other's engaged to Archibald London, Esquire, of the – Waou! Ee! Shut up, I'm going.' He fell between Maurice's knees.

'Well, why don't you go if you're going?'

'Because I can't go.'

It was the first time he had dared to play with Durham. Religion and relatives faded into the background, as he rolled him up in the hearth rug and fitted his head into the waste-paper basket. Hearing the noise, Fetherstonhaugh ran up and helped. There was nothing but ragging for many days after that, Durham becoming quite as silly as himself. Wherever they met, which was everywhere, they would butt and spar and embroil their friends. At last Durham got tired. Being the weaker he was hurt sometimes, and his chairs had been broken.

Maurice felt the change at once. His coltishness passed, but they had become demonstrative during it. They walked arm in arm or arm around shoulder now. When they sat it was nearly always in the same position – Maurice in a chair, and Durham at his feet, leaning against him. In the world of their friends this attracted no notice. Maurice would stroke Durham's hair.

And their range increased elsewhere. During this Lent term Maurice came out as a theologian. It was not humbug entirely. He believed that he believed, and felt genuine pain when anything he was accustomed to met criticism – the pain that masquerades among the middle classes as Faith. It was not Faith, being inactive. It gave him no support, no wider outlook. It didn't exist till opposition touched it, when it ached like a useless nerve. They all had these nerves at home, and regarded them as divine, though neither the Bible nor the Prayer Book nor the Sacraments nor Christian ethics nor anything spiritual were alive to them. 'But how can people?' they exclaimed, when anything was attacked, and subscribed to Defence Societies. Maurice's father was becoming a pillar of Church and Society when he died, and other things being alike Maurice would have stiffened too.

But other things were not to be alike. He had this overwhelming desire to impress Durham. He wanted to show his friend that he had something besides brute strength, and where his father would have kept canny silence he began to talk, talk. 'You think I don't think, but I can tell you I do.' Very often Durham made no reply and Maurice would be terrified lest he was losing him. He had heard it said, 'Durham's all right as long as you amuse him, then he drops you,' and feared lest by exhibiting his orthodoxy he was bringing on what he tried to avoid. But he could not stop. The craving for notice grew overwhelming, so he talked, talked.

One day Durham said, 'Hall, why this thusness?'

'Religion means a lot to me,' bluffed Maurice. 'Because I say so little you think I don't feel. I care a lot.'

'In that case come to coffee after hall.'

They were just going in. Durham, being a scholar, had to read grace, and there was cynicism in his accent. During the meal they looked at each other. They sat at different tables, but Maurice had contrived to move his seat so that he could glance at his friend. The phase of bread pellets was over. Durham looked severe this evening

46

and was not speaking to his neighbours. Maurice knew that he was thoughtful and wondered what about.

'You wanted to get it and you're going to,' said Durham, sporting the door.

Maurice went cold and then crimson. But Durham's voice, when he next heard it, was attacking his opinions on the Trinity. He thought he minded about the Trinity, yet it seemed unimportant, beside the fires of his terror. He sprawled in an armchair, all the strength out of him, with sweat on his forehead and hands. Durham moved about getting the coffee ready and saying, 'I knew you wouldn't like this, but you have brought it on yourself. You can't expect me to bottle myself up indefinitely. I must let out sometimes.'

'Go on,' said Maurice, clearing his throat.

'I never meant to talk, for I respect people's opinions too much to laugh at them, but it doesn't seem to me that you have any opinions to respect. They're all second-hand tags – no, tenth-hand.'

Maurice, who was recovering, remarked that this was pretty strong.

'You're always saying, "I care a lot."'

'And what right have you to assume that I don't?'

'You do care a lot about something, Hall, but it obviously isn't the Trinity.'

'What is it then?'

'Rugger.'

Maurice had another attack. His hand shook and he spilt the coffee on the arm of the chair. 'You're a bit unfair,' he heard himself saying. 'You might at least have the grace to suggest that I care about people.'

Durham looked surprised, but said, 'You care nothing about the Trinity, anyway.'

'Oh, damn the Trinity.'

He burst with laughter. 'Exactly, exactly. We will now pass on to my next point.'

'I don't see the use, and I've a rotten head any way – I mean a headache. Nothing's gained by – all this. No doubt I can't prove the thing – I mean the arrangement of Three Gods in One and One in Three. But it means a lot to millions of people, whatever you may say, and we aren't going to give it up. We feel about it very deeply. God is good. That is the main point. Why go off on a side track?'

'Why feel so deeply about a side track?'

47

'What?'

Durham tidied up his remarks for him.

'Well, the whole show all hangs together.'

'So that if the Trinity went wrong it would invalidate the whole show?'

'I don't see that. Not at all.'

He was doing badly, but his head really did ache, and when he wiped the sweat off it re-formed.

'No doubt I can't explain well, as I care for nothing but rugger.'

Durham came and sat humorously on the edge of his chair.

'Look out – you've gone into the coffee now.'

'Blast – so I have.'

While he cleaned himself, Maurice unsported and looked out into the court. It seemed years since he had left it. He felt disinclined to be longer alone with Durham and called to some men to join them. A coffee of the usual type ensued, but when they left Maurice felt equally disinclined to leave with them. He flourished the Trinity again. 'It's a mystery,' he argued.

'It isn't a mystery to me. But I honour anyone to whom it really is.'

Maurice felt uncomfortable and looked at his own thick brown hands. Was the Trinity really a mystery to him? Except at his confirmation had he given the institution five minutes' thought? The arrival of the other men had cleared his head, and, no longer emotional, he glanced at his mind. It appeared like his hands – serviceable, no doubt, and healthy, and capable of development. But it lacked refinement, it had never touched mysteries, nor a good deal else. It was thick and brown.

'My position's this,' he announced after a pause. 'I don't believe in the Trinity, I give in there, but on the other hand I was wrong when I said everything hangs together. It doesn't, and because I don't believe in the Trinity it doesn't mean I am not a Christian.'

'What do you believe in?' said Durham, unchecked.

'The – the essentials.'

'As?'

In a low voice Maurice said, 'The Redemption.' He had never spoken the words out of church before and thrilled with emotion. But he did not believe in them any more than in the Trinity, and knew that Durham would detect this. The Redemption was the highest card in the suit, but that suit wasn't trumps, and his friend could capture it with some miserable two.

All that Durham said at the time was, 'Dante did believe in the Trinity,' and going to the shelf found the concluding passage of the *Paradiso*. He read to Maurice about the three rainbow circles that intersect, and between their junctions is enshadowed a human face. Poetry bored Maurice, but towards the close he cried, 'Whose face was it?'

'God's, don't you see?'

'But isn't that poem supposed to be a dream?'

Hall was a muddle-headed fellow, and Durham did not try to make sense of this, nor knew that Maurice was thinking of a dream of his own at school, and of the voice that had said, 'That is your friend.'

'Dante would have called it an awakening, not a dream.'

'Then you think that sort of stuff's all right?'

'Belief's always right,' replied Durham, putting back the book. 'It's all right and it's also unmistakable. Every man has somewhere about him some belief for which he'd die. Only isn't it improbable that your parents and guardians told it to you? If there is one won't it be part of your own flesh and spirit? Show me that. Don't go hawking out tags like "The Redemption" or "The Trinity".'

'I've given up the Trinity.'

'The Redemption, then.'

'You're beastly hard,' said Maurice. 'I always knew I was stupid, it's no news. The Risley set are more your sort and you had better talk to them.'

Durham looked awkward. He was nonplussed for a reply at last, and let Maurice slouch off without protest. Next day they met as usual. It had not been a tiff but a sudden gradient, and they travelled all the quicker after the rise. They talked theology again, Maurice defending the Redemption. He lost. He realized that he had no sense of Christ's existence or of His goodness, and should be positively sorry if there was such a person. His dislike of Christianity grew and became profound. In ten days he gave up communicating, in three weeks he cut out all the chapels he dared. Durham was puzzled by the rapidity. They were both puzzled, and Maurice, although he had lost and yielded all his opinions, had a queer feeling that he was really winning and carrying on a campaign that he had begun last term.

49

For Durham wasn't bored with him now. Durham couldn't do without him, and would be found at all hours curled up in his room and spoiling to argue. It was so unlike the man, who was reserved and no great dialectician. He gave as his reason for attacking Maurice's opinions that 'They are so rotten, Hall, everyone else up here believes respectably.' Was this the whole truth? Was there not something else behind his new manner and furious iconoclasm? Maurice thought there was. Outwardly in retreat, he thought that his Faith was a pawn well lost; for in capturing it Durham had exposed his heart.

Towards the end of term they touched upon a yet more delicate subject. They attended the Dean's translation class, and when one of the men was forging quietly ahead Mr Cornwallis observed in a flat toneless voice: 'Omit: a reference to the unspeakable vice of the Greeks.' Durham observed afterwards that he ought to lose his fellowship for such hypocrisy.

Maurice laughed.

'I regard it as a point of pure scholarship. The Greeks, or most of them, were that way inclined, and to omit it is to omit the mainstay of Athenian society.'

'Is that so?'

'You've read the *Symposium*?'

Maurice had not, and did not add that he had explored Martial.

'It's all in there – not meat for babes, of course, but you ought to read it. Read it this vac.'

No more was said at the time, but he was free of another subject, and one that he had never mentioned to any living soul. He hadn't known it could be mentioned, and when Durham did so in the middle of the sunlit court a breath of liberty touched him.

8

ON reaching home he talked about Durham until the fact that he had a friend penetrated into the minds of his family. Ada wondered whether it was brother to a certain Miss Durham – not but what she was an only child – while Mrs Hall confused it with a don named Cumberland. Maurice was deeply wounded. One strong feeling arouses another, and a profound irritation against his womenkind set in. His relations with them hitherto had been trivial but stable, but it seemed iniquitous that anyone should mispronounce the name of the man who was more to him than all the world. Home emasculated everything.

It was the same with his atheism. No one felt as deeply as he expected. With the crudity of youth he drew his mother apart and said that he should always respect her religious prejudices and those of the girls, but that his own conscience permitted him to attend church no longer. She said it was a great misfortune.

'I knew you would be upset. I cannot help it, mother dearest. I am made that way and it is no good arguing.'

'Your poor father always went to church.'

'I'm not my father.'

'Morrie, Morrie, what a thing to say.'

'Well, he isn't,' said Kitty in her perky way. 'Really, mother, come.'

'Kitty, dear, you here,' cried Mrs Hall, feeling that disapproval was due and unwilling to bestow it on her son. 'We were talking about things not suited, and you are perfectly wrong besides, for Maurice is the image of his father – Dr Barry said so.'

'Well, Dr Barry doesn't go to church himself,' said Maurice, falling into the family habit of talking all over the shop.

'He is a most clever man,' said Mrs Hall with finality, 'and Mrs Barry's the same.'

This slip of their mother's convulsed Ada and Kitty. They would not stop laughing at the idea of Mrs Barry's being a man, and Maurice's atheism was forgotten. He did not communicate on Easter Sunday, and supposed the row would come then, as in Durham's case. But no one took any notice, for the suburbs no longer exact Christianity. This disgusted him; it made him look at society with new eyes. Did society, while professing to be so moral and sensitive, really mind anything?

He wrote often to Durham – long letters trying carefully to express shades of feeling. Durham made little of them and said so. His replies were equally long. Maurice never let them out of his pocket, changing them from suit to suit and even pinning them in his pyjamas when he went to bed. He would wake up and touch them and, watching the reflections from the street lamp, remember how he used to feel afraid as a little boy.

Episode of Gladys Olcott.

Miss Olcott was one of their infrequent guests. She had been good to Mrs Hall and Ada in some hydro, and, receiving an invitation, had followed it up. She was charming – at least the women said so, and male callers told the son of the house he was a lucky dog. He laughed, they laughed, and having ignored her at first he took to paying her attentions.

Now Maurice, though he did not know it, had become an attractive young man. Much exercise had tamed his clumsiness. He was heavy but alert, and his face seemed following the example of his body. Mrs Hall put it down to his moustache – 'Maurice's moustache will be the making of him' – a remark more profound than she realized. Certainly the little black line of it did pull his face together, and show up his teeth when he smiled, and his clothes suited him also: by Durham's advice he kept to flannel trousers, even on Sunday.

He turned his smile on Miss Olcott – it seemed the proper thing to do. She responded. He put his muscles at her service by taking her out in his new side-car. He sprawled at her feet. Finding she smoked, he persuaded her to stop behind with him in the dining-room and to look between his eyes. Blue vapour quivered and shredded and built dissolving walls, and Maurice's thoughts voyaged with it, to vanish as soon as a window was opened for fresh air. He saw that she was pleased, and his family, servants and all, intrigued; he determined to go further.

Something went wrong at once. Maurice paid her compliments, said that her hair etc. was ripping. She tried to stop him, but he was insensitive, and did not know that he had annoyed her. He had read that girls always pretended to stop men who complimented them. He haunted her. When she excused herself from riding with him on the last day he played the domineering male. She was his guest, she came, and having taken her to some scenery that he considered romantic he pressed her little hand between his own.

It was not that Miss Olcott objected to having her hand pressed. Others had done it and Maurice could have done it had he guessed how. But she knew something was wrong. His touch revolted her. It was a corpse's. Springing up she cried, 'Mr Hall, don't be silly. I mean *don't* be silly. I am not saying it to make you sillier.'

'Miss Olcott – Gladys – I'd rather die than offend –' growled the boy, trying to keep it up.

'I must go back by train,' she said, crying a little. 'I must, I'm awfully sorry.' She arrived home before him with a sensible little story about a headache and dust in her eyes, but his family also knew that something had gone wrong.

Except for this episode the vac passed pleasantly. Maurice did some reading, following his friend's advice rather than his tutor's, and he asserted in one or two ways his belief that he was grown up. At his instigation his mother dismissed the Howells who had long paralysed the outdoor department, and set up a motor-car instead of a carriage. Everyone was impressed, including the Howells. He also called upon his father's old partner. He had inherited some business aptitude and some money, and it was settled that when he left Cambridge he should enter the firm as an unauthorized clerk; Hill and Hall, Stock Brokers. Maurice was stepping into the niche that England had prepared for him.

9

DURING the previous term he had reached an unusual level mentally, but the vac pulled him back towards public-schoolishness. He was less alert, he again behaved as he supposed he was supposed to behave – a perilous feat for one who is not dowered with imagination. His mind, not obscured totally, was often crossed by clouds, and though Miss Olcott had passed, the insincerity that led him to her remained. His family were the main cause of this. He had yet to realize that they were stronger than he and influenced him incalculably. Three weeks in their company left him untidy, sloppy, victorious in every item, yet defeated on the whole. He came back thinking, and even speaking, like his mother or Ada.

Till Durham arrived he had not noticed the deterioration. Durham had not been well, and came up a few days late. When his face, paler than usual, peered round the door, Maurice had a spasm of despair, and tried to recollect where they stood last term, and to gather up the threads of the campaign. He felt himself slack, and afraid of action. The worst part of him rose to the surface, and urged him to prefer comfort to joy.

'Hullo, old man,' he said awkwardly.

Durham slipped in without speaking.

'What's wrong?'

'Nothing;' and Maurice knew that he had lost touch. Last term he would have understood this silent entrance.

'Anyhow, take a pew.'

Durham sat upon the floor beyond his reach. It was late afternoon. The sounds of the May term, the scents of the Cambridge year in flower, floated in through the window and said to Maurice, 'You are unworthy of us.' He knew that he was three parts dead, an alien, a yokel in Athens. He had no business here, nor with such a friend.

'I say, Durham –'

Durham came nearer. Maurice stretched out a hand and felt the head nestle against it. He forgot what he was going to say. The sounds

54

and scents whispered, 'You are we, we are youth.' Very gently he stroked the hair and ran his fingers down into it as if to caress the brain.

'I say, Durham, have you been all right?'

'Have you?'

'No.'

'You wrote you were.'

'I wasn't.'

The truth in his own voice made him tremble. 'A rotten vac and I never knew it,' and wondered how long he should know it. The mist would lower again, he felt sure, and with an unhappy sigh he pulled Durham's head against his kneee, as though it was a talisman for clear living. It lay there, and he had accomplished a new tenderness – stroked it steadily from temple to throat. Then, removing both hands, he dropped them on either side of him and sat sighing.

'Hall.'

Maurice looked.

'Is there some trouble?'

He caressed and again withdrew. It seemed as certain that he hadn't as that he had a friend.

'Anything to do with that girl?'

'No.'

'You wrote you liked her.'

'I didn't – don't.'

Deeper sighs broke from him. They rattled in his throat, turning to groans. His head fell back, and he forgot the pressure of Durham on his knee, forgot that Durham was watching his turbid agony. He stared at the ceiling with wrinkled mouth and eyes, understanding nothing except that man has been created to feel pain and loneliness without help from heaven.

Now Durham stretched up to him, stroked his hair. They clasped one another. They were lying breast against breast soon, head was on shoulder, but just as their cheeks met someone called 'Hall' from the court, and he answered: he always had answered when people called. Both started violently, and Durham sprang to the mantelpiece where he leant his head on his arm. Absurd people came thundering up the stairs. They wanted tea. Maurice pointed to it, then was drawn into their conversation, and scarcely noticed his friend's departure. It had been an ordinary talk, he told himself, but too sentimental, and he cultivated a breeziness against their next meeting.

This took place soon enough. With half a dozen others he was starting for the theatre after hall when Durham called him.

'I knew you read the *Symposium* in the vac,' he said in a low voice.

Maurice felt uneasy.

'Then you understand – without me saying more –'

'How do you mean?'

Durham could not wait. People were all around them, but with eyes that had gone intensely blue he whispered, 'I love you.'

Maurice was scandalized, horrified. He was shocked to the bottom of his suburban soul, and exclaimed, 'Oh, rot!' The words, the manner, were out of him before he could recall them. 'Durham, you're an Englishman. I'm another. Don't talk nonsense. I'm not offended, because I know you don't mean it, but it's the only subject absolutely beyond the limit as you know, it's the worst crime in the calendar, and you must never mention it again. Durham! a rotten notion really –'

But his friend was gone, gone without a word, flying across the court, the bang of his door heard through the sounds of spring.

10

A SLOW nature such as Maurice's appears insensitive, for it needs time even to feel. Its instinct is to assume that nothing either for good or evil has happened, and to resist the invader. Once gripped, it feels acutely, and its sensations in love are particularly profound. Given time, it can know and impart ecstasy; given time, it can sink to the heart of Hell. Thus it was that his agony began as a slight regret; sleepless nights and lonely days must intensify it into a frenzy that consumed him. It worked inwards, till it touched the root whence body and soul both spring, the 'I' that he had been trained to obscure, and, realized at last, doubled its power and grew superhuman. For it might have been joy. New worlds broke loose in him at this, and he saw from the vastness of the ruin what ecstasy he had lost, what a communion.

They did not speak again for two days. Durham would have made it longer, but most of their friends were now in common, and they were bound to meet. Realizing this, he wrote Maurice an icy note suggesting that it would be a public convenience if they behaved as if nothing had happened. He added, 'I shall be obliged if you will not mention my criminal morbidity to anyone. I am sure you will do this from the sensible way in which you took the news.' Maurice did not reply, but first put the note with the letters he had received during the vac and afterwards burnt them all.

He supposed the climax of agony had come. But he was fresh to real suffering as to reality of any kind. They had yet to meet. On the second afternoon they found themselves in the same four at tennis and the pain grew excruciating. He could scarcely stand or see; if he returned Durham's service the ball sent a throb up his arm. Then they were made to be partners; once they jostled, Durham winced, but managed to laugh in the old fashion.

Moreover, it proved convenient that he should come back to college in Maurice's side-car. He got in without demur. Maurice, who had not been to bed for two nights, went light-headed, turned the machine into a by-lane and travelled top speed. There was a wagon in front, full of women. He drove straight at them, but when they screamed stuck on his brakes, and just avoided disaster. Durham made no comment. As he indicated in his note, he only spoke when others were present. All other intercourse was to end.

That evening Maurice went to bed as usual. But as he laid his head on the pillows a flood of tears oozed from it. He was horrified. A man crying! Fetherstonhaugh might hear him. He wept stifled in the sheets, he sprang about kissing, then struck his head against the wall and smashed the crockery. Someone did come up the stairs. He grew quiet at once and did not recommence when the footsteps died away. Lighting a candle, he looked with surprise at his torn pyjamas and trembling limbs. He continued to cry, for he could not stop, but the suicidal point had been passed, and, remaking the bed, he lay down. His gyp was clearing away the ruins when he opened his eyes. It seemed queer to Maurice that a gyp should have been dragged in. He wondered whether the man suspected anything, then slept again. On waking the second time he found letters on the floor – one from old Mr Grace, his grandfather, about the party that was to be given when he came of age, another from a don's wife asking him to lunch ('Mr Durham is coming too, so you won't be shy'), another from Ada with mention of Gladys Olcott. Yet again he fell asleep.

Madness is not for everyone, but Maurice's proved the thunderbolt that dispels the clouds. The storm had been working up not for three days as he supposed, but for six years. It had brewed in the obscurities of being where no eye pierces, his surroundings had thickened it. It had burst and he had not died. The brilliancy of day was around him, he stood upon the mountain range that overshadows youth, he saw.

Most of the day he sat with open eyes, as if looking into the Valley he had left. It was all so plain now. He had lied. He phrased it 'been fed upon lies', but lies are the natural food of boyhood, and he had eaten greedily. His first resolve was to be more careful in the future. He would live straight, not because it mattered to anyone now, but for the sake of the game. He would not deceive himself so much. He would not – and this was the test – pretend to care about women when the only sex that attracted him was his own. He loved men and always had loved them. He longed to embrace them and mingle his being with theirs. Now that the man who returned his love had been lost, he admitted this.

II

AFTER this crisis Maurice became a man. Hitherto – if human beings can be estimated – he had not been worth anyone's affection, but conventional, petty, treacherous to others, because to himself. Now he had the highest gift to offer. The idealism and the brutality that ran through boyhood had joined at last, and twined into love. No one might want such love, but he could not feel ashamed of it, because it was 'he', neither body or soul, nor body and soul, but 'he' working through both. He still suffered, yet a sense of triumph had come else-where. Pain had shown him a niche behind the world's judgements, whither he could withdraw.

There was still much to learn, and years passed before he explored certain abysses in his being – horrible enough they were. But he dis-covered the method and looked no more at scratches in the sand. He had awoken too late for happiness, but not for strength, and could feel an austere joy, as of a warrior who is homeless but stands fully armed.

As the term went on he decided to speak to Durham. He valued words highly, having so lately discovered them. Why should he suffer and cause his friend suffering, when words might put all right? He heard himself saying, 'I really love you as you love me,' and Durham replying, 'Is that so? Then I forgive you,' and to the ardour of youth such a conversation seemed possible, though somehow he did not conceive it as leading to joy. He made several attempts, but partly through his own shyness, partly through Durham's, they failed. If he went round, the door was sported, or else there were people inside; should he enter, Durham left when the other guests did. He invited him to meals – he could never come; he offered to lift him again for tennis, but an excuse was made. Even if they met in the court, Durham would affect to have forgotten something and run past him or away. He was surprised their friends did not notice the change, but few undergraduates are observant – they have too much to discover within themselves and it was a don who remarked that Durham had stopped honeymooning with that Hall person.

He found his opportunity after a debating society to which both belonged. Durham – pleading his Tripos – had sent in his resignation, but had begged that the society might meet in his rooms first, as he wished to take his share of hospitality. This was like him; he hated to be under an obligation to anyone. Maurice went and sat through a tedious evening. When everyone, including the host, surged out into the fresh air, he remained, thinking of the first night he had visited that room, and wondering whether the past cannot return.

Durham entered, and did not at once see who it was. Ignoring him utterly, he proceeded to tidy up for the night.

'You're beastly hard,' blurted Maurice, 'you don't know what it is to have a mind in a mess, and it makes you very hard.'

Durham shook his head as one who refuses to listen. He looked so ill that Maurice had a wild desire to catch hold of him.

'You might give me a chance instead of avoiding me – I only want to discuss.'

'We've discussed the whole evening.'

'I mean the *Symposium*, like the ancient Greeks.'

'Oh Hall, don't be so stupid – you ought to know that to be alone with you hurts me. No, please don't reopen. It's over. It's over.' He went into the other room and began to undress. 'Forgive this discourtesy, but I simply can't – my nerves are all nohow after three weeks of this.'

'So are mine,' cried Maurice.

'Poor, poor chap!'

'Durham, I'm in Hell.'

'Oh, you'll get out. It's only the Hell of disgust. You've never done anything to be ashamed of, so you don't know what's really Hell.'

Maurice gave a cry of pain. It was so unmistakable that Durham, who was about to close the door between them, said, 'Very well, I'll discuss if you like. What's the matter? You appear to want to apologize about something. Why? You behave as if I'm annoyed with you. What have you done wrong? You've been thoroughly decent from first to last.'

In vain he protested.

'So decent that I mistook your ordinary friendliness. When you were so good to me, above all the afternoon I came up – I thought it was something else. I am more sorry than I can ever say. I had no right to move out of my books and music, which was what I did when I met you. You won't want my apology any more than anything else I could give, but, Hall, I do make it most sincerely. It is a lasting grief to have insulted you.'

His voice was feeble but clear, and his face like a sword. Maurice flung useless words about love.

'That's all, I think. Get married quickly and forget.'

'Durham, I love you.'

He laughed bitterly.

'I do – I have always –'

'Good night, good night.'

'I tell you, I do – I came to say it – in your very own way – I have always been like the Greeks and didn't know.'

'Expand the statement.'

Words deserted him immediately. He could only speak when he was not asked to.

'Hall, don't be grotesque.' He raised his hand, for Maurice had exclaimed. 'It's like the very decent fellow you are to comfort me, but there are limits; one or two things I can't swallow.'

'I'm not grotesque –'

'I shouldn't have said that. So do leave me. I'm thankful it's into your hands I fell. Most men would have reported me to the Dean or the Police.'

'Oh, go to Hell, it's all you're fit for,' cried Maurice, rushed into the court and heard once more the bang of the outer door. Furious he stood on the bridge in a night that resembled the first – drizzly with faint stars. He made no allowance for three weeks of torture unlike his own or for the poison which, secreted by one man, acts differently on another. He was enraged not to find his friend as he had left him. Twelve o'clock struck, one, two, and he was still planning what to say when there is nothing to say and the resources of speech are ended.

Then savage, reckless, drenched with the rain, he saw in the first glimmer of dawn the window of Durham's room, and his heart leapt alive and shook him to pieces. It cried 'You love and are loved.' He looked round the court. It cried 'You are strong, he weak and alone,' won over his will. Terrified at what he must do, he caught hold of the mullion and sprang.

'Maurice –'

As he alighted his name had been called out of dreams. The violence went out of his heart, and a purity that he had never imagined dwelt there instead. His friend had called him. He stood for a moment entranced, then the new emotion found him words, and laying his hand very gently upon the pillows he answered 'Clive!'

Part Two

12

CLIVE had suffered little from bewilderment as a boy. His sincere mind, with its keen sense of right and wrong, had brought him the belief that he was damned instead. Deeply religious, with a living desire to reach God and to please Him, he found himself crossed at an early age by this other desire, obviously from Sodom. He had no doubt as to what it was: his emotion, more compact than Maurice's, was not split into the brutal and the ideal, nor did he waste years in bridging the gulf. He had in him the impulse that destroyed the City of the Plain. It should not ever become carnal, but why had he out of all Christians been punished with it?

At first he thought God must be trying him, and if he did not blaspheme would recompense him like Job. He therefore bowed his head, fasted, and kept away from anyone whom he found himself inclined to like. His sixteenth year was ceaseless torture. He told no one, and finally broke down and had to be removed from school. During the convalescence he found himself falling in love with a cousin who walked by his bath chair, a young married man. It was hopeless, he was damned.

These terrors had visited Maurice, but dimly: to Clive they were definite, continuous, and not more insistent at the Eucharist than elsewhere. He never mistook them, in spite of the rein he kept on grossness. He could control the body; it was the tainted soul that mocked his prayers.

The boy had always been a scholar, awake to the printed word, and the horrors the Bible evoked for him were to be laid by Plato. Never could he forget his emotion at first reading the *Phaedrus*. He saw there his malady described exquisitely, calmly, as a passion which we can direct, like any other, towards good or bad. Here was no invitation to licence. He could not believe his good fortune at first – thought there must be some misunderstanding and that he and Plato were thinking of different things. Then he saw that the temperate pagan really did comprehend him, and, slipping past the Bible rather than opposing it, was offering a new guide for life. 'To make the most of what I have.' Not to crush it down, not vainly to wish that it was something else, but to cultivate it in such ways as will not vex either God or Man.

He was obliged however to throw over Christianity. Those who base their conduct upon what they are rather than upon what they ought to be, always must throw it over in the end, and besides, between Clive's temperament and that religion there is a secular feud. No clear-headed man can combine them. The temperament, to quote the legal formula, is 'not to be mentioned among Christians', and a legend tells that all who shared it died on the morning of the Nativity. Clive regretted this. He came of a family of lawyers and squires, good and able men for the most part, and he did not wish to depart from their tradition. He wished Christianity would compromise with him a little and searched the Scriptures for support. There was David and Jonathan; there was even the 'disciple that Jesus loved'. But the Church's interpretation was against him; he could not find any rest for his soul in her without crippling it, and withdrew higher into the classics yearly.

By eighteen he was unusually mature, and so well under control that he could allow himself to be friendly with anyone who attracted him. Harmony had succeeded asceticism. At Cambridge he cultivated tender emotions for other undergraduates, and his life, hitherto grey, became slightly tinged with delicate hues. Cautious and sane, he advanced, nor was there anything petty in his caution. He was ready to go further should he consider it right.

In his second year he met Risley, himself 'that way'. Clive did not return the confidence which was given rather freely, nor did he like Risley and his set. But he was stimulated. He was glad to know that there were more of his sort about, and their frankness braced him into telling his mother about his agnosticism; it was all he could tell her. Mrs Durham, a worldly woman, made little protest. It was at Christmas the trouble came. Being the only gentry in the parish, the Durhams communicated separately, and to have the whole village looking on while she and her daughters knelt without Clive in the middle of that long footstool cut her with shame and stung her into anger. They quarrelled. He saw her for what she really was – withered, unsympathetic, empty – and in his disillusion found himself thinking vividly of Hall.

Hall: he was only one of several men whom he rather liked. True he, also, had a mother and two sisters, but Clive was too level-headed to pretend this was the only bond between them. He must like Hall more than he realized – must be a little in love with him. And as soon as they met he had a rush of emotion that carried him into intimacy.

The man was bourgeois, unfinished and stupid – the worst of confidants. Yet he told about his home troubles, touched out of all proportion by his dismissal of Chapman. When Hall started teasing he was charmed. Others held off, regarding him as sedate, and he liked being thrown about by a powerful and handsome boy. It was delightful too when Hall stroked his hair: the faces of the two people in the room would fade: he leant back till his cheek brushed the flannel of the trousers and felt the warmth strike through. He was under no illusion on these occasions. He knew what kind of pleasure he was receiving, and received it honestly, certain that it brought no harm to either of them. Hall was a man who only liked women – one could tell that at a glance.

Towards the end of the term he noticed that Hall had acquired a peculiar and beautiful expression. It came only now and then, was subtle and lay far down; he noticed it first when they were squabbling about theology. It was affectionate, kindly, and to that extent a natural expression, but there was mixed in it something that he had not observed in the man, a touch of – impudence? He was not sure, but liked it. It recurred when they met suddenly or had been silent. It beckoned to him across intellect, saying, 'This is all very well, you're clever, we know – but come!' It haunted him so that he watched for it while his brain and tongue were busy, and when it came he felt himself replying, 'I'll come – I didn't know.'

'You can't help yourself now. You must come.'

'I don't want to help myself.'

'Come then.'

He did come. He flung down all the barriers – not at once, for he did not live in a house that can be destroyed in a day. All that term and through letters afterwards he made the path clear. Once certain that Hall loved him, he unloosed his own love. Hitherto it had been dalliance, a passing pleasure for body and mind. How he despised that now. Love was harmonious, immense. He poured into it the dignity as well as the richness of his being, and indeed in that well-tempered soul the two were one. There was nothing humble about Clive. He knew his own worth, and, when he had expected to go through life without love, he had blamed circumstances rather than himself. Hall, though attractive and beautiful, had not condescended. They would meet on an equality next term.

But books meant so much for him he forgot that they were a bewilderment to others. Had he trusted the body there would have been no disaster, but by linking their love to the past he linked it to the present, and roused in his friend's mind the conventions and the fear of the law. He realized nothing of this. What Hall said he must mean. Otherwise why should he say it? Hall loathed him – had said so, 'Oh, rot' – the words hurt more than any abuse, and rang in his ears for days. Hall was the healthy normal Englishman, who had never had a glimmer of what was up.

Great was the pain, great the mortification, but worse followed. So deeply had Clive become one with the beloved that he began to loathe himself. His whole philosophy of life broke down, and the sense of sin was reborn in its ruins, and crawled along corridors. Hall had said he was a criminal, and must know. He was damned. He dare never be friends with a young man again, for fear of corrupting him. Had he not lost Hall his faith in Christianity and attempted his purity besides?

During those three weeks Clive altered immensely, and was beyond the reach of argument when Hall – good, blundering creature – came to his room to comfort him, tried this and that without success and vanished in a gust of temper. 'Oh, go to Hell, it's all you're fit for.' Never a truer word but hard to accept from the beloved. Clive's defeat increased: his life had been blown to pieces, and he felt no inward strength to rebuild it and clear out evil. His conclusion was 'Ridiculous boy! I never loved him. I only had an image I made up in my polluted mind, and may God help me to get rid of it.'

But it was this image that visited his sleep, and caused him to whisper its name.

'Maurice . . .'

'Clive . . .'

'Hall!' he gasped, fully awake. Warmth was upon him. 'Maurice, Maurice, Maurice . . . Oh *Maurice* –'

'I know.'

'Maurice, I love you.'

'I you.'

They kissed, scarcely wishing it. Then Maurice vanished as he had come, through the window.

13

'I've missed two lectures already,' remarked Maurice, who was breakfasting in his pyjamas.

'Cut them all – he'll only gate you.'

'Will you come out in the side-car?'

'Yes, but a long way,' said Clive, lighting a cigarette. 'I can't stick Cambridge in this weather. Let's get right outside it ever so far and bathe. I can work as we go along – Oh damnation!' – for there were steps on the stairs. Joey Fetherstonhaugh looked in and asked one or other of them to play tennis with him that afternoon. Maurice accepted.

'Maurice! What did you do that for, you fool?'

'Cleared him out quickest. Clive, meet me at the garage in twenty minutes, bring your putrid books and borrow Joey's goggles. I must dress. Bring some lunch too.'

'What about horses instead?'

'Too slow.'

They met as arranged. Joey's goggles had offered no difficulty, as he had been out. But as they threaded Jesus Lane they were hailed by the Dean.

'Hall, haven't you a lecture?'

'I overslept,' called Maurice contemptuously.

'Hall! Hall! Stop when I speak.'

Maurice went on. 'No good arguing,' he observed.

'Not the least.'

They swirled across the bridge and into the Ely road. Maurice said, 'Now we'll go to Hell.' The machine was powerful, he reckless naturally. It leapt forward into the fens and the receding dome of the sky. They became a cloud of dust, a stench, and a roar to the world, but the air they breathed was pure, and all the noise they heard was the long drawn cheer of the wind. They cared for no one, they were outside humanity, and death, had it come, would only have continued their pursuit of a retreating horizon. A tower, a town – it had been

Ely – were behind them, in front the same sky, paling at last as though heralding the sea. 'Right turn,' again, then 'left,' 'right,' until all sense of direction was gone. There was a rip, a grate. Maurice took no notice. A noise arose as of a thousand pebbles being shaken together between his legs. No accident occurred, but the machine came to a standstill among the dark black fields. The song of the lark was heard, the trail of dust began to settle behind them. They were alone.

'Let's eat,' said Clive.

They ate on a grassy embankment. Above them the waters of a dyke moved imperceptibly, and reflected interminable willow trees. Man who had created the whole landscape was nowhere to be seen. After lunch Clive thought he ought to work. He spread out his books and was asleep in ten minutes. Maurice lay up by the water, smoking. A farmer's cart appeared, and it did occur to him to ask which county they were in. But he said nothing, nor did the farmer appear to notice him. When Clive awoke it was past three. 'We shall want some tea soon,' was his contribution.

'All right. Can you mend that bloody bike?'

'Oh yes, didn't something jam?' He yawned and walked down to the machine. 'No, I can't, Maurice, can you?'

'Rather not.'

They laid their cheeks together and began laughing. The smash struck them as extraordinarily funny. Grandpapa's present too! He had given it to Maurice against his coming of age in August. Clive said, 'How if we left it and walked?'

'Yes, who'd do it any harm? Leave the coats and things inside it. Likewise Joey's goggles.'

'What about my books?'

'Leave 'em too.'

'I shan't want them after hall?'

'Oh, I don't know. Tea's more important than hall. It stands to reason – well what are you giggling at? – that if we follow a dyke long enough we must come to a pub.'

'Why, they use it to water their beer!'

Maurice smote him on the ribs, and for ten minutes they played up among the strees, too silly for speech. Pensive again, they stood close together, then hid the bicycle behind dog roses, and started. Clive took his notebook away with him, but it did not survive in any useful form, for the dyke they were following branched.

'We must wade this,' he said. 'We can't go round or we shall never get anywhere. Maurice, look – we must keep in a bee line south.'

'All right.'

It did not matter which of them suggested what that day; the other always agreed. Clive took off his shoes and socks and rolled his trousers up. Then he stepped upon the brown surface of the dyke and vanished. He reappeared swimming.

'All that deep!' he spluttered, climbing out. 'Maurice, no idea! Had you?'

Maurice cried, 'I say, I must bathe properly.' He did so, while Clive carried his clothes. The light grew radiant. Presently they came to a farm.

The farmer's wife was inhospitable and ungracious, but they spoke of her afterwards as 'absolutely ripping'. She did in the end give them tea and allow Clive to dry near her kitchen fire. She 'left payment to them', and, when they overpaid her, grumbled. Nothing checked their spirits. They transmuted everything.

'Good-bye, we're greatly obliged,' said Clive. 'And if any of your men come across the bike: I wish we could describe where we left it better. Anyhow I'll give you my friend's card. Tie it on the bike if they will be so kind, and bring it down to the nearest station. Something of the sort, I don't know. The station master will wire to us.'

The station was five miles on. When they reached it the sun was low, and they were not back in Cambridge till after hall. All this last part of the day was perfect. The train, for some unknown reason, was full, and they sat close together, talking quietly under the hubbub, and smiling. When they parted it was in the ordinary way: neither had an impulse to say anything special. The whole day had been ordinary. Yet it had never come before to either of them, nor was it to be repeated.

14

THE Dean sent Maurice down.

Mr Cornwallis was not a severe official, and the boy had a tolerable record, but he could not overlook so gross a breach of discipline. 'And why did you not stop when I called you, Hall?' Hall made no answer, did not even look sorry. He had a smouldering eye, and Mr Cornwallis, though much annoyed, realized that he was confronted with a man. In a dead, bloodless way, he even guessed what had happened.

'Yesterday you cut chapel, four lectures, including my own translation class, and hall. You have done this sort of thing before. It's unnecessary to add impertinence, don't you think? Well? No reply? You will go down and inform your mother of the reason. I shall inform her too. Until you write me a letter of apology, I shall not recommend your readmission to the college in October. Catch the twelve o'clock.'

'All right.'

Mr Cornwallis motioned him out.

No punishment was inflicted on Durham. He had been let off all lectures in view of his Tripos, and even if he had been remiss the Dean would not have worried him; the best classical scholar of his year, he had won special treatment. A good thing he would no longer be distracted by Hall. Mr Cornwallis always suspected such friendships. It was not natural that men of different characters and tastes should be intimate, and although undergraduates, unlike schoolboys, are officially normal, the dons exercised a certain amount of watchfulness, and felt it right to spoil a love affair when they could.

Clive helped him pack, and saw him off. He said little, lest he depressed his friend, who was still in the heroics, but his heart sank. It was his last term, for his mother would not let him stay up a fourth year, which meant that he and Maurice would never meet in Cambridge again. Their love belonged to it, and particularly to their rooms, so that he could not conceive of their meeting anywhere else. He wished that Maurice had not taken up a strong line with the

Dean, but it was too late now, and that the side-car had not been lost. He connected that side-car with intensities – the agony of the tennis court, the joy of yesterday. Bound in a single motion, they seemed there closer to one another than elsewhere; the machine took on a life of its own, in which they met and realized the unity preached by Plato. It had gone, and when Maurice's train went also, actually tearing hand from hand, he broke down, and returning to his room wrote passionate sheets of despair.

Maurice received the letter the next morning. It completed what his family had begun, and he had his first explosion of rage against the world.

15

'I CAN'T apologize, mother – I explained last night there's nothing to apologize about. They had no right to send me down when everyone cuts lectures. It's pure spite, and you can ask anyone – Ada, do try turning on the coffee instead of the salt water.'

She sobbed, 'Maurice, you've upset mother: how can you be so unkind and brutal?'

'I'm sure I don't mean to be. I don't see I've been unkind. I shall go straight into the business now, like father did, without taking one of their rotten degrees. I see no harm in that.'

'You might have kept your poor father out, he never had any unpleasantness,' said Mrs Hall. 'Oh Morrie, my darling – and we did so look forward to Cambridge.'

'All this crying's a mistake,' announced Kitty, who aspired to the functions of a tonic. 'It only makes Maurice think he's important, which he isn't: he'll write to the Dean as soon as no one wants him to.'

'I shan't. It's unsuitable,' replied her brother, hard as iron.

'I don't see that.'

'Little girls don't see a good deal.'

'I'm not so sure!'

He glanced at her. But she only said that she saw a good deal more than some little boys who thought themselves little men. She was merely maundering, and the fear, tinged with respect, that had arisen in him died down. No, he couldn't apologize. He had done nothing wrong and wouldn't say he had, it was the first taste of honesty he had known for years, and honesty is like blood. In his unbending mood the boy thought it would be possible to live without compromise, and ignore all that didn't yield to himself and Clive! Clive's letter had maddened him. No doubt he is stupid – the sensible lover would apologize and get back to comfort his friend – but it was the stupidity of passion, which would rather have nothing than a little.

They continued talking and weeping. At last he rose, said, 'I can't eat to this accompaniment,' and went into the garden. His mother followed with a tray. Her very softness enraged him, for love develops the athlete. It cost her nothing to muck about with tender words and toast: she only wanted to make him soft too.

She wanted to know whether she had heard rightly, was he refusing to apologize? She wondered what her father would say, and incidentally learnt that the birthday gift was lying beside some East Anglian drove. She grew seriously concerned, for its loss was more intelligible to her than the loss of a degree. The girls minded too. They mourned the bicycle for the rest of the morning, and, though Maurice could always silence them or send them out of earshot, he felt that their pliancy might sap his strength again, as in the Easter vacation.

In the afternoon he had a collapse. He remembered that Clive and he had only been together one day! And they had spent it careering about like fools – instead of in one another's arms! Maurice did not know that they had thus spent it perfectly – he was too young to detect the triviality of contact for contact's sake. Though restrained by his friend, he would have surfeited passion. Later on, when his love took second strength, he realized how well Fate had served him. The one embrace in the darkness, the one long day in the light and the wind, were twin columns, each useless without the other. And all the agony of separation that he went through now, instead of destroying, was to fulfil.

He tried to answer Clive's letter. Already he feared to ring false. In the evening he received another, composed of the words 'Maurice! I love you.' He answered, 'Clive, I love you.' Then they wrote every day and for all their care created new images in each other's hearts. Letters distort even more quickly than silence. A terror seized Clive that something was going wrong, and just before his exam he got leave to run down to town. Maurice lunched with him. It was horrible. Both were tired, and they had chosen a restaurant where they could not hear themselves speak. 'I haven't enjoyed it,' said Clive when he wished good-bye. Maurice felt relieved. He had pretended to himself that he had enjoyed it, and thus increased his misery. They agreed that they would confine themselves to facts in their letters, and only write when anything was urgent. The emotional strain relaxed, and Maurice, nearer to brain fever than he supposed, had several dreamless nights that healed him. But daily life remained a poor business.

His position at home was anomalous: Mrs Hall wished that someone would decide it for her. He looked like a man and had turned out the Howells last Easter; but on the other hand he had been sent down from Cambridge and was not yet twenty-one. What was his place in her house? Instigated by Kitty, she tried to assert herself, but Maurice, after a genuine look of surprise, laid back his ears. Mrs Hall wavered, and, though fond of her son, took the unwise step of appealing to Dr Barry. Maurice was asked to go round one evening to be talked to.

'Well, Maurice, and how goes the career? Not quite as you expected, eh?'

Maurice was still afraid of their neighbour.

'Not quite as your mother expected, which is more to the point.'

'Not quite as anyone expected,' said Maurice, looking at his hands.

Dr Barry then said, 'Oh, it's all for the best. What do you want with a university degree? It was never intended for the suburban classes. You're not going to be either a parson or a barrister or a pedagogue. And you are not a county gentleman. Sheer waste of time. Get into harness at once. Quite right to insult the Dean. The city's your place. Your mother –' He paused and lit a cigar, the boy had been offered nothing. 'Your mother doesn't understand this. Worrying because you don't apologize. For my own part I think these things right themselves. You got into an atmosphere for which you are not suited, and you've very properly taken the first opportunity to get out of it.'

'How do you mean, sir?'

'Oh. Not sufficiently clear? I mean that the county gentleman would apologize by instinct if he found he had behaved like a cad. You've a different tradition.'

'I think I must be getting home now,' said Maurice, not without dignity.

'Yes, I think you must. I didn't invite you to have a pleasant evening, as I hope you have realized.'

'You've spoken straight – perhaps some day I shall too. I know I'd like to.'

This set the Doctor off, and he cried:

'How dare you bully your mother, Maurice. You ought to be horsewhipped. You young puppy! Swaggering about instead of asking her to forgive you! I know all about it. She came here with tears in her eyes and asked me to speak. She and your sisters are my respected neighbours, and as long as a woman calls me I'm at her

79

service. Don't answer me, sir, don't answer, I want none of your speech, straight or otherwise. You are a disgrace to chivalry. I don't know what the world is coming to. I don't know what the world – I'm disappointed and disgusted with you.'

Maurice, outside at last, mopped his forehead. He was ashamed in a way. He knew he had behaved badly to his mother, and all the snob in him had been touched to the raw. But somehow he could not retract, could not alter. Once out of the rut, he seemed out of it for ever. 'A disgrace to chivalry.' He considered the accusation. If a woman had been in that side-car, if then he had refused to stop at the Dean's bidding, would Dr Barry have required an apology from him? Surely not. He followed out this train of thought with difficulty. His brain was still feeble. But he was obliged to use it, for so much in current speech and ideas needed translation before he could understand them.

His mother met him, looking ashamed herself; she felt, as he did, that she ought to have done her own scolding. Maurice had grown up, she complained to Kitty; the children went from one; it was all very sad. Kitty asserted her brother was still nothing but a boy, but all these women had a sense of some change in his mouth and eyes and voice since he had faced Dr Barry.

16

THE Durhams lived in a remote part of England on the Wilts and Somerset border. Though not an old family they had held land for four generations, and its influence had passed into them. Clive's great-great-uncle had been Lord Chief Justice in the reign of George IV, and the nest he had feathered was Penge. The feathers were inclined to blow about now. A hundred years had nibbled into the fortune, which no wealthy bride had replenished, and both house and estate were marked, not indeed with decay, but with the immobility that precedes it.

The house lay among woods. A park, still ridged with the lines of vanished hedges, stretched around, giving light and air and pasture to horses and Alderney cows. Beyond it the trees began, most planted by old Sir Edwin, who had annexed the common lands. There were two entrances to the park, one up by the village, the other on the clayey road that went to the station. There had been no station in the old days, and the approach from it, which was undignified and led by the back premises, typified an afterthought of England's.

Maurice arrived in the evening. He had travelled straight from his grandfather's at Birmingham, where, rather tepidly, he had come of age. Though in disgrace, he had not been mulcted of his presents, but they were given and received without enthusiasm. He had looked forward so much to being twenty-one. Kitty implied that he did not enjoy it because he had gone to the bad. Quite nicely he pinched her ear for this and kissed her, which annoyed her a good deal. 'You have no *sense* of things,' she said crossly. He smiled.

From Alfriston Gardens, with its cousins and meat teas, the change to Penge was immense. County families, even when intelligent, have something alarming about them, and Maurice approached any seat with awe. True, Clive had met him and was with him in the brougham, but then so was a Mrs Sheepshanks, who had arrived by his train. Mrs Sheepshanks had a maid, following behind with her luggage and his in a cab, and he wondered whether he ought to have brought a servant too. The lodge gate was held by a little girl. Mrs Sheepshanks wished *everyone* curtsied. Clive trod on his foot when she said this, but he wasn't sure whether accidentally. He was sure of nothing. When they approached he mistook the back for the front, and prepared to open the door. Mrs Sheepshanks said, 'Oh, but that's complimentary.' Besides, there was a butler to open the door.

Tea, very bitter, was awaiting them, and Mrs Durham looked one way while she poured out the other. People stood about, all looking distinguished or there for some distinguished reason. They were doing things or causing others to do them: Miss Durham booked him to canvass tomorrow for Tariff Reform. They agreed politically; but the cry with which she greeted his alliance did not please him. 'Mother, Mr Hall *is* sound.' Major Western, a cousin also stopping in the house, would ask him about Cambridge. Did Army men mind one being sent down? . . . No, it was worse than the restaurant, for there Clive had been out of his element too.

'Pippa, does Mr Hall know his room?'

'The Blue Room, mamma.'

'The one with no fireplace,' called Clive. 'Show him up.' He was seeing off some callers.

Miss Durham passed Maurice on to the butler. They went up a side staircase, Maurice saw the main flight to the right, and wondered whether he was being slighted. His room was small, furnished cheaply. It had no outlook. As he knelt down to unpack, a feeling of Sunnington came over him, and he determined, while he was at Penge, to work through all his clothes. They shouldn't suppose he was unfashionable; he was as good as anyone. But he had scarcely reached this conclusion when Clive rushed in with the sunlight behind him. 'Maurice, I shall kiss you,' he said, and did so.

'Where – what's through there?'

'Our study –' He was laughing, his expression wild and radiant.

'Oh, so that's why –'

'Maurice! Maurice! you've actually come. You're here. This place'll never seem the same again, I shall love it at last.'

'It's jolly for me coming,' said Maurice chokily: the sudden rush of joy made his head swim.

'Go on unpacking. So I arranged it on purpose. We're up this staircase by ourselves. It's as like college as I could manage.'

'It's better.'

'I really feel it will be.'

There was a knock on the passage door. Maurice started, but Clive though still sitting on his shoulder said 'Come in!' indifferently. A housemaid entered with hot water.

'Except for meals we need never be in the other part of the house,' he continued. 'Either here or out of doors. Jolly, eh? I've a piano.' He drew him into the study. 'Look at the view. You may shoot rabbits out of this window. By the way, if my mother or Pippa tells you at dinner that they want you to do this or that tomorrow, you needn't worry. Say 'yes' to them if you like. You're actually going to ride with me, and they know it. It's only their ritual. On Sunday, when you haven't been to church they'll pretend afterwards you were there.'

'But I've no proper riding-breeches.'

'I can't associate with you in that case,' said Clive and bounded off.

When Maurice returned to the drawing-room he felt he had a greater right to be there than anyone. He walked up to Mrs Sheepshanks, opened his mouth before she could open hers and was encouraging to her. He took his place in the absurd octet that was forming to go in – Clive and Mrs Sheepshanks, Major Western and another woman, another man and Pippa, himself and his hostess. She apologized for the smallness of the party.

'Not at all,' said Maurice, and saw Clive glance at him maliciously: he had used the wrong tag. Mrs Durham then put him through his paces, but he did not care a damn whether he satisfied her or not. She had her son's features and seemed equally able, though not equally sincere. He understood why Clive should have come to despise her.

After dinner the men smoked, then joined the ladies. It was a suburban evening, but with a difference; these people had the air of settling something: they either just had arranged or soon would rearrange England. Yet the gateposts, the roads – he had noticed them on the way up – were in bad repair, and the timber wasn't kept properly, the windows stuck, the boards creaked. He was less impressed than he had expected by Penge.

When the ladies retired Clive said, 'Maurice, you look sleepy too.' Maurice took the hint, and five minutes afterwards they met again in

83

the study, with all the night to talk into. They lit their pipes. It was the first time they had experienced full tranquillity together, and exquisite words would be spoken. They knew this, yet scarcely wanted to begin.

'I'll tell you my latest now,' said Clive. 'As soon as I got home I had a row with mother and told her I should stop up a fourth year.'

Maurice gave a cry.

'What's wrong?'

'I've been sent down.'

'But you're coming back in October.'

'I'm not. Cornwallis said I must apologize, and I wouldn't – I thought you wouldn't be up, so I didn't care.'

'And I settled to stop because I thought you would be up. Comedy of Errors.'

Maurice stared gloomily before him.

'Comedy of Errors, not Tragedy. You can apologize now.'

'It's too late.'

Clive laughed. 'Why too late? It makes it simpler. You didn't like to apologize until the term in which your offence was committed had come to an end. "Dear Mr Cornwallis: Now that the term is over, I venture to write to you." I'll draft the letter tomorrow.'

Maurice pondered and finally exclaimed 'Clive, you're a devil.'

'I'm a bit of an outlaw, I grant, but it serves these people right. As long as they talk of the unspeakable vice of the Greeks they can't expect fair play. It served my mother right when I slipped up to kiss you before dinner. She would have no mercy if she knew, she wouldn't attempt, wouldn't want to attempt to understand that I feel to you as Pippa to her fiancé, only far more nobly, far more deeply, body and soul, no starved medievalism of course, only a – a particular harmony of body and soul that I don't think women have even guessed. But you know.'

'Yes. I'll apologize.'

There was a long interval: they discussed the motor bicycle, which had never been heard of again. Clive made coffee.

'Tell me, what made you wake me that night after the Debating Society? Describe.'

'I kept on thinking of something to say, and couldn't, so at last I couldn't even think, so I just came.'

'Sort of thing you would do.

'Are you ragging?' asked Maurice shyly.

'My God!' There was a silence. 'Tell me now about the night I first came up. Why did you make us both so unhappy?'

'I don't know, I say. I can't explain anything. Why did you mislead me with that rotten Plato? I was still in a muddle. A lot of things hadn't joined up in me that since have.'

'But hadn't you been getting hold of me for months? Since first you saw me at Risley's, in fact.'

'Don't ask me.'

'It's a queer business, anyway.'

'It's that.'

Clive laughed delightedly, and wriggled in his chair. 'Maurice, the more I think it over the more certain I am that it's you who are the devil.'

'Oh, all right.'

'I should have gone through life half awake if you'd had the decency to leave me alone. Awake intellectually, yes, and emotionally in a way; but here –' He pointed with his pipe stem to his heart; and both smiled. 'Perhaps we woke up one another. I like to think that anyway.'

'When did you first care about me?'

'Don't ask me,' echoed Clive.

'Oh, be a bit serious – well – what was it in me you first cared about?'

'Like really to know?' asked Clive, who was in the mood Maurice adored – half mischievous, half passionate; a mood of supreme affection.

'Yes.'

'Well, it was your beauty.'

'My what?'

'Beauty . . . I used to admire that man over the bookcase most.'

'I can give points to a picture, I dare say,' said Maurice, having glanced at the Michelangelo. 'Clive, you're a silly little fool, and since you've brought it up I think you're beautiful, the only beautiful person I've ever seen. I love your voice and everything to do with you, down to your clothes or the room you are sitting in. I adore you.'

Clive went crimson. 'Sit up straight and let's change the subject,' he said, all the folly out of him.

'I didn't mean to annoy you at all –'

'Those things must be said once, or we should never know they were in each other's hearts. I hadn't guessed, not so much at least. You've done all right, Maurice.' He did not change the subject but developed it into another that had interested him recently, the precise influence of Desire upon our aesthetic judgements. 'Look at that picture, for instance. I love it because, like the painter himself, I love the subject. I don't judge it with eyes of the normal man. There seem two roads for arriving at Beauty – one is in common, and all the world has reached Michelangelo by it, but the other is private to me and a few more. We come to him by both roads. On the other hand Greuze – his subject matter repels me. I can only get to him down one road. The rest of the world finds two.'

Maurice did not interrupt: it was all charming nonsense to him.

'These private roads are perhaps a mistake,' concluded Clive. 'But as long as the human figure is painted they will be taken. Landscape is the only safe subject – or perhaps something geometric, rhythmical, inhuman absolutely. I wonder whether that is what the Mohammedans were up to and old Moses – I've just thought of this. If you introduce the human figure you at once arouse either disgust or desire. Very faintly sometimes, but it's there. "Thou shalt not make for thyself any graven image" – because one couldn't possibly make it for all other people too. Maurice, shall we rewrite history? "The Aesthetic Philosophy of the Decalogue." I've always thought it remarkable of God not to have damned you or me in it. I used to put it down to him for righteousness, though now I suspect he was merely ill-informed. Still I might make out a case. Shall I choose it for a Fellowship Dissertation?'

'I can't follow, you know,' said Maurice, a little ashamed.

And their love scene drew out, having the inestimable gain of a new language. No tradition overawed the boys. No convention settled what was poetic, what absurd. They were concerned with a passion that few English minds have admitted, and so created untrammelled. Something of exquisite beauty arose in the mind of each at last, something unforgettable and eternal, but built of the humblest scraps of speech and from the simplest emotions.

'I say, will you kiss me?' asked Maurice, when the sparrows woke in the eaves above them, and far out in the woods the ringdoves began to coo.

Clive shook his head, and smiling they parted, having established perfection in their lives, at all events for a time.

17

It seems strange that Maurice should have won any respect from the Durham family, but they did not dislike him. They only disliked people who wanted to know them well – it was a positive mania – and the rumour that a man wished to enter county society was a sufficient reason for excluding him from it. Inside (region of high interchange and dignified movements that meant nothing) were to be found several who, like Mr Hall, neither loved their fate nor feared it, and would depart without a sigh if necessary. The Durhams felt they were conferring a favour on him by treating him as one of themselves, yet were pleased he should take it as a matter of course, gratitude being mysteriously connected in their minds with ill breeding.

Wanting only his food and his friend, Maurice did not observe he was a success, and was surprised when the old lady claimed him for a talk towards the end of his visit. She had questioned him about his family and discovered the nakedness thereof, but this time her manner was deferential: she wanted his opinion of Clive.

'Mr Hall, we wish you to help us: Clive thinks so much of you. Do you consider it wise for him to stop up a fourth year at Cambridge?'

Maurice was wanting to wonder which horse he should ride in the afternoon: he only half attended, which gave an appearance of profundity.

'After the deplorable exhibition he has made of himself in the Tripos – is it wise?'

'He means to,' said Maurice.

Mrs Durham nodded. 'There you have gone to the root of the matter. Clive means to. Well, he is his own master. This place is his. Did he tell you?'

'No.'

'Oh, Penge is his absolutely, under my husband's will. I must move to the dower house as soon as he marries –'

Maurice started; she looked at him and saw that he had coloured. 'So there *is* some girl,' she thought. Neglecting the point for a

88

moment, she returned to Cambridge, and observed how little a fourth year would profit a 'yokel' – she used the word with gay assurance – and how desirable it was that Clive should take his place in the countryside. There was the game, there were his tenants, there were finally politics. 'His father represented the division, as you doubtless know.'

'No.'

'What does he talk to you about?' she laughed. 'Anyhow, my husband was a member for seven years, and though a Lib is in now, one knows that cannot last. All our old friends are looking to him. But he must take his place, he must fit himself, and what on earth is the good of all this – I forget what – advanced work. He ought to spend the year travelling instead. He must go to America and if possible the Colonies. It has become absolutely indispensable.'

'He speaks of travelling after Cambridge. He wants me to go.'

'I trust you will – but not Greece, Mr Hall. That is travelling for play. Do dissuade him from Italy and Greece.'

'I'd prefer America myself.'

'Naturally – anyone sensible would; but he's a student – a dreamer – Pippa says he writes verse. Have you seen any?'

Maurice had seen a poem to himself. Conscious that life grew daily more amazing, he said nothing. Was he the same man who eight months back had been puzzled by Risley? What had deepened his vision? Section after section the armies of humanity were coming alive. Alive, but slightly absurd; they misunderstood *him* so utterly: they exposed their weakness when they thought themselves most acute. He could not help smiling.

'You evidently have . . .' Then suddenly: 'Mr Hall, is there anyone? Some Newnham girl? Pippa declares there is.'

'Pippa had better ask then,' Maurice replied.

Mrs Durham was impressed. He had met one impertinence with another. Who would have expected such skill in a young man? He seemed even indifferent to his victory, and was smiling to one of the other guests, who approached over the lawn to tea. In the tones that she reserved for an equal she said, 'Impress on him about America anyhow. He needs reality. I noticed that last year.'

Maurice duly impressed, when they were riding through the glades alone.

'I thought you were going down,' was Clive's comment. 'Like them. They wouldn't look at Joey.' Clive was in full reaction against his family, he hated the worldliness that they combined with complete ignorance of the World. 'These children will be a nuisance,' he remarked during a canter.

'What children?'

'Mine! The need of an heir for Penge. My mother calls it marriage, but that was all she was thinking of.'

Maurice was silent. It had not occurred to him before that neither he nor his friend would leave life behind them.

'I shall be worried eternally. They've always some girl staying in the house as it is.'

'Just go on growing old –'

'Eh, boy?'

'Nothing,' said Maurice, and reined up. An immense sadness – he believed himself beyond such irritants – had risen up in his soul. He and the beloved would vanish utterly – would continue neither in Heaven nor on Earth. They had won past the conventions, but Nature still faced them, saying with even voice, 'Very well, you are thus; I blame none of my children. But you must go the way of all sterility.' The thought that he was sterile weighed on the young man with a sudden shame. His mother or Mrs Durham might lack mind or heart, but they had done visible work; they had handed on the torch their sons would tread out.

He had meant not to trouble Clive, but out it all came as soon as they lay down in the fern. Clive did not agree. 'Why children?' he asked. 'Why always children? For love to end where it begins is far more beautiful, and Nature knows it.'

'Yes, but if everyone –'

Clive pulled him back into themselves. He murmured something about Eternity in an hour: Maurice did not understand, but the voice soothed him.

18

DURING the next two years Maurice and Clive had as much happiness as men under that star can expect. They were affectionate and consistent by nature, and, thanks to Clive, extremely sensible. Clive knew that ecstasy cannot last, but can carve a channel for something lasting, and he contrived a relation that proved permanent. If Maurice made love it was Clive who preserved it, and caused its rivers to water the garden. He could not bear that one drop should be wasted, either in bitterness or in sentimentality, and as time went on they abstained from avowals ('we have said everything') and almost from caresses. Their happiness was to be together; they radiated something of their calm among others, and could take their place in society.

Clive had expanded in this direction ever since he had understood Greek. The love that Socrates bore Phaedo now lay within his reach, love passionate but temperate, such as only finer natures can understand, and he found in Maurice a nature that was not indeed fine, but charmingly willing. He led the beloved up a narrow and beautiful path, high above either abyss. It went on until the final darkness – he could see no other terror – and when that descended they would at all events have lived more fully than either saint or sensualist, and would have extracted to their utmost the nobility and sweetness of the world. He educated Maurice, or rather his spirit educated Maurice's spirit, for they themselves became equal. Neither thought 'Am I led; am I leading?' Love had caught him out of triviality and Maurice out of bewilderment in order that two imperfect souls might touch perfection.

So they proceeded outwardly like other men. Society received them, as she receives thousands like them. Behind Society slumbered the Law. They had their last year at Cambridge together, they travelled in Italy. Then the prison house closed, but on both of them. Clive was working for the bar, Maurice harnessed to an office. They were together still.

19

By this time their families had become acquainted. 'They will never get on,' they had agreed. 'They belong to different sections of society.' But, perhaps out of perversity, the families did get on, and Clive and Maurice found amusement in seeing them together. Both were misogynists, Clive especially. In the grip of their temperaments, they had not developed the imagination to do duty instead, and during their love women had become as remote as horses or cats; all that the creatures did seemed silly. When Kitty asked to hold Pippa's baby, when Mrs Durham and Mrs Hall visited the Royal Academy in unison, they saw a misfit in nature rather than in society, and gave wild explanations. There was nothing strange really: they themselves were sufficient cause. Their passion for each other was the strongest force in either family, and drew everything after it as a hidden current draws a boat. Mrs Hall and Mrs Durham came together because their sons were friends; 'and now,' said Mrs Hall, 'we are friends too.'

Maurice was present the day their 'friendship' began. The matrons met in Pippa's London house. Pippa had married a Mr London, a coincidence that made a great impression on Kitty, who hoped she would not think of it and laugh during tea. Ada, as too silly for a first visit, had been left at home by Maurice's advice. Nothing happened. Then Pippa and her mother motored out to return the civility. He was in town but again nothing seemed to have happened, except that Pippa had praised Kitty's brains to Ada and Ada's beauty to Kitty, thus offending both girls, and Mrs Hall had warned Mrs Durham against installing hot air at Penge. Then they met again, and as far as he could see it was always like this; nothing, nothing, and still nothing.

Mrs Durham had of course her motives. She was looking out wives for Clive, and put down the Hall girls on her list. She had a theory one ought to cross breeds a bit, and Ada, though suburban, was healthy. No doubt the girl was a fool, but Mrs Durham did not propose to retire to the dower house in practice, whatever she might do in theory, and believed she could best manage Clive through his wife. Kitty had fewer qualifications. She was less foolish, less beautiful, and less rich. Ada would inherit the whole of her grandfather's fortune, which was considerable, and had always inherited his good humour. Mrs Durham met old Mr Grace once, and rather liked him.

Had she supposed the Halls were also planning she would have drawn back. Like Maurice they held her by their indifference. Mrs Hall was too idle to scheme, the girls too innocent. Mrs Durham regarded Ada as a favourable line and invited her to Penge. Only Pippa, into whose mind a breath of modernity had blown, began to think her brother's coldness odd. 'Clive, *are* you going to marry?' she asked suddenly. But his reply, 'No, do tell mother,' dispelled her suspicions: it is the sort of reply a man who is going to marry would make.

No one worried Maurice. He had established his power at home, and his mother began to speak of him in the tones she had reserved for her husband. He was not only the son of the house, but more of a personage than had been expected. He kept the servants in order, understood the car, subscribed to this and not to that, tabooed certain of the girls' acquaintances. By twenty-three he was a promising suburban tyrant, whose rule was the stronger because it was fairly just and mild. Kitty protested, but she had no backing and no experience. In the end she had to say she was sorry and to receive a kiss. She was no match for this good-humoured and slightly hostile young man, and she failed to establish the advantage that his escapade at Cambridge had given her.

Maurice's habits became regular. He ate a large breakfast and caught the 8.36 to town. In the train he read the *Daily Telegraph*. He worked till 1.0, lunched lightly, and worked again through the afternoon. Returning home, he had some exercise and a large dinner, and in the evening he read the evening paper, or laid down the law, or played billiards or bridge.

But every Wednesday he slept at Clive's little flat in town. Weekends were also inviolable. They said at home, 'You must never interfere with Maurice's Wednesdays or with his weekends. He would be most annoyed.'

20

CLIVE got through his bar exams successfully, but just before he was called he had a slight touch of influenza with fever. Maurice came to see him as he was recovering, caught it, and went to bed himself. Thus they saw little of one another for several weeks, and when they did meet Clive was still white and nervy. He came down to the Halls', preferring their house to Pippa's, and hoping that the good food and quiet would set him up. He ate little, and when he spoke his theme was the futility of all things.

'I'm a barrister because I may enter public life,' he said in reply to a question of Ada's. 'But why should I enter public life? Who wants me?'

'Your mother says the country does.'

'If the county wants anyone it wants a Radical. But I've talked to more people than my mother, and they're weary of us leisured classes coasting round in motor-cars and asking for something to do. All this solemn to and fro between great houses – it's a game without gaiety. You don't find it played outside England. (Maurice, I'm going to Greece.) No one wants us, or anything except a comfortable home.'

'But to give a comfortable home's what public life is,' shrilled Kitty.

'Is, or ought to be?'

'Well, it's all the same.'

'Is and ought to be are not the same,' said her mother, proud of grasping the distinction. 'You ought to be not interrupting Mr Durham, whereas you –'

'– is,' supplied Ada, and the family laugh made Clive jump.

'We are and we ought to be,' concluded Mrs Hall. 'Very different.'

'Not always,' contradicted Clive.

'Not always, remember that, Kitty,' she echoed, vaguely admonitory: on other occasions he had not minded her. Kitty cried back to her first assertion. Ada was saying anything, Maurice nothing. He was eating away placidly, too used to such table talk to see that it worried his friend. Between the courses he told an anecdote. All were silent to listen to him. He spoke slowly, stupidly, without attending to his words or taking the trouble to be interesting. Suddenly Clive cut in with 'I say – I'm going to faint,' and fell off his chair.

'Get a pillow, Kitty: Ada, eau de Cologne,' said their brother. He loosened Clive's collar. 'Mother, fan him; no; fan him . . .'

'Silly it is,' murmured Clive.

As he spoke, Maurice kissed him.

'I'm all right now.'

The girls and a servant came running in.

'I can walk,' he said, the colour returning to his face.

'Certainly not,' cried Mrs Hall. 'Maurice'll carry you – Mr Durham, put your arms round Maurice.'

'Come along, old man. The doctor: somebody telephone.' He picked up his friend, who was so weak that he began to cry.

'Maurice – I'm a fool.'

'Be a fool,' said Maurice, and carried him, upstairs, undressed him, and put him to bed. Mrs Hall knocked, and going out to her he said quickly, 'Mother, you needn't tell the others I kissed Durham.'

'Oh, certainly not.'

'He wouldn't like it. I was rather upset and did it without thinking. As you know, we are great friends, relations almost.'

It sufficed. She liked to have little secrets with her son; it reminded her of the time when she had been so much to him. Ada joined them with a hot water bottle, which he took in to the patient.

'The doctor'll see me like this,' Clive sobbed.

'I hope he will.'

'Why?'

Maurice lit a cigarette, and sat on the edge of the bed. 'We want him to see you at your worst. Why did Pippa let you travel?'

'I was supposed to be well.'

'Hell take you.'

'Can we come in?' called Ada through the door.

'No. Send the doctor alone.'

'He's here,' cried Kitty in the distance. A man, little older then themselves, was announced.

'Hullo, Jowitt,' said Maurice, rising. 'Just cure me this chap. He's had influenza, and is supposed to be well. Result he's fainted, and can't stop crying.'

'We know all about that,' remarked Mr Jowitt, and stuck a thermometer into Clive's mouth. 'Been working hard?'

'Yes, and now wants to go to Greece.'

'So he shall. You clear out now. I'll see you downstairs.'

Maurice obeyed, convinced that Clive was seriously ill. Jowitt followed in about ten minutes, and told Mrs Hall it was nothing much – a bad relapse. He wrote prescriptions, and said he would send in a nurse. Maurice followed him into the garden, and, laying a hand on his arm, said, 'Now tell me how ill he is. This isn't a relapse. It's something more. Please tell me the truth.'

'*He's* all right,' said the other; somewhat annoyed, for he piqued himself on telling the truth. 'I thought you realized that. He's stopped the hysteria and is getting off to sleep. It's just an ordinary relapse. He will have to be more careful this time than the other, that's all.'

'And how long will these ordinary relapses, as you call them, go on? At any moment may he have this appalling pain?'

'He's only a bit uncomfortable – caught a chill in the car, he thinks.'

'Jowitt, you don't tell me. A grown man doesn't cry, unless he's gone pretty far.'

'That is only the weakness.'

'Oh, give it your own name,' said Maurice, removing his hand. 'Besides, I'm keeping you.'

'Not a bit, my young friend, I'm here to answer any difficulties.'

'Well, if it's so slight, why are you sending in a nurse?'

'To amuse him. I understand he's well off.'

'And can't we amuse him?'

'No, because of the infection. You were there when I told your mother none of you ought to go into the room.'

'I thought you meant my sisters.'

'You equally – more, for you've already caught it from him once.'

'I won't have a nurse.'

'Mrs Hall has telephoned to the Institute.'

'Why is everything done in such a damned hurry?' said Maurice, raising his voice. 'I shall nurse him myself.'

'Have you wheeling the baby next.'

'I beg your pardon?'

Jowitt went off laughing.

In tones that admitted no argument Maurice told his mother he should sleep in the patient's room. He would not have a bed taken in, lest Clive woke up, but lay down on the floor with his head on a foot-stool, and read by the rays of a candle lamp. Before long Clive stirred and said feebly, 'Oh damnation, oh damnation.'

'Want anything?' Maurice called.

'My inside's all wrong.'

Maurice lifted him out of bed and put him on the night stool. When relief had come he lifted him back.

'I can walk: you mustn't do this sort of thing.'

'You'd do it for me.'

He carried the stool down the passage and cleaned it. Now that Clive was undignified and weak, he loved him as never before.

'You mustn't,' repeated Clive, when he came back. 'It's too filthy.'

'Doesn't worry me,' said Maurice, lying down. 'Get off to sleep again.'

'The doctor told me he'd send a nurse.'

'What do you want with a nurse? It's only a touch of diarrhoea. You can keep on all night as far as I'm concerned. Honestly, it doesn't worry me – I don't say this to please you. It just doesn't.'

'I can't possibly – your office –'

'Look here, Clive, would you rather have a trained nurse or me? One's coming tonight, but I left word she was to be sent away again, because I'd rather chuck the office and look after you myself, and thought you'd rather.'

Clive was silent so long that Maurice thought him asleep. At last he sighed, 'I suppose I'd better have the nurse.'

'Right: she will make you more comfortable than I can. Perhaps you're right.'

Clive made no reply.

Ada had volunteered to sit up in the room below, and, according to arrangement, Maurice tapped three times, and while waiting for her studied Clive's blurred and sweaty face. It was useless the doctor talking: his friend was in agony. He longed to embrace him, but remembered this had brought on the hysteria, and besides, Clive was restrained, fastidious almost. As Ada did not come he went downstairs, and found that she had fallen asleep. She lay, the picture of health, in a big leather chair, with her hands dropped on either side and her feet stretched out. Her bosom rose and fell, her heavy black hair served as a cushion to her face, and between her lips he saw teeth and a scarlet tongue. 'Wake up,' he cried irritably.

Ada woke.

'How do you expect to hear the front door when the nurse comes?'

'How is poor Mr Durham?'

'Very ill; dangerously ill.'

'Oh Maurice! Maurice!'

'The nurse is to stop. I called you, but you never came. Go off to bed now, as you can't even help that much.'

'Mother said I must sit up, because the nurse mustn't be let in by a man – it wouldn't look well.'

'I can't think how you have time to think of such rubbish,' said Maurice.

'We must keep the house a good name.'

He was silent, then laughed in the way the girls disliked. At the bottom of their hearts they disliked him entirely, but were too confused mentally to know this. His laugh was the only grievance they avowed.

'Nurses are not nice. No nice girl would be a nurse. If they are you may be sure they do not come from nice homes, or they would stop at home.'

'Ada, how long were you at school?' asked her brother, as he helped himself to a drink.

'I call going to school stopping at home.'

He set down his glass with a clank, and left her. Clive's eyes were open, but he did not speak or seem to know that Maurice had returned, nor did the coming of the nurse arouse him.

21

IT was plain in a few days that nothing serious was amiss with the visitor. The attack, despite its dramatic start, was less serious than its predecessor, and soon allowed his removal to Penge. His appearance and spirits remained poor, but that must be expected after influenza, and no one except Maurice felt the least uneasiness.

Maurice thought seldom about disease and death, but when he did it was with strong disapproval. They could not be allowed to spoil his life or his friend's, and he brought all his youth and health to bear on Clive. He was with him constantly, going down uninvited to Penge for weekends or for a few days' holiday, and trying by example rather than precept to cheer him up. Clive did not respond. He could rouse himself in company, and even affect interest in a right of way question that had arisen between the Durhams and the British Public, but when they were alone he relapsed into gloom, would not speak, or spoke in a half serious, half joking way that tells of mental exhaustion. He determined to go to Greece. That was the only point on which he held firm. He would go, though the month would be September, and he alone. 'It must be done,' he said. 'It is a vow. Every barbarian must give the Acropolis its chance once.'

Maurice had no use for Greece. His interest in the classics had been slight and obscene, and had vanished when he loved Clive. The stories of Harmodius and Aristogeiton, of Phaedrus, of the Theban Band were well enough for those whose hearts were empty, but no substitute for life. That Clive should occasionally prefer them puzzled him. In Italy, which he liked well enough in spite of the food and the frescoes, he had refused to cross to the yet holier land beyond the Adriatic. 'It sounds out of repair' was his argument. 'A heap of old stones without any paint on. At all events this' – he indicated the library of Siena Cathedral – 'you may say what you like, but it is in working order.' Clive, in his amusement, jumped up and down upon the Piccolomini tiles, and the custodian laughed too instead of scolding them. Italy had been very jolly – as much as one wants in the way of sight-seeing surely – but in these latter days Greece had cropped up again. Maurice hated the very word, and by a curious inversion connected it with morbidity and death. Whenever he wanted to plan, to play tennis, to talk nonsense, Greece intervened. Clive saw his antipathy, and took to teasing him about it, not very kindly.

For Clive wasn't kind: it was to Maurice the most serious of all the symptoms. He would make slightly malicious remarks, and use his intimate knowledge to wound. He failed: i.e., his knowledge was incomplete, or he would have known the impossibility of vexing athletic love. If Maurice sometimes parried outwardly it was because he felt it human to respond: he always had been put off Christ turning the other cheek. Inwardly nothing vexed him. The desire for union was too strong to admit resentment. And sometimes, quite cheerfully, he would conduct a parallel conversation, hitting out at Clive at times in acknowledgement of his presence, but going his own way towards light, in hope that the beloved would follow.

Their last conversation took place on these lines. It was the evening before Clive's departure, and he had the whole of the Hall family to dine with him at the Savoy, as a return for their kindness to him, and had sandwiched them out between some other friends. 'We shall know what it is if you fall *this* time,' cried Ada, nodding at the champagne. 'Your health!' he replied. 'And the health of all ladies. Come, Maurice!' It pleased him to be slightly old-fashioned. Healths were drunk, and only Maurice detected the underlying bitterness.

After the banquet he said to Maurice, 'Are you sleeping at home?'
'No.'

'I thought you might want to see your people home.'

'Not he, Mr Durham,' said his mother. 'Nothing I can do or say can make him miss a Wednesday. Maurice is a regular old bachelor.'

'My flat's upside down with packing,' remarked Clive. 'I leave by the morning train, and go straight through to Marseilles.'

Maurice took no notice, and came. They stood yawning at each other, while the lift descended for them, then sped upwards, climbed another stage on their feet and went down a passage that recalled the approach to Risley's rooms at Trinity. The flat, small, dark and silent, lay at the end. It was, as Clive said, littered with rubbish, but his housekeeper, who slept out, had made up Maurice's bed as usual, and had arranged drinks.

'Yet again,' remarked Clive.

Maurice liked alcohol, and had a good head.

'I'm going to bed. I see you've found what you wanted.'

'Take care of yourself. Don't overdo the ruins. By the way –' He took a phial out of his pocket. 'I knew you'd forget this. Chlorodyne.'

'Chlorodyne! Your contribution!'

He nodded.

'Chlorodyne for Greece . . . Ada has been telling me that you thought I was going to die. Why on earth do you worry about my health? There's no fear. I shan't ever have so clean and clear an experience as death.'

'I know I shall die some time and I don't want to, nor you to. If either of us goes, nothing's left for both. I don't know if you call that clean and clear?'

'Yes, I do.'

'Then I'd rather be dirty,' said Maurice, after a pause.

Clive shivered.

'Don't you agree?'

'Oh, you're getting like everyone else. You will have a theory. We can't go quietly ahead, we must always be formulating, though every formula breaks down. "Dirt at all costs" is to be yours. I say there are cases when one gets too dirty. Then Lethe, if there is such a river, will wash it away. But there may not be such a river. The Greeks assumed little enough, yet too much perhaps. There may be no forgetfulness beyond the grave. This wretched equipment may continue. In other words, beyond the grave there may be Hell.'

'Oh, balls.'

Clive generally enjoyed his metaphysics. But this time he went on. 'To forget everything – even happiness. Happiness! A casual tickling of someone or something against oneself – that's all. Would that we had never been lovers! For then, Maurice, you and I should have lain still and been quiet. We should have slept, then had we been at rest with kings and counsellors of the earth, which built desolate places for themselves –'

'What on earth are you talking about?'

'– or as an hidden untimely birth, we had not been: as infants which never saw light. But as it is – Well, don't look so serious.'

'Don't try to be funny then,' said Maurice. 'I never did think anything of your speeches.'

'Words conceal thought. That theory?'

'They make a silly noise. I don't care about your thoughts either.'

'Then what do you care about in me?'

Maurice smiled: as soon as this question was asked, he felt happy, and refused to answer it.

'My beauty?' said Clive cynically. 'These somewhat faded charms. My hair is falling out. Are you aware?'

'Bald as an egg by thirty.'

'As an addled egg. Perhaps you like me for my mind. During and after my illness I must have been a delightful companion.'

Maurice looked at him with tenderness. He was studying him, as in the earliest days of their acquaintance. Only then it was to find out what he was like, now what had gone wrong with him. Something was wrong. The diseases still simmered, vexing the brain, and causing it to be gloomy and perverse, and Maurice did not resent this: he hoped to succeed where the doctor had failed. He knew his own strength. Presently he would put it forth as love, and heal his friend, but for the moment he investigated.

'I expect you do like me for my mind – for its feebleness. You always knew I was inferior. You're wonderfully considerate – give me plenty of rope and never snub me as you did your family at dinner.'

It was as if he wanted to pick a quarrel.

'Now and then you call me to heel –' He pinched him, pretending to be playful. Maurice started. 'What is wrong now? Tired?'

'I'm off to bed.'

'I.e., you're tired. Why can't you answer a question? I didn't say "tired of me", though I might have.'

'Have you ordered your taxi for the nine o'clock?'

'No, nor got my ticket. I shan't go to Greece at all. Perhaps it'll be as intolerable as England.'

'Well, good night, old man.' He went, deeply concerned, to his room. Why would everyone declare Clive was fit to travel? Clive even knew he wasn't himself. So methodical as a rule, he had put off taking his ticket till the last moment. He might still not go, but to express the hope was to defeat it. Maurice undressed, and catching sight of himself in the glass thought, 'A mercy I'm fit.' He saw a well-trained serviceable body and a face that contradicted it no longer. Virility had harmonized them and shaded either with dark hair. Slipping on his pyjamas, he sprang into bed, concerned, yet profoundly happy, because he was strong enough to live for two. Clive had helped him. Clive would help him again when the pendulum swung, meanwhile he must help Clive, and all through life they would alternate thus: as he dozed off he had a further vision of love, that was not far from the ultimate.

There was a knock at the wall that divided their rooms.

'What is it?' he called; then, 'Come in!' for Clive was now at the door.

'Can I come into your bed?'

'Come along,' said Maurice, making room.

'I'm cold and miserable generally. I can't sleep. I don't know why.'

Maurice did not misunderstand him. He knew and shared his opinions on this point. They lay side by side without touching. Presently Clive said, 'It's no better here. I shall go.' Maurice was not sorry, for he could not get to sleep either, though for a different reason, and he was afraid Clive might hear the drumming of his heart, and guess what it was.

CLIVE sat in the theatre of Dionysus. The stage was empty, as it had been for many centuries, the auditorium empty; the sun had set though the Acropolis behind still radiated heat. He saw barren plains running down to the sea, Salamiss, Aegina, mountains, all blended in a violet evening. Here dwelt his gods – Pallas Athene in the first place: he might if he chose imagine her shrine untouched, and her statue catching the last of the glow. She understood all men, though motherless and a virgin. He had been coming to thank her for years because she had lifted him out of the mire.

But he saw only dying light and a dead land. He uttered no prayer, believed in no deity and knew that the past was devoid of meaning like the present, and a refuge for cowards.

Well, he had written to Maurice at last. His letter was journeying down to the sea. Where one sterility touched another, it would embark and voyage past Sunium and Cythera, would land and embark, would land again. Maurice would get it as he was starting for his work. 'Against my will I have become normal. I cannot help it.' The words had been written.

He descended the theatre wearily. Who could help anything? Not only in sex, but in all things men have moved blindly, have evolved out of slime to dissolve into it when this accident of consequences is over. μὴ φῦναι τὸν ἅπαντα νικᾷ λόγον, sighed the actors in this very place two thousand years before. Even that remark, though further from vanity than most, was vain.

Dear Clive,

Please come back on receiving this. I have looked out your connections, and you can reach England on Tuesday week if you start at once. I am very anxious about you on account of your letter, as it shows how ill you are. I have waited to hear from you for a fortnight and now comes two sentences, which I suppose mean that you cannot love anyone of your own sex any longer. We will see whether this is so as soon as you arrive!

I called upon Pippa yesterday. She was full of the lawsuit, and thinks your mother made a mistake in closing the path. Your mother has told the village she is not closing it against them. I called to get news of you, but Pippa had not heard either. You will be amused to hear that I have been learning some classical music lately – also golf. I get on as well as can be expected at Hill and Hall's. My mother has gone to Birmingham after changing backwards and forwards for a week. Now you have all the news. Wire on getting this, and again on reaching Dover.

Maurice.

Clive received this letter and shook his head. He was going with some hotel acquaintances up Pentelicus, and tore it to pieces on the top of the mountain. He had stopped loving Maurice and should have to say so plainly.

HE stopped a week more at Athens, lest by any possibility he was wrong. The change had been so shocking that sometimes he thought Maurice was right, and that it was the finish of his illness. It humiliated him, for he had understood his soul, or, as he said, himself, ever since he was fifteen. But the body is deeper than the soul and its secrets inscrutable. There had been no warning – just a blind alteration of the life spirit, just an announcement, 'You who loved men, will henceforward love women. Understand or not, it's the same to me.' Whereupon he collapsed. He tried to clothe the change with reason, and understand it, in order that he might feel less humiliated: but it was of the nature of death or birth, and he failed.

It came during illness – possibly through illness. During the first attack, when he was severed from ordinary life and feverish, it seized an opportunity that it would have taken some time or other. He noticed how charming his nurse was and enjoyed obeying her. When he went a drive his eye rested on women. Little details, a hat, the way a skirt is held, scent, laughter, the delicate walk across mud – blended into a charming whole, and it pleased him to find that the women often answered his eye with equal pleasure. Men had never responded – they did not assume he admired them, and were either unconscious or puzzled. But women took admiration for granted. They might be offended or coy, but they understood, and welcomed him into a world of delicious interchange. All through the drive Clive was radiant. How happy normal people made their lives! On how little had he existed for twenty-four years! He chatted to his nurse, and felt her his for ever. He noticed the statues, the advertisements, the daily papers. Passing a cinema palace, he went in. The film was unbearable artistically, but the man who made it, the men and the women who looked on – they knew, and he was one of them.

In no case could the exaltation have lasted. He was like one whose ears have been syringed; for the first few hours he hears super-normal sounds, which vanish when he adjusts himself to the human tradition.

He had not gained a sense, but rearranged one, and life would not have appeared as a holiday for long. It saddened at once, for on his return Maurice was waiting for him, and a seizure resulted: like a fit, it struck at him from behind the brain. He murmured that he was too tired to talk, and escaped, and Maurice's illness gave him a further reprieve, during which he persuaded himself that their relations had not altered, and that he might without disloyalty contemplate women. He wrote affectionately and accepted the invitation to recruit, without misgivings.

He said he caught cold in the car; but in his heart he believed that the cause of his relapse was spiritual: to be with Maurice or anyone connected with him was suddenly revolting. The heat at dinner! The voices of the Halls! Their laughter! Maurice's anecdote! It mixed with the food – was the food. Unable to distinguish matter from spirit, he fainted.

But when he opened his eyes it was to the knowledge that love had died, so that he wept when his friend kissed him. Each kindness increased his suffering, until he asked the nurse to forbid Mr Hall to enter the room. Then he recovered and could fly to Penge, where he loved him as much as ever until he turned up. He noticed the devotion, the heroism even, but his friend bored him. He longed for him to go back to town, and actually said so, so near the surface had the rock risen. Maurice shook his head and stopped.

Clive did not give in to the life spirit without a struggle. He believed in the intellect and tried to think himself back into the old state. He averted his eyes from women, and when that failed adopted childish and violent expedients. The one was this visit to Greece, the other – he could not recall it without disgust. Not until all emotion had ebbed would it have been possible. He regretted it deeply, for Maurice now inspired him with a physical dislike that made the future more difficult, and he wished to keep friends with his old lover, and to help him through the approaching catastrophe. It was all so complicated. When love flies it is remembered not as love but as something else. Blessed are the uneducated, who forget it entirely, and are never conscious of folly or pruriency in the past, of long aimless conversations.

25

CLIVE did not wire, nor start at once. Though desirous to be kind and training himself to think reasonably of Maurice, he refused to obey orders as of old. He returned to England at his leisure. He did wire from Folkestone to Maurice's office, and expected to be met at Charing Cross, and when he was not he took a train on to the suburbs, in order to explain as quickly as possible. His attitude was sympathetic and calm.

It was an October evening; the falling leaves, the mist, the hoot of an owl, filled him with pleasing melancholy. Greece had been clear but dead. He liked the atmosphere of the North, whose gospel is not truth, but compromise. He and his friend would arrange something that should include women. Sadder and older, but without a crisis, they would slip into a relation, as evening into night. He liked the night also. It had graciousness and repose. It was not absolutely dark. Just as he was about to lose his way up from the station, he saw another street lamp, and then past that another. There were chains in every direction, one of which he followed to his goal.

Kitty heard his voice, and came from the drawing-room to welcome him. He had always cared for Kitty least of the family – she was not a true woman, as he called it now – and she brought the news that Maurice was away for the night on business. 'Mother and Ada are in church,' she added. 'They have had to walk because Maurice would take the car.'

'Where has he gone?'

'Don't ask me. He leaves his address with the servants. We know even less about Maurice than when you were last here, if you think that possible. He has become a most mysterious person.' She gave him tea, humming a tune.

Her lack of sense and of charm produced a not unwelcome reaction in her brother's favour. She continued to complain of him in the cowed fashion that she had inherited from Mrs Hall.

'It's only five minutes to church,' remarked Clive.

'Yes, they would have been in to receive you if he had let us know. He keeps everything so secret, and then laughs at girls.'

'It was I who did not let him know.'

'What's Greece like?'

He told her. She was as bored as her brother would have been, and had not his gift of listening beneath words. Clive remembered how often he had held forth to Maurice and felt at the end an access of intimacy. There was a good deal to be saved out of the wreck of that passion. Maurice was big, and so sensible when once he understood.

Kitty proceeded, sketching her own affairs in a slightly clever way. She had asked to go to an Institute to acquire Domestic Economy, and her mother would have allowed her, but Maurice had put his foot down when he heard that the fees were three guineas a week. Kitty's grievances were mainly financial: she wanted an allowance. Ada had one. Ada, as heiress-apparent, had to 'learn the value of money. But I am not to learn anything.' Clive decided that he would tell his friend to treat the girl better; once before he had interfered, and Maurice, charming to the core, had made him feel he could say anything.

A deep voice interrupted them; the churchgoers were back. Ada came in, dressed in a jersey, tam o'shanter and grey skirt; the autumn mist had left a delicate bloom upon her hair. Her cheeks were rosy, her eyes bright; she greeted him with obvious pleasure, and though her exclamations were the same as Kitty's they produced a different effect. 'Why didn't you let us know?' she cried. 'There will be nothing but the pie. We would have given you a real English dinner.'

He said he must return to town in a few minutes but Mrs Hall insisted he should sleep. He was glad to do this. The house now filled with tender memories, especially when Ada spoke. He had forgotten she was so different from Kitty.

'I thought you were Maurice,' he said to her. 'Your voices are wonderfully alike.'

'It's because I have a cold,' she said, laughing.

'No, they are alike,' said Mrs Hall. 'Ada has Maurice's voice, his nose, by which of course I mean the mouth too, and his good spirits and good health. Three things, I often think of it. Kitty on the other hand has his brain.'

All laughed. The three women were evidently fond of one another.

Clive saw relations that he had not guessed, for they were expanding in the absence of their man. Plants live by the sun, yet a few of them flower at night-fall, and the Halls reminded him of the evening primroses that starred a deserted alley at Penge. When talking to her mother and sister, even Kitty had beauty, and he determined to rebuke Maurice about her; not unkindly, for Maurice was beautiful too, and bulked largely in this new vision.

The girls had been incited by Dr Barry to join an ambulance class, and after dinner Clive submitted his body to be bound. Ada tied up his scalp, Kitty his ankle, while Mrs Hall, happy and careless, repeated, 'Well, Mr Durham, this is a better illness than the last anyhow.'

'Mrs Hall, I wish you would call me by my Christian name.'

'Indeed I will. But Ada and Kitty – not you.'

'I wish Ada and Kitty would too.'

'Clive, then!' said Kitty.

'Kitty, then!'

'Clive.'

'Ada – that's better.' But he was blushing. 'I hate formalities.'

'So do I,' came the chorus. 'I care nothing for anyone's opinion – never did,' and fixed him with candid eyes.

'Maurice on the other hand,' from Mrs Hall, 'is very particular.'

'Maurice is a rip really – Waow, you're hurting my head.'

'Waow, waow,' Ada imitated.

There was a ring at the telephone.

'He has had your wire from the office,' announced Kitty. 'He wants to know whether you're here.'

'Say I am.'

'He's coming back tonight, then. Now he wants to talk to you.'

Clive took the receiver, but only a burr arrived. They had been disconnected. They could not ring Maurice up as they did not know where he was, and Clive felt relieved, for the approach of reality alarmed him. He was so happy being bandaged: his friend would arrive soon enough. Now Ada bent over him. He saw features that he knew, with a light behind that glorified them. He turned from the dark hair and eyes to the unshadowed mouth or to the curves of the body, and found in her the exact need of his transition. He had seen more seductive women, but none that promised such peace. She was the compromise between memory and desire, she was the quiet evening that Greece had never known. No argument touched her, because she was tenderness, who reconciles present with past. He had not supposed there was such a creature except in Heaven, and he did not believe in Heaven. Now much had become possible suddenly. He lay looking into her eyes, where some of his hope lay reflected. He knew that he might make her love him, and the knowledge lit him with temperate fire. It was charming – he desired no more yet, and his only anxiety was lest Maurice should arrive, for a memory should remain a memory. Whenever the others ran out of the room to see whether that noise was the car, he kept her with him, and soon she understood that he wished this, and stopped without his command.

'If you knew what it is to be in England!' he said suddenly.

'Is Greece not nice?'

'Horrible.'

She was distressed and Clive also sighed. Their eyes met.

'I'm so sorry, Clive.'

'Oh, it's all over.'

'What exactly was it –'

'Ada, it was this. While in Greece I had to reconstruct my life from the bottom. Not an easy task, but I think I've done it.'

'We often talked of you. Maurice said you would like Greece.'

'Maurice doesn't know – no one knows as much as you! I've told you more than anyone. Can you keep a secret?'

'Of course.'

Clive was nonplussed. The conversation had become impossible. But Ada never expected continuity. To be alone with Clive, whom she innocently admired, was enough. She told him how thankful she was he had returned. He agreed, with vehemence. 'Especially to return here.'

'The car!' Kitty shrieked.

'Don't go!' he repeated, catching her hand.

'I must – Maurice –'

'Bother Maurice,' He held her. There was a tumult in the hall. 'Where's he gone?' his friend was roaring. 'Where've you put him?'

'Ada, take me a walk tomorrow. See more of me . . . That's settled.'

Her brother burst in. Seeing the bandages, he thought there had been an accident, then laughed at his mistake. 'Come out of that,

Clive. Why did you let them? I say, he looks well. You look well. Good man. Come and have a drink. I'll unpick you. No, girls, not you.' Clive followed him, but, turning, had an imperceptible nod from Ada.

Maurice looked like an immense animal in his fur coat. He slipped it off as soon as they were alone, and came up smiling. 'So you don't love me?' he challenged.

'All that must be tomorrow,' said Clive, averting his eyes.

'Quite so. Have a drink.'

'Maurice, I don't want a row.'

'I do.'

He waved the glass aside. The storm must burst. 'But you mustn't talk to me like this,' he continued. 'It increases my difficulties.'

'I want a row and I'll have it.' He came in his oldest manner and thrust a hand into Clive's hair. 'Sit down. Now why did you write me that letter?'

Clive did not reply. He was looking with growing dismay into the face he had once loved. The horror of masculinity had returned, and he wondered what would happen if Maurice tried to embrace him.

'Why? Eh? Now you're fit again, tell me.'

'Go off my chair, and I will.' Then he began one of the speeches he had prepared. It was scientific and impersonal, as this would wound Maurice least, 'I have become normal – like other men, I don't know how, any more than I know how I was born. It is outside reason, it is against my wish. Ask any questions you like. I have come down here to answer them, for I couldn't go into details in my letter. But I wrote the letter because it was true.'

'True, you say?'

'Was and is the truth.'

'You say that you care for women only, not men?'

'I care for men, in the real sense, Maurice, and always shall.'

'All that presently.'

He too was impersonal, but he had not got off the chair. His fingers remained on Clive's head, touching the bandages, his mood had changed from gaiety to quiet concern. He was neither angry nor afraid, he only wanted to heal, and Clive, in the midst of repulsion, realized what a triumph of love was ruining, and how feeble or how ironical must be the power that governs Man.

'Who made you change?'

He disliked the form of the question. 'No one. It was a change in me merely physical.' He began to relate his experiences.

'Evidently the nurse,' said Maurice thoughtfully. 'I wish you had told me before . . . I knew something had gone wrong and thought of several things, but not this. One oughtn't to keep secrets, or they get worse. One ought to talk, talk, talk – provided one has someone to talk to, as you and I have. If you'd have told me, you would have been right by now.'

'Why?'

'Because I should have made you right.'

'How?'

'You'll see,' he said smiling.

'It's not the least good – I've changed.'

'Can the leopard change his spots? Clive, you're in a muddle. It's part of your general health. I'm not anxious now, because you're well otherwise, you even look happy, and the rest must follow. I see you were afraid to tell me, lest it gave me pain, but we've got past sparing each other. You ought to have told me. What else am I here for? You can't trust anyone else. You and I are outlaws. All this' – he pointed to the middle-class comfort of the room – 'would be taken from us if people knew.'

He groaned. 'But I've changed, I've changed.'

We can only interpret by our experiences. Maurice could understand muddle, not change. 'You only think you've changed,' he said, smiling. 'I used to think I had when Miss Olcott was here, but it all went when I returned to you.'

'I know my own mind,' said Clive, getting warm and freeing himself from the chair. 'I was never like you.'

'You are now. Do you remember how I pretended –'

'Of course I remember. Don't be childish.'

'We love each other, and know it. Then what else –'

'Oh, for God's sake, Maurice, hold your tongue. If I love anyone it's Ada.' He added, 'I take her at random as an example.'

But an example was the one thing Maurice could realize. 'Ada?' he said, with a change of tone.

'Only to prove to you the sort of thing.'

'You scarcely know Ada.'

'Nor did I know my nurse or the other women I've mentioned. As I said before, it's no special person, only a tendency.'

'Who was in when you arrived?'

'Kitty.'

'But it's Ada, not Kitty.'

'Yes, but I don't mean – Oh, don't be stupid!'

'What do you mean?'

'Anyhow, you understand, now,' said Clive, trying to keep impersonal, and turning to the comforting words with which his discourse should have concluded. 'I've changed. Now I want you to understand too that the change won't spoil anything in our friendship that is real. I like you enormously – more than any man I've ever met.' (He did not feel this as he said it.) 'I most enormously respect and admire you. It's character, not passion, that is the real bond.'

'Did you say something to Ada just before I came in? Didn't you hear my car come up? Why did Kitty and my mother come out and not you? You must have heard my noise. You knew I flung up my work for you. You never talked to me down the telephone. You didn't write or come back from Greece. How much did you see of her when you were here before?'

'Look here, old man, I can't be cross-questioned.'

'You said you could.'

'Not about your sister.'

'Why not?'

'You must shut up, I say. Come back to what I was saying about character – the real tie between human beings. You can't build a house on the sand, and passion's sand. We want bed rock . . .'

'Ada!' he called, suddenly deliberate.

Clive shouted in horror. 'What for?'

'Ada! Ada!'

He rushed at the door and locked it. 'Maurice, it mustn't end like this – not a row,' he implored. But as Maurice approached he pulled out the key and clenched it, for chivalry had awoken at last. 'You can't drag in a woman,' he breathed; 'I won't have it.'

'Give that up.'

'I mustn't. Don't make it worse. No – no.'

Maurice bore down on him. He escaped: they dodged round the big chair, arguing for the key in whispers.

They touched with hostility, then parted for ever, the key falling between them.

'Clive, did I hurt you?'

'No.'

'My darling, I didn't mean to.'

'I'm all right.'

They looked at one another for a moment before beginning new lives. 'What an ending,' he sobbed, 'what an ending.'

'I do rather love her,' said Clive, very pale.

'What's going to happen?' said Maurice, sitting down and wiping his mouth. 'Arrange . . . I'm done for.'

Since Ada was in the passage Clive went out to her: to Woman was his first duty. Having appeased her with vague words, he returned to the smoking-room, but the door was now locked between them. He heard Maurice turn out the electric light and sit down with a thud.

'Don't be an ass anyway,' he called nervously. There was no reply. Clive scarcely knew what to do. At any rate he could not stop in the house. Asserting a man's prerogative, he announced that he must sleep in town after all, in which the women acquiesced. He left the darkness within for that without: the leaves fell as he went to the station, the owls hooted, the mist enveloped him. It was so late that the lamps had been extinguished in the suburban roads, and total night without compromise weighed on him, as on his friend. He too suffered and exclaimed, 'What an ending!' but he was promised a dawn. The love of women would rise as certainly as the sun, scorching up immaturity and ushering the full human day, and even in his pain he knew this. He would not marry Ada – she had been transitional – but some goddess of the new universe that had opened to him in London, someone utterly unlike Maurice Hall.

Part Three

26

FOR three years Maurice had been so fit and happy that he went on automatically for a day longer. He woke with the feeling that it must be all right soon. Clive would come back, apologizing or not as he chose, and he would apologize to Clive. Clive must love him, because his whole life was dependent on love and here it was going on as usual. How could he sleep and rest if he had no friend? When he returned from town to find no news, he remained for a little calm, and allowed his family to speculate on Clive's departure. But he began to watch Ada. She looked sad – even their mother noticed it. Shading his eyes, he watched her. Save for her, he would have dismissed the scene as 'one of Clive's long speeches', but she came into that speech as an example. He wondered why she was sad.

'I say –' he called when they were alone; he had no idea what he was going to say, though a sudden blackness should have warned him. She replied, but he could not hear her voice. 'What's wrong with you?' he asked, trembling.

'Nothing.'

'There is – I can see it. You can't take me in.'

'Oh no – really, Maurice, nothing.'

'Why did – what did he say?'

'Nothing.'

'Who said nothing?' he yelled, crashing both fists on the table. He had caught her.

'Nothing – only Clive.'

The name on her lips opened Hell. He suffered hideously and before he could stop himself had spoken words that neither ever forgot. He accused his sister of corrupting his friend. He let her suppose that Clive had complained of her conduct and gone back to town on that account. Her gentle nature was so outraged that she could not defend herself, but sobbed and sobbed, and implored him not to speak to her mother, just as if she were guilty. He assented: jealousy had maddened him.

'But when you see him – Mr Durham – tell him I didn't mean – say there's no one whom I'd rather –'

'– go wrong with,' he supplied: not till later did he understand his own blackguardism.

Hiding her face, Ada collapsed.

'I shall not tell him. I shall never see Durham again to tell. You've the satisfaction of breaking up that friendship.'

She sobbed, 'I don't mind that – you've always been so unkind to us, always.' He drew up at last. Kitty had said that sort of thing to him, but never Ada. He saw that beneath their obsequious surface his sisters disliked him: he had not even succeeded at home. Muttering 'It's not my fault,' he left her.

A refined nature would have behaved better and perhaps have suffered less. Maurice was not intellectual, nor religious, nor had he that strange solace of self-pity that is granted to some. Except on one point his temperament was normal, and he behaved as would the average man who after two years of happiness had been betrayed by his wife. It was nothing to him that Nature had caught up this dropped stitch in order to continue her pattern. While he had love he had kept reason. Now he saw Clive's change as treachery and Ada as its cause, and returned in a few hours to the abyss where he had wandered as a boy.

After this explosion his career went forward. He caught the usual train to town, to earn and spend money in the old manner; he read the old papers and discussed strikes and the divorce laws with his friends. At first he was proud of his self-control: did not he hold Clive's reputation in the hollow of his hand? But he grew more bitter, he wished that he had shouted while he had the strength and smashed down this front of lies. What if he too were involved? His family, his position in society – they had been nothing to him for years. He was an outlaw in disguise. Perhaps among those who took to the greenwood in old time there had been two men like himself – two. At times he entertained the dream. Two men can defy the world.

Yes: the heart of his agony would be loneliness. He took time to realize this, being slow. The incestuous jealousy, the mortification, the rage at his past obtuseness – these might pass, and having done much harm they did pass. Memories of Clive might pass. But the loneliness remained. He would wake and gasp 'I've no one!' or 'Oh Christ, what a world!' Clive took to visiting him in dreams. He knew there was no one, but Clive, smiling in his sweet way, said 'I'm genuine this time,' to torture him. Once he had a dream about the dream of the face and the voice, a dream about it, no nearer. Also old dreams of the other sort, that tried to disintegrate him. Days followed nights. An immense silence, as of death, encircled the young man, and as he was going up to town one morning it struck him that he really was dead. What was the use of money-grubbing, eating and playing games? That was all he did or had ever done.

'Life's a damn poor show,' he exclaimed, crumpling up the *Daily Telegraph*.

The other occupants of the carriage who liked him began to laugh.

'I'd jump out of the window for twopence.'

Having spoken, he began to contemplate suicide. There was nothing to deter him. He had no initial fear of death, and no sense of a world beyond it, nor did he mind disgracing his family. He knew that loneliness was poisoning him, so that he grew viler as well as more unhappy. Under these circumstances might he not cease? He began to compare ways and means, and would have shot himself but for an unexpected event. This event was the illness and death of his grandfather, which induced a new state of mind.

Meanwhile, he had received letters from Clive, but they always contained the sentence, 'We had better not meet just yet.' He grasped the situation now – his friend would do anything for him except be with him; it had been thus ever since the first illness, and on these lines he was offered friendship in the future. Maurice did not cease to love, but his heart had been broken; he never had wild thoughts of winning Clive back. What he grasped he grasped with a firmness that the refined might envy, and suffered up to the hilt.

He answered these letters, oddly sincere. He still wrote what was true, and confided that he was unbearably lonely and should blow out his brains before the year ended. But he wrote without emotion. It was more a tribute to their heroic past, and accepted by Durham as such. His replies were unemotional also, and it was plain that, however much help he was given and however hard he tried, he could no longer penetrate into Maurice's mind.

27

Maurice's grandfather was an example of the growth that may come with old age. Throughout life he had been the ordinary business man – hard and touchy – but he retired not too late, and with surprising results. He took to 'reading', and though the direct effects were grotesque, a softness was generated that transformed his character. The opinions of others – once to be contradicted or ignored – appeared worthy of note, and their desires worth humouring. Ida, his unmarried daughter, who kept house for him, had dreaded the time 'when my father will have nothing to do', and herself impervious, did not realize that he had changed until he was about to leave her.

The old gentleman employed his leisure in evolving a new religion – or rather a new cosmogony, for it did not contradict chapel. The chief point was that God lives inside the sun, whose bright envelope consists of the spirits of the blessed. Sunspots reveal God to men, so that when they occurred Mr Grace spent hours at his telescope, noting the interior darkness. The incarnation was a sort of sunspot.

He was glad to discuss his discovery with anyone, but did not proselytize, remarking that each must settle for himself: Clive Durham, with whom he had once had a long talk, knew as much about his opinions as anyone. They were those of the practical man who tries to think spiritually – absurd and materialistic, but first hand. Mr Grace had rejected the tasteful accounts of the unseen that are handed out by the churches, and for that reason the hellenist had got on with him.

Now he was dying. A past of questionable honesty had faded, and he looked forward to joining those he loved and to be joined in due season by those whom he left behind. He summoned his late employees – men without illusions, but they 'humoured the old hypocrite'. He summoned his family, whom he had always treated well. His last days were very beautiful. To inquire into the causes of beauty were to inquire too closely, and only a cynic would dispel the blended Sorrow and Peace that perfumed Alfriston Gardens while a dear old man lay dying.

The relations came separately, in parties of two and three. All, except Maurice, were impressed. There was no intrigue, as Mr Grace had been open about his will, and each knew what to expect. Ada, as the favourite grandchild, shared the fortune with her aunt. The rest had legacies. Maurice did not propose to receive his. He did nothing to force Death on, but it waited to meet him at the right moment, probably when he returned.

But the sight of a fellow-traveller disconcerted him. His grandfather was getting ready for a journey to the sun, and, garrulous with illness, poured out to him one December afternoon. 'Maurice, you read the papers. You've seen the new theory –' It was that a meteor swarm impinged on the rings of Saturn, and chipped pieces off them that fell into the sun. Now Mr Grace located the wicked in the outer planets of our system, and since he disbelieved in eternal damnation had been troubled how to extricate them. The new theory explained this. They were chipped off and reabsorbed into the good! Courteous and grave, the young man listened until a fear seized him that this tosh might be true. The fear was momentary, yet started one of those rearrangements that affect the whole character. It left him with the conviction that his grandfather was convinced. One more human being had come alive. He had accomplished an act of creation, and as he did so Death turned her head away. 'It's a great thing to believe as you do,' he said very sadly. 'Since Cambridge I believe in nothing – except in a sort of darkness.'

'Ah, when I was your age – and now I see a bright light – no electric light can compare to it.'

'When you were my age, grandfather, what?'

But Mr Grace did not answer questions. He said, 'Brighter than magnesium wire – the light within,' then drew a stupid parallel between God, dark inside the glowing sun, and the soul, invisible inside the visible body. 'The power within – the soul: let it out, but not yet, not till the evening.' He paused. 'Maurice, be good to your mother; to your sisters; to your wife and children; to your clerks, as I have.' He paused again and Maurice grunted, but not disrespectfully. He was caught by the phrase, 'not till the evening, do not let it out till the evening.' The old man rambled ahead. One ought to be good – kind – brave: all the old advice. Yet it was sincere. It came from a living heart.

'Why?' he interrupted. 'Grandpapa, why?'

'The light within –'

'I haven't one.' He laughed lest emotion should master him. 'Such light as I had went out six weeks ago. I don't want to be good or kind or brave. If I go on living I shall be – not those things: the reverse of them. I don't want that either; I don't want anything.'

'The light within –'

Maurice had neared confidences, but they would not have been listened to. His grandfather didn't, couldn't understand. He was only to get 'the light within – be kind', yet the phrase continued the rearrangement that had begun inside him. Why *should* one be kind and good? For someone's sake – for the sake of Clive or God or the sun? But he had no one. No one except his mother mattered and she only a little. He was practically alone, and why should he go on living? There was really no reason, yet he had a dreary feeling he should, because he had not got Death either; she, like Love, had glanced at him for a minute, then turned away, and left him to 'play the game'. And he might have to play as long as his grandfather, and retire as absurdly.

28

HIS change, then, cannot be described as a conversion. There was nothing edifying about it. When he came home and examined the pistol he would never use, he was seized with disgust; when he greeted his mother no unfathomable love for her welled up. He lived on, miserable and misunderstood, as before, and increasingly lonely. One cannot write those words too often: Maurice's loneliness: it increased.

But a change there had been. He set himself to acquire new habits, and in particular those minor arts of life that he had neglected when with Clive. Punctuality, courtesy, patriotism, chivalry even – here were a few. He practised a severe self-discipline. It was necessary not only to acquire the art, but to know when to apply it, and gently to modify his behaviour. At first he could do little. He had taken up a line to which his family and the world were accustomed, and any deviation worried them. This came out very strongly in a conversation with Ada.

Ada had become engaged to his old chum Chapman, and his hideous rivalry with her could end. Even after his grandfather's death he had feared she might marry Clive, and gone hot with jealousy. Clive would marry someone. But the thought of him with Ada remained maddening, and he could scarcely have behaved properly unless it had been removed

The match was excellent, and having approved of it publicly he took her aside, and said, 'Ada, I behaved so badly to you, dear, after Clive's visit. I want to say so now and ask you to forgive me. It's given a lot of pain since. I'm very sorry.'

She looked surprised and not quite pleased; he saw that she still disliked him. She muttered, 'That's all over – I love Arthur now.'

'I wish I had not gone mad that evening, but I happened to be very much worried about something. Clive never said what I let you think he said either. He never blamed you.'

'I don't care whether he did. It doesn't signify.'

Her brother's apologies were so rare that she seized the opportunity to trample on him. 'When did you last see him?' – Kitty had suggested they had quarrelled.

'Not for some time.'

'Those weekends and Wednesdays seem to have quite stopped.'

'I wish you happiness. Old Chappie's a good fellow. For two people who are in love to marry strikes me as very jolly.'

'It's very kind of you to wish me happiness, Maurice, I'm sure. I hope I shall have it whether I am wished it or not.' (This was described to Chapman afterwards as a 'repartee'.) 'I'm sure I wish you the same sort of thing you've been wishing me all along equally.' Her face reddened. She had suffered a good deal, and was by no means indifferent to Clive, whose withdrawal had hurt her.

Maurice guessed as much and looked gloomily at her. Then he changed the subject, and, being without memory, she recovered her temper. But she could not forgive her brother: indeed it was not right that one of her temperament should, since he had insulted her centrally, and marred the dawning of a love.

Similar difficulties arose with Kitty. She also was on his conscience, but was displeased when he made amends. He offered to pay her fees at the Domestic Institute whereon her soul had been so long set, and, though she accepted, it was ungraciously, and with the remark, 'I expect I'm too old now to properly learn anything.' She and Ada incited each other to thwart him in little things. Mrs Hall was shocked at first and rebuked them, but finding her son too indifferent to protect himself, she grew indifferent too. She was fond of him, but would not fight for him any more than she would fight against him when he was rude to the Dean. And so it happened that he was considered less in the house, and during the winter rather lost the position he had won at Cambridge. It began to be 'Oh, Maurice won't mind – he can walk – sleep on the camp bed – smoke without a fire.' He raised no objection – this was the sort of thing he now lived for – but he noted the subtle change and how it coincided with the coming of loneliness.

The world was likewise puzzled. He joined the Territorials – hitherto he had held off on the ground that the country can only be saved by conscription. He supported the social work even of the Church. He gave up Saturday golf in order to play football with the youths of the College Settlement in South London, and his Wednesday evenings in order to teach arithmetic and boxing to them. The railway carriage felt a little suspicious. Hall had turned serious, what! He cut down his expenses that he might subscribe more largely to charities – to preventive charities: he would not give a halfpenny to rescue work. What with all this and what with his stockbroking he managed to keep on the go.

Yet he was doing a fine thing – proving on how little the soul can exist. Fed neither by Heaven nor by Earth he was going forward, a lamp that would have blown out, were materialism true. He hadn't a God, he hadn't a lover – the two usual incentives to virtue. But on he struggled with his back to ease, because dignity demanded it. There was no one to watch him, nor did he watch himself, but struggles like his are the supreme achievements of humanity, and surpass any legends about Heaven.

No reward awaited him. This work, like much that had gone before, was to fall ruining. But he did not fall with it, and the muscles it had developed remained for another use.

29

THE crash came on a Sunday in spring – exquisite weather. They sat round the breakfast table, in mourning because of Grandpa, but otherwise worldly. Beside his mother and sisters, there was impossible Aunt Ida, who lived with them now, and a Miss Tonks, a friend whom Kitty had made at the Domestic Institute, and who indeed seemed its only tangible product. Between Ada and himself stood an empty chair.

'Oh, Mr Durham's engaged to be married,' cried Mrs Hall, who was reading a letter. 'How friendly of his mother to tell me. Penge, a county estate,' she explained to Miss Tonks.

'That won't impress Violet, mother. She's a socialist.'

'Am I, Kitty? Good news.'

'You mean bad news, Miss Tonks,' said Aunt Ida.

'Mother, who toom?'

'You will say "Who toom" as a joke too often.'

'Oh mother, get on, who is she?' asked Ada, having stifled a regret.

'Lady Anne Woods. You can read the letter for yourselves. He met her in Greece. Lady Anne Woods. Daughter of Sir H. Woods.'

There was an outcry among the well-informed. It was subsequently found that Mrs Durham's sentence ran, 'I will now tell you the name of the lady: Anne Woods: daughter of Sir H. Woods.' But even then it was remarkable, and owing to Greece romantic.

'Maurice!' said his aunt across the hubbub.

'Hullo!'

'That boy's late.'

Leaning back in his chair he shouted 'Dickie!' at the ceiling: they were putting up Dr Barry's young nephew for the weekend, to oblige.

'He doesn't even sleep above, so that's no good,' said Kitty.

'I'll go up.'

He smoked half a cigarette in the garden and returned. The news had nearly upset him after all. It had come so brutally, and – what hurt him as much – no one behaved as if it were his concern. Nor was it. Mrs Durham and his mother were the principals now. Their friendship had survived the heroic.

He was thinking, 'Clive might have written: for the sake of the past he might', when his aunt interrupted him. 'That boy's never come,' she complained.

He rose with a smile. 'My fault. I forgot.'

'Forgot!' Everyone concentrated on him. 'Forgot when you went out specially? Oh Morrie, you are a funny boy.' He left the room, pursued by humorous scorn, and almost forgot again. 'In there's my work,' he thought, and a deadly lassitude fell on him.

He went upstairs with the tread of an older man, and drew breath at the top. He stretched his arms wide. The morning was exquisite – made for others: for them the leaves rustled and the sun poured into the house. He banged at Dickie Barry's door, and, as that seemed no use, opened it.

The boy, who had been to a dance the night before, remained asleep. He lay with his limbs uncovered. He lay unashamed, embraced and penetrated by the sun. The lips were parted, the down on the upper was touched with gold, the hair broken into countless glories, the body was a delicate amber. To anyone he would have seemed beautiful, and to Maurice who reached him by two paths he became the World's desire.

'It's past nine,' he said as soon as he could speak.

Dickie groaned and pulled up the bedclothes to his chin.

'Breakfast – wake up.'

'How long have you been here?' he asked, opening his eyes, which were all of him that was now visible, and gazing into Maurice's.

'A little,' he said, after a pause.

'I'm awfully sorry.'

'You can be as late as you like – it's only I didn't want you to miss the jolly day.'

Downstairs they were revelling in snobbery. Kitty asked him whether he had known about Miss Woods. He answered 'Yes' – a lie that marked an epoch. Then his aunt's voice arrived, was that boy never coming?

'I told him not to hurry,' said Maurice, trembling all over.

'Maurice, you're not very practical, dear,' said Mrs Hall.

'He's on a visit.'

Auntie remarked that the first duty of a visitor was to conform to the rules of the house. Hitherto he had never opposed her, but now he said, 'The rule of this house is that everyone does what they like.'

'Breakfast is at half past eight.'

'For those who like. Those who are sleepy like breakfast at nine or ten.'

'No house could go on, Maurice. No servants would stop, as you will find.'

'I'd rather servants went than my guests were treated like schoolboys.'

'A schoolboy! Haw! He *is* one!'

'Mr Barry's now at Woolwich,' said Maurice shortly.

Aunt Ida snorted, but Miss Tonks shot him a glance of respect. The others had not listened, intent on poor Mrs Durham, who would now only have the dower house. The loss of his temper left him very happy. In a few minutes Dickie joined them, and he rose to greet his god. The boy's hair was now flat from the bath, and his graceful body hidden beneath clothes, but he remained extraordinarily beautiful. There was a freshness about him – he might have arrived with the flowers – and he gave the impression of modesty and of good will. When he apologized to Mrs Hall, the note of his voice made Maurice shiver. And this was the child he wouldn't protect at Sunnington! This the guest whose arrival last night he had felt rather a bore.

So strong was the passion, while it lasted, that he believed the crisis of his life had come. He broke all engagements, as in the old days. After breakfast he saw Dickie to his uncle's, got arm in arm with him, and exacted a promise for tea. It was kept. Maurice abandoned himself to joy. His blood heated. He would not attend to the talk, yet even this advantaged him, for when he said 'What?' Dickie came over to the sofa. He passed an arm round him . . . The entrance of Aunt Ida may have averted disaster, yet he thought he saw response in the candid eyes.

They met once more – at midnight. Maurice was not happy now, for during the hours of waiting his emotion had become physical.

'I'd a latch key,' said Dickie, surprised at finding his host up.

'I know.'

There was a pause. Both uneasy, they were glancing at each other and afraid to meet a glance.

'Is it a cold night out?'

'No.'

'Can I get you anything before I go up?'

'No, thanks.'

Maurice went to the switches and turned on the landing light. Then he turned out the lights in the hall and sprang after Dickie, overtaking him noiselessly.

'This is my room,' he whispered. 'I mean generally. They've turned me out for you.' He added, 'I sleep here alone.' He was conscious that words were escaping him. Having removed Dickie's overcoat he stood holding it, saying nothing. The house was so quiet that they could hear the women breathing in the other rooms.

The boy said nothing either. The varieties of development are endless, and it so happened that he understood the situation perfectly. If Hall insisted, he would not kick up a row, but he had rather not: he felt like that about it.

'I'm above,' panted Maurice, not daring. 'In the attic over this – if you want anything – all night alone. I always am.'

Dickie's impulse was to bolt the door after him, but he dismissed it as unsoldierly, and awoke to the ringing of the breakfast bell, with the sun on his face and his mind washed clean.

30

THIS episode burst Maurice's life to pieces. Interpreting it by the past, he mistook Dickie for a second Clive, but three years are not lived in a day, and the fires died down as quickly as they had risen, leaving some suspicious ashes behind them. Dickie left on the Monday, and by Friday his image had faded. A client then came into the office, a lively and handsome young Frenchman, who implored Monsieur 'All not to swindle him. While they chaffed, a familiar feeling arose, but this time he smelt attendant odours from the abyss. 'No, people like me must keep our noses to the grindstone, I'm afraid,' he replied, in answer to the Frenchman's prayer to lunch with him, and his voice was so British that it produced shouts of laughter and a pantomime.

When the fellow had gone he faced the truth. His feeling for Dickie required a very primitive name. He would have sentimentalized once and called it adoration, but the habit of honesty had grown strong. What a stoat he had been! Poor little Dickie! He saw the boy leaping from his embrace, to smash through the window and break his limbs, or yelling like a maniac until help came. He saw the police –

'Lust.' He said the word out loud.

Lust is negligible when absent. In the calm of his office Maurice expected to subdue it, now that he had found its name. His mind, ever practical, wasted no time in theological despair, but advanced to the grindstone. He had been forewarned, and therefore forearmed, and had only to keep away from boys and young men to ensure success. Yes, from other young men. Certain obscurities of the last six months became clear. For example, a pupil at the Settlement – He wrinkled his nose, as one who needs no further proof. The feeling that can impel a gentleman towards a person of lower class stands self-condemned.

He did not know what lay ahead. He was entering into a state that would only end with impotence or death. Clive had postponed it. Clive had influenced him, as always. It had been understood between them that their love, though including the body, should not gratify it, and the understanding had proceeded – no words were used – from Clive. He had been nearest to words on the first evening at Penge, when he refused Maurice's kiss, or on the last afternoon there, when they lay amid deep fern. Then had been framed the rule that brought the golden age, and would have sufficed till death. But to Maurice, despite his content, there had been something hypnotic about it. It had expressed Clive, not him, but now that he was alone he cracked hideously, as once at school. And it was not Clive who would heal him. That influence, even if exerted, would have failed, for a relation such as theirs cannot break without transforming both men for ever.

But he could not realize all this. The ethereal past had blinded him, and the highest happiness he could dream was a return to it. As he sat in his office working, he could not see the vast curve of his life, still less the ghost of his father sitting opposite. Mr Hall senior had neither fought nor thought; there had never been any occasion; he had supported society and moved without a crisis from illicit to licit love. Now, looking across at his son, he is touched with envy, the only pain that survives in the world of shades. For he sees the flesh educating the spirit, as his has never been educated, and developing the sluggish heart and the slack mind against their will.

Presently Maurice was called to the telephone. He raised it to his ear, and, after six months' silence, heard the voice of his only friend.

'Hullo,' he began, 'hullo, you will have heard my news, Maurice.'

'Yes, but you didn't write, so I didn't.'

'Quite so.'

'Where are you now?'

'Off to a restaurant. We want you to come round there. Will you?'

'I'm afraid I can't. I've just refused one invitation to lunch.'

'Are you too busy to talk a little?'

'Oh no.'

Clive resumed, evidently relieved by the atmosphere. 'My young woman's with me. Presently she'll talk too.'

'Oh, all right. Tell me all your plans.'

'The wedding's next month.'

'Best of luck.'

Neither could think of anything to say.

'Now for Anne.'

'I'm Anne Woods,' said a girl's voice.

'My name's Hall.'

'What?'

'Maurice Christopher Hall.'

'Mine's Anne Clare Wilbraham Woods, but I can't think of anything to say.'

'No more can I.'

'You're the eighth friend of Clive I've talked to in this way this morning.'

'The eighth?'

'I can't hear.'

'I said the eighth.'

'Oh yes, now I'll give Clive a turn. Good-bye.'

Clive resumed. 'By the way, can you come down to Penge next week? It's short notice, but later all will be chaos.'

'I'm afraid I can't do that very well. Mr Hill's getting married too, so that I'm more or less busy here.'

'What, your old partner?'

'Yes, and after him Ada to Chapman.'

'So I heard. How about August? Not September, that's almost certainly the by-election. But come in August and see us through that awful Park v. Village cricket match.'

'Thanks, I probably could. You had better write nearer the time.'

'Oh, of course. By the way, Anne has a hundred pounds in her pocket. Will you invest it for her?'

'Certainly. What does she fancy?'

'You'd better choose. She's not allowed to fancy more than four per cent.'

Maurice quoted a few securites.

'I'd like the last one,' said Anne's voice. 'I didn't catch its name.'

'You'll see it on the Contract Note. What's your address, please?'

She informed him.

'All right. Send the cheque when you hear from us. Perhaps I'd better ring off and buy at once.'

He did so. Their intercourse was to run on these lines. However pleasant Clive and his wife were to him, he always felt that they stood at the other end of the the telephone wire. After lunch he chose their wedding present. His instinct was to give a thumper, but since he was only eighth on the list of the bridegroom's friends, this would seem out of place. While paying three guineas he caught sight of himself in the glass behind the counter. What a solid young citizen he looked – quiet, honourable, prosperous without vulgarity. On such does England rely. Was it conceivable that on Sunday last he had nearly assaulted a boy?

31

As the spring wore away, he decided to consult a doctor. The decision – most alien to his temperament – was forced on him by a hideous experience in the train. He had been brooding in an ill-conditioned way, and his expression aroused the suspicions and hopes of the only other person in the carriage. This person, stout and greasy-faced, made a lascivious sign, and, off his guard, Maurice responded. Next moment both rose to their feet. The other man smiled, where-upon Maurice knocked him down. Which was hard on the man, who was elderly and whose nose streamed with blood over the cushions, and the harder because he was now consumed with fear and thought Maurice would pull the alarm cord. He spluttered apologies, offered money. Maurice stood over him, black-browed, and saw in this disgusting and dishonourable old age his own.

He loathed the idea of a doctor, but he had failed to kill lust single-handed. As crude as in his boyhood, it was many times as strong, and raged in his empty soul. He might 'keep away from young men', as he had naïvely resolved, but he could not keep away from their images, and hourly committed sin in his heart. Any punishment was prefer-able, for he assumed a doctor would punish him. He could undergo any course of treatment on the chance of being cured, and even if he wasn't he would be occupied and have fewer minutes for brooding.

Whom should he consult? Young Jowitt was the only doctor he knew well, and the day after that railway journey he managed to remark to him in casual tones, 'I say, in your rounds here, do you come across unspeakables of the Oscar Wilde sort?' But Jowitt re-plied, 'No, that's in the asylum work, thank God,' which was dis-couraging, and perhaps it might be better to consult someone whom he should never see again. He thought of specialists, but did not know whether there were any for his disease, nor whether they would keep faith if he confided in them. On all other subjects he could com-mand advice, but on this, which touched him daily, civilization was silent.

In the end he braved a visit to Dr Barry. He knew he should have a bad time, but the old man, though a bully and a tease, was absolutely trustworthy, and had been better disposed to him since his civilities to Dickie. They were in no sense friends, which made it easier, and he went so seldom to the house that it would make little difference were he forbidden it for ever.

He went on a cold evening in May. Spring had turned into a mockery, and a wretched summer was expected also. It was exactly three years since he had come here under balmy skies, to receive his lecture about Cambridge, and his heart beat quicker, remembering how severe the old man had been then. He found him in an agreeable mood, playing bridge with his daughter and wife, and urgent that Maurice should make a fourth in their party.

'I'm afraid I want to speak to you, sir,' he said with an emotion so intense that he felt he should never accomplish the real words at all.

'Well, speak away.'

'I mean professionally.'

'Lord, man, I've retired from practice for the last six years. You go to Jericho or Jowitt. Sit down, Maurice. Glad to see you, shouldn't have guessed you were dying. Polly! Whisky for this fading flower.'

Maurice remained standing, then turned away so oddly that Dr Barry followed him into the hall and said, 'Hi, Maurice, can I seriously do anything for you?'

'I should think you can!'

'I've not even a consulting-room.'

'It's an illness too awfully intimate for Jowitt – I'd rather come to you – you're the only doctor alive I dare tell. Once before I said to you I hoped I'd learn to speak out. It's about that.'

'A secret trouble, eh? Well, come along.'

They went into the dining-room, which was still strewn with dessert. The Venus de Medici in bronze stood on the mantelpiece, copies of Greuze hung on the walls. Maurice tried to speak and failed, poured out some water, failed again, and broke into a fit of sobbing.

'Take your time,' said the old man quite kindly, 'and remember of course that this is professional. Nothing you say will ever reach your mother's ears.'

The ugliness of the interview overcame him. It was like being back in the train. He wept at the hideousness into which he had been forced, he who had meant to tell no one but Clive. Unable to say the right words, he muttered, 'It's about women–'

Dr Barry leapt to a conclusion – indeed he had been there ever since they spoke in the hall. He had had a touch of trouble himself when young, which made him sympathetic about it. 'We'll soon fix that up,' he said.

Maurice stopped his tears before more than a few had issued, and felt the rest piled in an agonizing bar across his brain. 'Oh, fix me for God's sake,' he said, and sank into a chair, arms hanging. 'I'm close on done for.'

'Ah, women! How well I remember when you spouted on the platform at school . . . the year my poor brother died it was . . . you gaped at some master's wife . . . he's a lot to learn and life's a hard school, I remember thinking. Only women can teach us and there are bad women as well as good. Dear, dear!' He cleared his throat. 'Well, boy, don't be afraid of me. Only tell me the truth, and I'll get you well. When did you catch the beastly thing? At the Varsity?'

Maurice did not understand. Then his brow went damp. 'It's nothing as filthy as that,' he said explosively. 'In my own rotten way I've kept clean.'

Dr Barry seemed offended. He locked the door, saying 'Impotent, eh? Let's have a look,' rather contemptuously.

Maurice stripped, throwing the garments from him in a rage. He had been insulted as he had insulted Ada.

'You're all right,' was the verdict.

'What d'ye mean, sir, by all right?'

'What I say. You're a clean man. Nothing to worry about here.'

He sat down by the fire, and, dulled though he was to impressions, Dr Barry noted the pose. It wasn't artistic, yet it could have been called superb. He sat in his usual position, and his body as well as his face seemed gazing indomitably at the flames. He wasn't going to knuckle under – somehow he gave that impression. He might be slow and clumsy, but if once he got what he wanted he would hold to it till Heaven and Earth blushed crimson.

'You're all right,' repeated the other. 'You can marry tomorrow if you like, and if you take an old man's advice you will. Cover up now, it's so draughty. What put all this into your head?'

'So you've never guessed,' he said, with a touch of scorn in his terror. 'I'm an unspeakable of the Oscar Wilde sort.' His eyes closed, and driving clenched fists against them he sat motionless, having appealed to Caesar.

At last judgement came. He could scarcely believe his ears. It was 'Rubbish, rubbish!' He had expected many things, but not this; for if his words were rubbish his life was a dream.

'Dr Barry, I can't have explained –'

'Now listen to me, Maurice, never let that evil hallucination, that temptation from the devil, occur to you again.'

The voice impressed him, and was not Science speaking?

'Who put that lie into your head? You whom I see and know to be a decent fellow! We'll never mention it again. No – I'll not discuss. I'll not discuss. The worst thing I could do for you is to discuss it.'

'I want advice,' said Maurice, struggling against the overwhelming manner. 'It's not rubbish to me, but my life.'

'Rubbish,' came the voice authoritatively.

'I've been like this ever since I can remember without knowing why. What is it? Am I diseased? If I am, I want to be cured, I can't put up with the loneliness any more, the last six months specially. Anything you tell me, I'll do. That's all. You must help me.'

He fell back into his original position, gazing body and soul into the fire.

'Come! Dress yourself.'

'I'm sorry,' he murmured, and obeyed. Then Dr Barry unlocked the door and called, 'Polly! Whisky!' The consultation was over.

32

DR BARRY had given the best advice he could. He had read no scientific works on Maurice's subject. None had existed when he walked the hospitals, and any published since were in German, and therefore suspect. Averse to it by temperament, he endorsed the verdict of society gladly; that is to say, his verdict was theological. He held that only the most depraved could glance at Sodom, and so, when a man of good antecedents and physique confessed the tendency, 'Rubbish, rubbish!' was his natural reply. He was quite sincere. He believed that Maurice had heard some remark by chance, which had generated morbid thoughts, and that the contemptuous silence of a medical man would at once dispel them.

And Maurice went away not unimpressed. Dr Barry was a great name at home. He had twice saved Kitty and had attended Mr Hall through his last illness, and he was so honest and independent and never said what he did not feel. He had been their ultimate authority for nearly twenty years – seldom appealed to, but known to exist and to judge righteousness, and now that he pronounced 'rubbish', Maurice wondered whether it might not be rubbish, though every fibre in him protested. He hated Dr Barry's mind; to tolerate prostitution struck him as beastly. Yet he respected it and went away inclined for another argument with destiny.

He was the more inclined for a reason that he could not tell to the doctor. Clive had turned towards women soon after he reached the age of twenty-four. He himself would be twenty-four in August. Was it possible that he would turn also . . . and now that he came to think, few men married before twenty-four. Maurice had the Englishman's inability to conceive variety. His troubles had taught him that other people are alive, but not yet that they are different, and he attempted to regard Clive's development as a forerunner of his own.

It would be jolly certainly to be married, and at one with society and the law. Dr Barry, meeting him on another day, said, 'Maurice, you get the right girl – there'll be no more trouble then.' Gladys Olcott recurred to him. Of course he was not a crude undergraduate now. He had suffered and explored himself, and knew he was abnormal. But hopelessly so? Suppose he met a woman who was sympathetic in other ways? He wanted children. He was capable of begetting children – Dr Barry had said so. Was marriage impossible after all? The topic was in the air at home, owing to Ada, and his mother would often suggest that he should find someone for Kitty and Kitty someone for him. Her detachment was amazing. The words, 'marriage', 'love', 'a family' had lost all meaning to her during widowhood. A concert ticket sent by Miss Tonks to Kitty revealed possibilities. Kitty could not use it, and offered it round the table. Maurice said he should like to go. She reminded him that it was his Club night, but he said he would cut that. He went, and it happened to be the symphony of Tchaikovsky Clive had taught him to like. He enjoyed the piercing and the tearing and the soothing – the music did not mean more to him than that – and they induced a warm feeling of gratitude towards Miss Tonks. Unfortunately, after the concert he met Risley.

'Symphonie Pathique,' said Risley gaily.

'Symphony Pathetic,' corrected the Philistine.

'Symphonie Incestueuse et Pathique.' And he informed his young friend that Tchaikovsky had fallen in love with his own nephew, and dedicated his masterpiece to him. 'I come to see all respectable London flock. Isn't it *supreme*!'

'Queer things you know,' said Maurice stuffily. It was odd that when he had a confidant he didn't want one. But he got a life of Tchaikovsky out of the library at once. The episode of the composer's marriage conveys little to the normal reader, who vaguely assumes incompatibility, but it thrilled Maurice. He knew what the disaster meant and how near Dr Barry had dragged him to it. Reading on, he made the acquaintance of 'Bob', the wonderful nephew to whom Tchaikovsky turns after the breakdown, and in whom is his spiritual and musical resurrection. The book blew off the gathering dust and he respected it as the one literary work that had ever helped him. But it only helped him backwards. He was where he had been in the train, having gained nothing except the belief that doctors are fools.

Now every avenue seemed blocked, and in his despair he turned to the practices he had abandoned as a boy, and found they did bring him a degraded kind of peace, did still the physical urge into which all his sensations were contracting, and enable him to do his work. He was an average man, and could have won an average fight, but Nature had pitted him against the extraordinary, which only saints can subdue unaided, and he began to lose ground. Shortly before his visit to Penge a new hope dawned, faint and unlovely. It was hypnotism. Mr Cornwallis, Risley told him, had been hypnotized. A doctor had said, 'Come, come, you are no eunuch!' and lo! he had ceased to be one. Maurice procured the doctor's address, but did not suppose anything would come of it: one interview with the science sufficed him, and he always felt Risley knew too much; his voice when he gave the address was friendly but slightly amused.

33

Now that Clive Durham was safe from intimacy, he looked forward to helping his friend, who must have had a pretty rough time since they parted in the smoking-room. Their correspondence had ceased several months ago. Maurice's last had been written after Birmingham, and announced he should not kill himself. Clive had never supposed he would, and was glad the melodrama was over. When they talked down the telephone he heard a man whom he might respect at the other end of it – a fellow who sounded willing to let bygones be bygones and passion acquaintanceship. There was no affectation of ease; poor Maurice sounded shy, a bit huffy even, exactly the condition Clive deemed natural, and felt he could ameliorate.

He was anxious to do what he could. Though the quality of the past escaped him he remembered its proportions, and acknowledged that Maurice had once lifted him out of aestheticism into the sun and wind of love. But for Maurice he would never have developed into being worthy of Anne. His friend had helped him through three barren years, and he would be ungrateful indeed if he did not help his friend. Clive did not like gratitude. He would rather have helped out of pure friendliness. But he had to use the only tool he had, and if all went well, if Maurice kept unemotional, if he remained at the end of a telephone, if he was sound as regarded Anne, if he was not bitter, or too serious or too rough – then they might be friends again, though by a different route and in a different manner. Maurice had admirable qualities – he knew this, and the time might be returning when he would feel it also.

Such thoughts as the above occurred to Clive rarely and feebly. The centre of his life was Anne. Would Anne get on with his mother? Would Anne like Penge, she who had been brought up in Sussex, near the sea? Would she regret the lack of religious opportunities there? And the presence of politics? Besotted with love, he gave her his body and soul, he poured out at her feet all that an earlier passion had taught him, and could only remember with an effort for whom that passion had been.

In the first glow of his engagement, when she was the whole world to him, the Acropolis included, he thought of confessing to her about Maurice. She had confessed a peccadillo to him. But loyalty to his friend withheld him, and he was glad afterwards, for, immortal as Anne proved, she was not Pallas Athene, and there were many points on which he could not touch. Their own union became the chief of these. When he arrived in her room after marriage, she did not know what he wanted. Despite an elaborate education, no one had told her about sex. Clive was as considerate as possible, but he scared her terribly, and left feeling she hated him. She did not. She welcomed him on future nights. But it was always without a word. They united in a world that bore no reference to the daily, and this secrecy drew after it much else of their lives. So much could never be mentioned. He never saw her naked, nor she him. They ignored the reproductive and the digestive functions. So there would never be any question of this episode of his immaturity.

It was unmentionable. It didn't stand between him and her. She stood between him and it, and on second thoughts he was glad, for though not disgraceful it had been sentimental and deserved oblivion.

Secrecy suited him, at least he adopted it without regret. He had never itched to call a spade a spade, and though he valued the body the actual deed of sex seemed to him unimaginative, and best veiled in night. Between men it is inexcusable, between man and woman it may be practised since nature and society approve, but never discussed nor vaunted. His ideal of marriage was temperate and graceful, like all his ideals, and he found a fit helpmate in Anne, who had refinement herself, and admired it in others. They loved each other tenderly. Beautiful conventions received them – while beyond the barrier Maurice wandered, the wrong words on his lips and the wrong desires in his heart, and his arms full of air.

34

MAURICE took a week's holiday in August and reached Penge according to invitation three days before the Park v. Village cricket match. He arrived in an odd and bitter mood. He had been thinking over Risley's hypnotist, and grew much inclined to consult him. It was such a nuisance. For instance, as he drove up through the park he saw a gamekeeper dallying with two of the maids, and felt a pang of envy. The girls were damned ugly, which the man wasn't: somehow this made it worse, and he stared at the trio, feeling cruel and respectable; the girls broke away giggling, the man returned the stare furtively and then thought it safer to touch his cap; he had spoilt that little game. But they would meet again when he had passed, and all over the world girls would meet men, to kiss them and be kissed; might it not be better to alter his temperament and toe the line? He would decide after his visit – for against hope he was still hoping for something from Clive.

'Clive's out,' said the young hostess. 'He sends you his love or something, and will be in to dinner. Archie London will look after you, but I don't believe you want looking after.'

Maurice smiled and accepted some tea. The drawing-room had its old air. Groups of people stood about with the air of arranging something, and though Clive's mother no longer presided she remained in residence, owing to the dower house drains. The sense of dilapidation had increased. Through pouring rain he had noticed gate posts crooked, trees stifling, and indoors some bright wedding presents showed as patches on a threadbare garment. Miss Woods had brought no money to Penge. She was accomplished and delightful, but she belonged to the same class as the Durhams, and every year England grew less inclined to pay her highly.

'Clive's canvassing,' she continued, 'there'll be a by-election in the autumn. He has at last induced them to induce him to stand;' she had the aristocratic knack of anticipating criticism. 'But seriously, it will be a wonderful thing for the poor if he gets in. He is their truest friend, if only they knew it.'

Maurice nodded. He felt disposed to discuss social problems. 'They want drilling a bit,' he said.

'Yes, they need a leader,' said a gentle but distinguished voice, 'and until they find one they will suffer.' Anne introduced the new rector, Mr Borenius. He was her own importation. Clive did not mind whom he appointed if the man was a gentleman and devoted himself to the village. Mr Borenius fulfilled both conditions, and as he was High Church might strike a balance against the outgoing incumbent, who had been Low.

'Oh Mr Borenius, how interesting!' the old lady cried from across the room. 'But I suppose in your opinion we all want a leader. I quite agree.' She darted her eyes hither and thither. 'All of you want a leader, I repeat.' And Mr Borenius's eyes followed hers, perhaps looking for something he did not find, for he soon took leave.

'He can't have anything to do at the Rectory,' said Anne thoughtfully, 'but he always is like that. He comes up to scold Clive about the housing, and won't stop to dinner. You see, he's so sensitive; he worries about the poor.'

'I've had to do with the poor too,' said Maurice, taking a piece of cake, 'but I can't worry over them. One must give them a leg up for the sake of the country generally, that's all. They haven't our feelings. They don't suffer as we should in their place.'

Anne looked disapproval, but she felt she had entrusted her hundred pounds to the right sort of stockbroker.

'Caddies and a college mission in the slums is all I know. Still, I've learned a little. The poor don't want pity. They only really like me when I've got the gloves on and am knocking them about.'

'Oh, you teach them boxing.'

'Yes, and play football . . . they're rotten sportsmen.'

'I suppose they are. Mr Borenius says they want love,' said Anne after a pause.

'I've no doubt they do, but they won't get it.'

'Mr Hall!'

Maurice wiped his moustache and smiled.

'You're *horrible*.'

'I didn't think. I suppose that does sound so.'

'But do you like being horrible?'

'One gets used to anything,' he said, suddenly turning, for the door had blown open behind.

'Well, good gracious me, I scold Clive for being cynical, but you outdo him.'

'I get used to being horrible, as you call it, as the poor do to their slums. It's only a question of time.' He was speaking rather freely; a biting recklessness had come to him since his arrival. Clive hadn't bothered to be in to receive him. Very well! 'After you've banged about a bit you get used to your particular hole. Everyone yapping at the start like a lot of puppies, Waou! Waou!' His unexpected imitation made her laugh. 'At last you learn that everyone's far too busy to listen to you, so you stop yapping. That's a fact.'

'A man's view,' she said, nodding her head. 'I'll never let Clive hold it. I believe in sympathy . . . in bearing one another's burdens. No doubt I'm unfashionable. Are you a disciple of Nietzsche?'

'Ask me another!'

Anne liked this Mr Hall, whom Clive had warned her she might find unresponsive. So he was in a way, but evidently he had personality. She understood why her husband had found him a good travelling companion in Italy. 'Now why don't you like the poor?' she asked suddenly.

'I don't dislike them. I just don't think about them except when I'm obliged. These slums, syndicalism, all the rest of it, are a public menace, and one has to do one's little bit against them. But not for love. Your Mr Borenius won't face facts.'

She was silent, then asked him how old he was.

'Twenty-four tomorrow.'

'Well, you're very hard for your age.'

'Just now you said I was horrible. You're letting me off very easily, Mrs Durham!'

'Anyhow, you're set, which is worse.'

She saw him frown, and, fearing she had been impertinent, turned the talk on to Clive. She had expected Clive to be back by now, she said, and it was the more disappointing because tomorrow Clive would have to be really away. The agent, who knew the constituency, was showing him round. Mr Hall must be forgiving, and he must help them in the cricket match.

'It rather depends upon some other plans . . . I might have to . . .'

She glanced at his face with a sudden curiosity, then said, 'Wouldn't you like to see your room? – Archie, take Mr Hall to the Russet Room.'

'Thanks . . Is there a post out?'

'Not this evening, but you can wire. Wire you'll stop . . . Or oughtn't I to interfere?'

'I may have to wire – I'm not quite sure. Thanks frightfully.' Then he followed Mr London to the Russet Room, thinking 'Clive might have . . . for the sake of the past he might have been here to greet me. He ought to have known how wretched I should feel.' He didn't care for Clive, but he could suffer from him. The rain poured out of a leaden sky on to the park, the woods were silent. As twilight fell, he entered a new circle of torment.

He stopped up in the room till dinner, fighting with ghosts he had loved. If this new doctor could alter his being, was it not his duty to go, though body and soul would be violated? With the world as it is, one must marry or decay. He was not yet free of Clive and never would be until something greater intervened.

'Is Mr Durham back?' he inquired, when the housemaid brought hot water.

'Yes, sir.'

'Just in?'

'No. About half an hour, sir.'

She drew the curtains and hid the sight but not the sound of the rain. Meanwhile Maurice scribbled a wire. ' "Lasker Jones, 6 Wigmore Place, W.," ' he read. ' "Please make appointment Thursday. Hall. C/o Durham, Penge, Wiltshire." '

'Yes, sir.'

'Thanks so much,' he said deferentially, and grimaced as soon as he was alone. There was now a complete break between his public and private actions. In the drawing-room he greeted Clive without a tremor. They shook hands warmly, Clive saying, 'You look awfully fit. Do you know whom you are going to take in?' and introducing him to a girl. Clive had become quite the squire. All his grievances against society had passed since his marriage. Agreeing politically, they had plenty to talk about.

On his side, Clive was pleased with his visitor. Anne had reported him as 'rough, but very nice' – a satisfactory condition. There was a coarseness of fibre about him, but that didn't matter now: that horrible scene about Ada could be forgotten. Maurice also got on well with Archie London – important, for Archie bored Anne and was the sort of man who could fix on to someone. Clive assigned them to each other, for the visit.

In the drawing-room they talked politics again, convinced every one of them that radicals are untruthful, and socialists mad. The rain poured down with a monotony nothing could disturb. In the lulls of conversation its whisper entered the room, and towards the end of the evening there was 'tap, tap' on the lid of the piano.

'The family ghost again,' said Mrs Durham with a bright smile.

'There's the sweetest hole in the ceiling,' cried Anne. 'Clive, can't we leave it?'

'We shall have to,' he remarked, ringing the bell. 'Let's shift our pianoforte though. It won't stand much more.'

'How about a saucer?' said Mr London. 'Clive, how about a saucer? Once the rain came through the ceiling of the club. I rang the bell and the servant brought a saucer.'

'I ring the bell and the servant brings nothing,' said Clive, pealing again. 'Yes, we'll have a saucer, Archie, but we must move the piano too. Anne's dear little hole may grow in the night. There's only a lean-to roof over this part of the room.'

'Poor Penge!' said his mother. All had risen to their feet, and were gazing at the leak, Anne began to probe the piano's entrails with blotting paper. The evening had broken up, and they were well content to make fun about the rain, which had sent them this hint of its presence.

'Bring a basin, will you,' said Clive, when the bell was answered, 'and a duster, and get one of the men to help shift the piano and take up the carpet in the bay. The rain's come through again.'

'We had to ring twice, ring twice,' remarked his mother. 'Le delai s'explique,' she added, for when the parlourmaid returned it was with the keeper as well as the valet. 'C'est toujours comme ça quand – we have our little idylls below stairs too, you know.'

'You men, what do you want to do tomorrow?' said Clive to his guests. 'I must go canvassing. Don't come too. It's beyond words dull. Like to take out a gun or what?'

'Very nice,' said Maurice and Archie.

'Scudder, do you hear?'

'Le bonhomme est distrait,' said his mother. The piano had rucked up a rug, and the servants, not liking to raise their voices before gentlefolk, misunderstood one another's orders, and whispered 'What?'

'Scudder, the gentlemen'll shoot tomorrow – I'm sure I don't know what, but come round at ten. Shall we turn in now?'

'Early to bed's the rule here, as you know, Mr Hall,' said Anne. Then she wished the three servants good night and led the way upstairs. Maurice lingered to choose a book. Might Lecky's *History of Rationalism* fill a gap? The rain dripped into the basin, the men muttered over the carpet in the bay, and, kneeling, seemed to celebrate some obsequy.

'Damnation, isn't there anything, anything?'

'– ish, he's not talking to us,' said the valet to the gamekeeper.

Lecky it was, but his mind proved unequal, and after a few minutes he threw it on the bed and brooded over the telegram. In the dreariness of Penge his purpose grew stronger. Life had proved a blind alley, with a muck heap at the end of it, and he must cut back and start again. One could be absolutely transformed, Risley implied, provided one didn't care a damn for the past. Farewell, beauty and warmth. They ended in muck and must go. Drawing the curtains, he gazed long into the rain, and sighed, and struck his own face, and bit his own lips.

35

THE next day was even drearier and the only thing to be said in its favour was that it had the unreality of a nightmare. Archie London chattered, the rain dribbled, and in the sacred name of sport they were urged after rabbits over the Penge estate. Sometimes they shot the rabbits, sometimes missed them, sometimes they tried ferrets and nets. The rabbits needed keeping down and perhaps that was why the entertainment had been forced on them: there was a prudent strain in Clive. They returned to lunch, and Maurice had a thrill: his telegram had arrived from Mr Lasker Jones, granting him an appointment for tomorrow. But the thrill soon passed, Archie thought they had better go after the bunnies again, and he was too depressed to refuse. The rain was now less, on the other hand the mist was thicker, the mud stickier, and towards tea time they lost a ferret. The keeper made out this was their fault, Archie knew better, and explained the matter to Maurice in the smoking-room with the aid of diagrams. Dinner arrived at eight, so did the politicians, and after dinner the drawing-room ceiling dripped into basins and saucers. Then in the Russet Room, the same weather, the same despair, and the fact that now Clive sat on his bed talking intimately did not make any difference. The talk might have moved him had it come earlier, but he had been so pained by the inhospitality, he had spent so lonely and so imbecile a day, that he could respond to the past no longer. His thoughts were all with Mr Lasker Jones, and he wanted to be alone to compose a written statement about his case.

Clive felt the visit had been a failure, but, as he remarked, 'Politics can't wait, and you happen to coincide with the rush.' He was vexed too at forgetting that today was Maurice's birthday – and was urgent that their guest should stop over the match. Maurice said he was frightfully sorry, but now couldn't, as he had this urgent and unexpected engagement in town.

'Can't you come back after keeping it? We're shocking hosts, but it's such a pleasure having you. Do treat the house as an hotel – go your way, and we'll go ours.'

'The fact is I'm hoping to get married,' said Maurice, the words flying from him as if they had independent life.

'I'm awfully glad,' said Clive, dropping his eyes. 'Maurice, I'm awfully glad. It's the greatest thing in the world, perhaps the only one –'

'I know.' He was wondering why he had spoken. His sentence flew out into the rain; he was always conscious of the rain and the decaying roofs at Penge.

'I shan't bother you with talk, but I must just say that Anne guessed it. Women are extraordinary. She declared all along that you had something up your sleeve. I laughed, but now I shall have to give in.' His eyes rose. 'Oh Maurice, I'm so glad. It's very good of you to tell me – it's what I've always wished for you.'

'I know you have.'

There was a silence. Clive's old manner had come back. He was generous, charming.

'It's wonderful, isn't it? – the – I'm so glad. I wish I could think of something else to say. Do you mind if I just tell Anne?'

'Not a bit. Tell everyone,' cried Maurice, with a brutality that passed unnoticed. 'The more the better.' He courted external pressure. 'If the girl I want won't, there's others.'

Clive smiled a little at this, but was too pleased to be squeamish. He was pleased partly for Maurice, but also because it rounded off his own position. He hated queerness, Cambridge, the Blue Room, certain glades in the park were – not tainted, there had been nothing disgraceful – but rendered subtly ridiculous. Quite lately he had turned up a poem written during Maurice's first visit to Penge, which might have hailed from the land through the looking-glass, so fatuous it was, so perverse. 'Shade from the old hellenic ships.' Had he addressed the sturdy undergraduate thus? And the knowledge that Maurice had equally outgrown such sentimentality purified it, and from him also words burst as if they had been alive.

'I've thought more often of you than you imagine, Maurice my dear. As I said last autumn, I care for you in the real sense, and always shall. We were young idiots, weren't we? – but one can get something even out of idiocy. Development. No, more than that, intimacy. You and I know and trust one another just because we were once idiots. Marriage has made no difference. Oh, that's jolly, I do think –'

'You give me your blessing then?'

'I should think so!'

'Thanks.'

Clive's eyes softened. He wanted to convey something warmer than development. Dare he borrow a gesture from the past?

'Think of me all tomorrow,' said Maurice, 'and as for Anne – she may think of me too.'

So gracious a reference decided him to kiss the fellow very gently on his big brown hand.

Maurice shuddered.

'You don't mind?'

'Oh no.'

'Maurice dear, I wanted just to show I hadn't forgotten the past. I quite agree – don't let's mention it ever again, but I wanted to show just this once.'

'All right.'

'Aren't you thankful it's ended properly?'

'How properly?'

'Instead of that muddle last year.'

'Oh with you.'

'Quits, and I'll go.'

Maurice applied his lips to the starched cuff of a dress shirt. Having functioned, he withdrew, leaving Clive more friendly than ever, and insistent he should return to Penge as soon as circumstances allowed this. Clive stopped talking late while the water gurgled over the dormer. When he had gone Maurice drew the curtains and fell on his knees, leaning his chin upon the window sill and allowing the drops to sprinkle his hair.

'Come!' he cried suddenly, surprising himself. Whom had he called? He had been thinking of nothing and the word had leapt out. As quickly as possible he shut out the air and the darkness, and re-enclosed his body in the Russet Room. Then he wrote his statement. It took some time, and, though far from imaginative, he went to bed with the jumps. He was convinced that someone had looked over his shoulder while he wrote. He wasn't alone. Or again, that he hadn't personally written. Since coming to Penge he seemed a bundle of voices, not Maurice, and now he could almost hear them quarrelling inside him. But none of them belonged to Clive: he had got that far.

36

ARCHIE LONDON was also returning to town, and very early next morning they stood in the hall together waiting for the brougham, while the man who had taken them after rabbits waited outside for a tip.

'Tell him to boil his head,' said Maurice crossly. 'I offered him five bob and he wouldn't take it. Damned cheek!'

Mr London was scandalized. What were servants coming to? Was it to be nothing but gold? If so, one might as well shut up shop, and say so. He began a story about his wife's monthly nurse. Pippa had treated that woman more than an equal, but what can you expect with half educated people? Half an education is worse than none.

'Hear, hear,' said Maurice, yawning.

All the same, Mr London wondered whether noblesse didn't oblige.

'Oh, try if you want to.'

He stretched a hand into the rain.

'Hall, he took it all right, you know.'

'Did he, the devil?' said Maurice. 'Why didn't he take mine? I suppose you gave more.'

With shame Mr London confessed this was so. He had increased the tip through fear of a snub. The fellow was the limit evidently, yet he couldn't think it was good taste in Hall to take the matter up. When servants are rude one should merely ignore it.

But Maurice was cross, tired, and worried about his appointment in town, and he felt the episode part of the ungraciousness of Penge. It was in the spirit of revenge that he strolled to the door, and said in his familiar yet alarming way, 'Hullo! So five shillings aren't good enough! So you'll only take gold!' He was interrupted by Anne, who had come to see them off.

'Best of luck,' she said to Maurice with a very sweet expression, then paused, as if inviting confidences. None came, but she added, 'I'm so glad you're not horrible.'

'Are you?'

'Men like to be thought horrible. Clive does. Don't you, Clive? Mr Hall, men are very funny creatures.' She took hold of her necklace and smiled. 'Very funny. Best of luck.' By now she was delighted with Maurice. His situation, and the way he took it, struck her as appropriately masculine. 'Now a woman in love,' she explained to Clive on the doorstep, as they watched their guests start: 'now a woman in love never bluffs – I wish I knew the girl's name.'

Interfering with the house-servants, the keeper carried out Maurice's case to the brougham, evidently ashamed. 'Stick it in then,' said Maurice coldly. Amid wavings from Anne, Clive and Mrs Durham, they started, and London recommenced the story of Pippa's monthly nurse.

'How about a little air?' suggested the victim. He opened the window and looked at the dripping park. The stupidity of so much rain! What did it *want* to rain for? The indifference of the universe to man! Descending into woods, the brougham toiled along feebly. It seemed impossible that it should ever reach the station, or Pippa's misfortune cease.

Not far from the lodge there was a nasty little climb, and the road, always in bad condition, was edged with dog roses that scratched the paint. Blossom after blossom crept past them, draggled by the ungenial year: some had cankered, others would never unfold: here and there beauty triumphed, but desperately, flickering in a world of gloom. Maurice looked into one after another, and though he did not care for flowers the failure irritated him. Scarcely anything was perfect. On one spray every flower was lopsided, the next swarmed with caterpillars, or bulged with galls. The indifference of nature! And her incompetence! He leant out of the window to see whether she couldn't bring it off once, and stared straight into the bright brown eyes of a young man.

'God, why there's that keeper chap again!'

'Couldn't be, couldn't have got here. We left him up at the house.'

'He could have if he'd run.'

'Why should he have run?'

'That's true, why should he have?' said Maurice, then lifted the flap at the back of the brougham and peered through it into the rose bushes, which a haze already concealed.

'Was it?'

'I couldn't see.' His companion resumed the narrative at once, and talked almost without ceasing until they parted at Waterloo.

In the taxi Maurice read over his statement, and its frankness alarmed him. He, who could not trust Jowitt, was putting himself into the hands of a quack; despite Risley's assurances, he connected hypnotism with séances and blackmail, and had often growled at it from behind the *Daily Telegraph*; had he not better retire?

But the house seemed all right. When the door opened, the little Lasker Joneses were playing on the stairs – charming children, who mistook him for 'Uncle Peter', and clung to his hands; and when he was shut into the waiting room with *Punch* the sense of the normal grew stronger. He went to his fate calmly. He wanted a woman to secure him socially and diminish his lust and bear children. He never thought of that woman as a positive joy – at the worst, Dickie had been that – for during the long struggle he had forgotten what Love is, and sought not happiness at the hands of Mr Lasker Jones, but repose.

That gentleman further relieved him by coming up to his idea of what an advanced scientific man ought to be. Sallow and expressionless, he sat in a large pictureless room before a roll-top desk. 'Mr Hall?' he said, and offered a bloodless hand. His accent was slightly American. 'Well, Mr Hall, and what's the trouble?' Maurice became detached too. It was as if they met to discuss a third party. 'It's all down here,' he said, producing the statement. 'I've consulted one doctor and he could do nothing. I don't know whether you can.'

The statement was read.

'I'm not wrong in coming to you, I hope?'

'Not at all, Mr Hall. Seventy-five per cent of my patients are of your type. Is that statement recent?'

'I wrote it last night.'

'And accurate?'

'Well, names and places are a bit changed, naturally.'

Mr Lasker Jones did not seem to think it natural. He asked several questions about 'Mr Cumberland', Maurice's pseudonym for Clive, and wished to know whether they had ever united: on his lips it was curiously inoffensive. He neither praised nor blamed nor pitied: he paid no attention to a sudden outburst of Maurice's against society.

And though Maurice yearned for sympathy – he had not had a word of it for a year – he was glad none came, for it might have shattered his purpose.

He asked, 'What's the name of my trouble? Has it one?'

'Congenital homosexuality.'

'Congenital how much? Well, can anything be done?'

'Oh, certainly, if you consent.'

'The fact is I've an old-fashioned prejudice against hypnotism.'

'I'm afraid you may possibly retain that prejudice after trying, Mr Hall. I cannot promise a cure. I spoke to you of my other patients – seventy-five per cent – but in only fifty per cent have I been successful.'

The confession gave Maurice confidence, no quack would have made it. 'We may as well have a shot,' he said, smiling. 'What must I do?'

'Merely remain where you are. I will experiment to see how deeply the tendency is rooted. You will return (if you wish) for regular treatment later. Mr Hall! I shall try to send you into a trance, and if I succeed I shall make suggestions to you which will (we hope) remain, and become part of your normal state when you wake. You are not to resist me.'

'All right, go ahead.'

Then Mr Lasker Jones left his desk and sat in an impersonal way on the arm of Maurice's chair. Maurice felt he was going to have a tooth out. For a little time nothing happened, but presently his eye caught a spot of light on the fire irons, and the rest of the room went dim. He could see whatever he was looking at, but little else, and he could hear the doctor's voice and his own. Evidently he was going into a trance, and the achievement gave him a feeling of pride.

'You're not quite off yet, I think.'

'No, I'm not.'

He made some more passes. 'How about now?'

'I'm nearer off now.'

'Quite?'

Maurice agreed, but did not feel sure. 'Now that you're quite off, how do you like my consulting-room?'

'It's a nice room.'

'Not too dark?'

'Rather dark.'

'You can see the picture though, can't you?'

Maurice then saw a picture on the opposite wall, yet he knew that there was none.

'Have a look at it, Mr Hall. Come nearer. Take care of that crack in the carpet though.'

'How broad is the crack?'

'You can jump it.'

Maurice immediately located a crack, and jumped, but he was not convinced of the necessity.

'Admirable – now what do you suppose this picture is of, whom is it of –?'

'Whom is it of –'

'Edna May.'

'Mr Edna May.'

'No, Mr Hall, Miss Edna May.'

'It's Mr Edna May.'

'Isn't she beautiful?'

'I want to go home to my mother.' Both laughed at this remark, the doctor leading.

'Miss Edna May is not only beautiful, she is attractive.'

'She doesn't attract me,' said Maurice pettishly.

'Oh Mr Hall, what an ungallant remark. Look at her lovely hair.'

'I like short hair best.'

'Why?'

'Because I can stroke it –' and he began to cry. He came to himself in the chair. Tears were wet on his cheeks, but he felt as usual, and started talking at once.

'I say, I had a dream when you woke me up. I'd better tell it you. I thought I saw a face and heard someone say, "That's your friend." Is that all right? I often feel it – I can't explain – sort of walking towards me through sleep, though it never gets up to me, that dream.'

'Did it get near now?'

'Jolly near. Is that a bad sign?'

'No, oh no – you're open to suggestion, you're open – I made you see a picture on the wall.'

Maurice nodded: he had quite forgotten. There was a pause,

during which he produced two guineas, and asked for a second appointment. It was arranged that he should telephone next week, and in the interval Mr Lasker Jones wanted him to remain where he was in the country, quietly.

Maurice could not doubt that Clive and Anne would welcome him, nor that their influence would be suitable. Penge was an emetic. It helped him to get rid of the old poisonous life that had seemed so sweet, it cured him of tenderness and humanity. Yes, he'd go back, he said: he would wire to his friends and catch the afternoon express.

'Mr Hall, take exercise in moderation. A little tennis, or stroll about with a gun.'

Maurice lingered to say, 'On second thoughts perhaps I won't go back.'

'Why so?'

'Well, it seems rather foolish to make that long journey twice in a day.'

'You prefer then to stop in your own home?'

'Yes – no – no, all right, I will go back to Penge.'

37

ON his return he was amused to find that the young people were just off for twenty-four hours' electioneering. He now cared less for Clive than Clive for him. That kiss had disillusioned. It was such a trivial prudish kiss, and alas! so typical. The less you had the more it was supposed to be – that was Clive's teaching. Not only was the half greater than the whole – at Cambridge Maurice would just accept this – but now he was offered the quarter and told it was greater than the half. Did the fellow suppose he was made of paper?

Clive explained how he wouldn't be going had Maurice held out hopes of returning, and how he would be back for the match any way. Anne whispered, 'Was the luck good?' Maurice replied 'So-so', whereupon she covered him with her wing and offered to invite his young lady down to Penge. 'Mr Hall, is she very charming? I am convinced she has bright brown eyes.' But Clive called her off, and Maurice was left to an evening with Mrs Durham and Mr Borenius.

Unusual restlessness was on him. It recalled the initial night at Cambridge, when he had been to Risley's rooms. The rain had stopped during his dash to town. He wanted to walk about in the evening and watch the sun set and listen to the dripping trees. Ghostly but perfect, the evening primroses were expanding in the shrubbery, and stirred him by their odours. Clive had shown him evening primroses in the past, but had never told him they smelt. He liked being out of doors, among the robins and bats, stealing hither and thither bare-headed, till the gong should summon him to dress for yet another meal, and the curtains of the Russet Room close. No, he wasn't the same; a rearrangement of his being had begun as surely as at Birmingham, when death had looked away, and to Mr Lasker Jones be all credit! Deeper than conscious effort there was a change, which might land him with luck in the arms of Miss Tonks.

As he wandered about, the man whom he had reprimanded in the morning came up, touched his cap and inquired whether he would shoot tomorrow. Obviously he wouldn't, since it was the cricket match, but the question had been asked in order to pave the way for an apology. 'I'm sure I'm very sorry I failed to give you and Mr London full satisfaction, sir,' was its form. Maurice, vindictive no longer, said, 'That's all right, Scudder.' Scudder was an importation – part of the larger life that had come into Penge with politics and Anne; he was smarter than old Mr Ayres the head keeper, and knew it. He implied that he hadn't taken the five shillings because it was too much; he didn't say why he had taken the ten! He added, 'Glad to see you down again so soon, sir,' which struck Maurice as subtly unsuitable, so he repeated, 'That's all right, Scudder,' and went in.

It was a dinner-jacket evening – not tails, because they would only be three – and though he had respected such niceties for years he found them suddenly ridiculous. What did clothes matter as long as you got your food, and the other people were good sorts – which they wouldn't be? And as he touched the carapace of his dress shirt a sense of ignominy came over him, and he felt he had no right to criticize anyone who lived in the open air. How dry Mrs Durham seemed – she was Clive with the sap perished. And Mr Borenius – how dry! Though to do Mr Borenius justice he contained surprises. Contemptuous of all parsons, Maurice had paid little attention to this one, and was startled when he came out strong after dessert. He had assumed that as rector of the parish he would be helping Clive in the election. But 'I vote for no one who is not a communicant, as Mr Durham understands.'

'The Rads are attacking your church, you know,' was all he could think of.

'That is why I do not vote for the Radical candidate. He is a Christian, so naturally I should have done.'

'Bit particular, sir, if I may say so. Clive will do all the things you want done. You may be lucky he isn't an atheist. There are a certain amount of those about, you know!'

He smiled in response, saying, 'The atheist is nearer the Kingdom of Heaven than the hellenist. "Unless ye become as little children" – and what is the atheist but a child?'

Maurice looked at his hands, but before he could frame a reply the valet came in to ask whether he had any orders for the keeper.

'I saw him before dinner. Simcox. Nothing, thanks. Tomorrow's the match. I did tell him.

'Yes, but he wonders whether you'd care to go down to the pond between the innings for a bathe, sir, now that the weather has altered. He has just baled out the boat.'

'Very good of him.'

'If that's Mr Scudder may I speak to him?' asked Mr Borenius.

'Will you tell him, Simcox? Also tell him I shan't be bathing.' When the valet had gone he said, 'Would you rather speak to him here? Have him in as far as I'm concerned.'

'Thank you, Mr Hall, but I'll go out. He'll prefer the kitchen.'

'He'll prefer it no doubt. There are fair young females in the kitchen.'

'Ah! Ah!' He had the air of one to whom sex occurs for the first time. 'You don't happen to know whether he has anyone in view matrimonially, do you?'

' 'Fraid I don't . . . saw him kissing two girls at once on my arrival if that's any help.'

'It sometimes happens that those men get confidential out shooting. The open air, the sense of companionship –'

'They don't get confidential with me. Archie London and I got rather fed up with him yesterday as a matter of fact. Too anxious to boss the show. We found him a bit of a swine.'

'Excuse the inquiry.'

'What's there to excuse?' said Maurice, annoyed with the rector for alluding so smugly to the open air.

'Speaking frankly, I should be glad to see that particular young man settled with a helpmate before he sails.' Smiling gently, he added, 'And all young men.'

'What's he sailing for?'

'He is to emigrate.' And intoning 'to emigrate' in a particular irritating way, he repaired to the kitchen.

Maurice strolled for five minutes in the shrubbery. Food and wine had heated him, and he thought with some inconsequence that even old Chapman had sown some wild oats. He alone – Clive admonishing – combined advanced thought with the conduct of a Sunday scholar. He wasn't Methuselah – he'd a right to a fling. Oh those jolly scents, those bushes where you could hide, that sky as black as the bushes! They were turning away from him. Indoors was his place and there he'd moulder, a respectable pillar of society who has never had the chance to misbehave. The alley that he was pacing opened through a swing gate into the park, but the damp grass there might dull his pumps, so he felt bound to return. As he did so he struck against corduroys, and was held for a moment by both elbows; it had been Scudder escaping from Mr Borenius. Released, he continued his dreamings. Yesterday's shoot, which at the time had made little impression on him, began faintly to glow, and he realized that even during its boredom he had been alive. He felt back from it to the incidents of his arrival, such as the piano-moving: then forwards to the incidents of today, beginning with the five shillings' tip and ending with now. And when he reached 'now', it was as if an electric current had passed through the chain of insignificant events so that he dropped it and let it smash back into darkness. 'Damnation, what a night,' he resumed while puffs of air touched him and one another. Then the swing gate in the distance, which had been tinkling for a little, seemed to slam against freedom, and he went indoors.

'Oh Mr Hall!' cried the old lady. 'How exquisite is your coiffure.'

'My coiffure?' He found that his head was all yellow with evening primrose pollen.

'Oh, don't brush it off. I like it on your black hair. Mr Borenius, is he not quite bacchanalian?'

The clergyman raised sightless eyes. He had been interrupted in the middle of a serious talk. 'But Mrs Durham,' he persisted. 'I understood so distinctly from you that all your servants had been confirmed.'

'I thought so, Mr Borenius, I did think so.'

'Yet I go into the kitchen, and straight away I discover Simcox, Scudder and Mrs Wetherall. For Simcox and Mrs Wetherall I can make arrangements. Scudder is the serious case, because I have not time to prepare him properly before he sails, even if the bishop could be prevailed upon.'

Mrs Durham tried to be grave, but Maurice, whom she rather liked, was laughing. She suggested that Mr Borenius should give Scudder a note to some clergyman abroad – there was bound to be one.

'Yes, but will he present it? He shows no hostility to the Church, but will he be bothered? Had I only been told which of your servants had been confirmed and which had not, this crisis would not have arisen.'

'Servants are so inconsiderate,' said the old lady. 'They tell me nothing. Why, Scudder sprung his notice on Clive in just the same way. His brother invites him. So off he goes. Now Mr Hall, let's have your advice over this crisis: what would you do?'

'Our young friend condemns the entire Church, militant and triumphant.'

Maurice roused himself. If the parson hadn't looked so damned ugly he wouldn't have bothered, but he couldn't stand that squinny face sneering at youth. Scudder cleaned a gun, carried a suitcase, baled out a boat, emigrated – did something anyway, while gentle-folk squatted on chairs finding fault with his soul. If he did cadge for tips it was natural, and if he didn't, if his apology was genuine – why then he was a fine fellow. He'd speak anyhow. 'How do you know he'll communicate if he's confirmed?' he said. 'I don't communicate.' Mrs Durham hummed a tune; this was going too far.

'But you were given the opportunity. The priest did what he could for you. He has not done what he could for Scudder and consequently the Church is to blame. That is why I make so much of a point which must appear very trivial to you.'

'I'm awfully stupid, but I think I see: you want to make sure that he and not the Church shall be to blame in the future. Well, sir, that may be your idea of religion but it isn't mine and it wasn't Christ's.'

It was as smart a speech as he had ever made; since the hypnotism his brain had known moments of unusual power. But Mr Borenius was unassailable. He replied pleasantly, 'The unbeliever has always such a very clear idea as to what Belief ought to be, I wish I had half his certainty.' Then he arose and went, and Maurice walked him through the short cut through the kitchen garden. Against the wall leant the subject of their deliberations, no doubt awaiting one of the maids; he appeared to be haunting the premises this evening. Maurice would have seen nothing, so thick now was the darkness; it was Mr Borenius who exacted a low 'Good night, sir' for them both. A delicate scent of fruit perfumed the air; it had further to be feared that the young man had stolen an apricot. Scents were everywhere that night, despite the cold, and Maurice returned via the shrubbery, that he might inhale the evening primroses.

Again he heard the cautious 'Good night, sir', and feeling friendly to the reprobate replied, 'Good night, Scudder, they tell me you're emigrating.'

'That's my idea, sir,' came the voice.

'Well, good luck to you.'

'Thank you, sir, it seems rather strange.'

'Canada or Australia, I suppose.'

'No, sir, the Argentine.'

'Ah, ah, a fine country.'

'Have you visited it, yourself, sir?'

'Rather not, England for me,' said Maurice, strolling on and again colliding with corduroys. Dull talk, unimportant meeting, yet they harmonized with the darkness, the quietness of the hour, they suited him, and as he walked away he was followed by a sense of well-being which lasted until he reached the house. Through its window he could see Mrs Durham all relaxed and ugly. Her face clicked into position as he entered, so did his own, and they exchanged a few affected remarks about his day in town, before parting for bed.

He had taken to sleeping badly during the past year, and knew as soon as he lay down that this would be a night of physical labour. The events of the last twelve hours had excited him, and clashed against one another in his mind. Now it was the early start, now the journey with London, the interview, the return; and at the back of all lurked a fear that he had not said something at that interview that he ought to have said, that he had missed out something vital from his confession to the doctor. Yet what was it? He had drawn up the statement yesterday in this very room, and been satisfied at the time. He began to worry – which Mr Lasker Jones had forbidden him to do, because the introspective are more difficult to heal: he was supposed to lie fallow to the suggestions sown during the trance, and never wonder whether they would germinate or not. But he could not help worrying, and Penge, instead of numbing, seemed more stimulating than most places. How vivid, if complex, were its impressions, how the tangle of flowers and fruit wreathed his brain! Objects he had never seen, such as rain water baled from a boat, he could see tonight, though curtained in tightly. Ah to get out to them! Ah for darkness – not the darkness of a house which coops up a man among furniture, but the darkness where he can be free! Vain wish! He had paid a doctor two guineas to draw the curtains tighter, and presently, in the brown cube of such a room, Miss Tonks would lie prisoned beside him. And, as the yeast of the trance continued to work, Maurice had the illusion of a portrait that changed, now at his will, now against it, from male to female, and came leaping down the football-field where he bathed . . . He moaned, half asleep. There was something better in life than this rubbish, if only he could get to it – love – nobility – big spaces where passion clasped peace, spaces no science could reach, but they existed for ever, full of woods some of them, and arched with majestic sky and a friend . . .

He really was asleep when he sprang up and flung wide the curtains with a cry of 'Come!' The action awoke him; what had he done that for? A mist covered the grass of the park, and the tree trunks rose out of it like the channel marks in the estuary near his old private school. It was jolly cold. He shivered and clenched his fists. The moon had risen. Below him was the drawing-room, and the men who were repairing the tiles on the roof of the bay had left their ladder resting against his window sill. What had they done that for? He shook the ladder and glanced into the woods, but the wish to go into them vanished as soon as he could go. What use was it? He was too old for fun in the damp.

But as he returned to his bed a little noise sounded, a noise so intimate that it might have arisen inside his own body. He seemed to crackle and burn and saw the ladder's top quivering against the moon-lit air. The head and the shoulders of a man rose up, paused, a gun was leant against the window sill very carefully, and someone he scarcely knew moved towards him and knelt beside him and whispered, 'Sir, was you calling out for me? . . . Sir, I know . . . I know,' and touched him.

Part Four

38

'HAD I best be going now, sir?'

Abominably shy, Maurice pretended not to hear.

'We mustn't fall asleep though, awkward if anyone came in,' he continued, with a pleasant blurred laugh that made Maurice feel friendly but at the same time diffident and sad. He managed to reply, 'You mustn't call me Sir,' and the laugh sounded again, as if brushing aside such problems. There seemed to be charm and insight, yet his discomfort increased.

'May I ask your name?' he said awkwardly.

'I'm Scudder.'

'I know you're Scudder – I meant your other name.'

'Only Alec just.'

'Jolly name to have.'

'It's only my name.'

'I'm called Maurice.'

'I saw you when you first drove up, Mr Hall, wasn't it Tuesday, I did think you looked at me angry and gentle both together.'

'Who were those people with you?' said Maurice, after a pause.

'Oh that wor only Mill, that wor Milly's cousin. Then do you remember the piano got wet the same evening, and you had great trouble to suit yourself over a book, didn't read it, did you either?'

'How ever did you know I didn't read my book?'

'Saw you leaning out of the window instead. I saw you the next night too. I was out on the lawn.'

'Do you mean you were out in all that infernal rain?'

'Yes ... watching ... oh, that's nothing, you've got to watch, haven't you ... see, I've not much longer in this country, that's how I kep putting it.'

'How beastly I was to you this morning!'

'Oh that's nothing – Excuse the question but is that door locked?'

'I'll lock it.' As he did so, the feeling of awkwardness returned. Whither was he tending, from Clive into what companionship?

Presently they fell asleep.

They slept separate at first, as if proximity harassed them, but towards morning a movement began, and they woke deep in each other's arms. 'Had I best be going now?' he repeated, but Maurice, through whose earlier night had threaded the dream 'Something is a little wrong and had better be,' was resting utterly at last, and murmured 'No, no.'

'Sir, the church has gone four, you'll have to release me.'

'Maurice, I'm Maurice.'

'But the church has –'

'Damn the church.'

He said, 'I've the cricket pitch to help roll for the match,' but did not move, and seemed in the faint grey light to be smiling proudly. 'I have the young birds too – the boat's done – Mr London and Mr Fetherstonhaugh dived splack into the water lilies – they told me all young gentlemen can dive – I never learned to. It seems more natural like not to let the head get under the water. I call that drowning before your day.'

'I was taught I'd be ill if I didn't wet my hair.'

'Well, you was taught what wasn't the case.'

'I expect so – it's a piece with all else I was taught. A master I used to trust as a kid taught me it. I can still remember walking on the beach with him . . . oh dear! And the tide came up, all beastly grey . . ." He shook himself fully awake, as he felt his companion slip from him. 'Don't, why did you?'

'There's the cricket –'

'No, there's not the cricket – You're going abroad.'

'Well, we'll find another opportunity before I do.'

'If you'll stop, I'll tell you my dream. I dreamt of an old grandfather of mine. He was a queer card. I wonder what you'd have made of him. He used to think dead people went to the sun, but he treated his own employees badly.'

'I dreamt the Reverend Borenius was trying to drown me, and now really I must go, I can't talk about dreams, don't you see, or I'll catch it from Mr Ayres.'

'Did you ever dream you'd a friend, Alec? Nothing else but just "my friend", he trying to help you and you him. A friend,' he repeated, sentimental suddenly. 'Someone to last your whole life

172

and you his. I suppose such a thing can't really happen outside sleep.'

But the moment for speech had passed. Class was calling, the crack in the floor must reopen at sunrise. When he reached the window Maurice called 'Scudder', and he turned like a well-trained dog.

'Alec, you're a dear fellow and we've been very happy.'

'You get some sleep, there's no hurry in your case,' he said kindly, and took up the gun that had guarded them through the night. The tips of the ladder quivered against the dawn as he descended, then were motionless. There was a tiny crackle from the gravel, a tiny clink from the fence that divided garden and park: then all was as if nothing had been, and silence absolute filled the Russet Room, broken after a time by the sounds of a new day.

39

HAVING unlocked the door, Maurice dashed back into bed.

'Curtains drawn, sir, nice air, nice day for the match,' said Simcox entering in some excitement with the tea. He looked at the head of black hair that was all the visitor showed. No answer came, and, disappointed of the morning chat Mr Hall had hitherto accorded, he gathered up the dinner-jacket and its appurtenances, and took them away to brush.

Simcox and Scudder; two servants. Maurice sat up and drank a cup of tea. He would have to give Scudder some handsome present now, indeed he would like to, but what should it be? What could one give a man in that position? Not a motor-bike. Then he remembered that he was emigrating, which made the problem easier. But the anxious look remained on his face, for he was wondering whether Simcox had been surprised at finding the door locked. Also had he meant anything by 'Curtains drawn, sir'? Voices sounded under his window. He tried to drowse again, but the acts of other men had impinged.

'Now what will you wear, sir, I wonder?' inquired Simcox, returning. 'You'll put on your cricketing flannels straight away perhaps; that rather than the tweed.'

'All right.'

'College blazer with them, sir?'

'No – never mind.'

'Very good, sir.' He straightened out a pair of socks and continued meditatively: 'Oh, they've moved that ladder at last, I see. About time.' Maurice then saw that the tips against the sky had disappeared. 'I could have sworn it was here when I brought in your tea, sir. Still, one can never be certain.'

'No, one can't,' agreed Maurice, speaking with difficulty and with the sense that he had lost his bearings. He felt relief when Simcox had left, but it was overshadowed by the thought of Mrs Durham and the breakfast table, and by the problem of a suitable present for his late companion. It couldn't be a cheque, lest suspicions were aroused when it was cashed. As he dressed, the trickle of discomfort gathered force. Though not a dandy, he had the suburban gentleman's usual show of toilet appliances, and they all seemed alien. Then the gong boomed, and just as he was going down to breakfast he saw a flake of mud close to the window sill. Scudder had been careful, but not careful enough. He was headachy and faint when, clothed all in white, he at last descended to take his place in society.

Letters – a pile of them, and all subtly annoying. Ada, most civil. Kitty, saying his mother looked done up. Aunt Ida – a postcard – wanting to know whether the chauffeur was supposed to obey orders, or had one misunderstood?, business fatuities, circulars about the College Mission, the Territorial training, the Golf Club, and the Property Defence Association. He bowed humorously over them to his hostess. When she scarcely responded, he went hot round his mouth. It was only that Mrs Durham's own letters worried her. But he did not know this, and was carried out further by the current. Each human being seemed new, and terrified him: he spoke to a race whose nature and numbers were unknown, and whose very food tasted poisonous.

After breakfast Simcox returned to the charge, 'Sir, in Mr Durham's absence the servants feel – we should be so honoured if you would captain us against the Village in the forthcoming Park versus Village match.'

'I'm not a cricketer, Simcox. Who's your best bat?'

'We have no one better than the under gamekeeper.'

'Then make the under gamekeeper captain.'

Simcox lingered to say, 'Things always go better under a gentleman.'

'Tell him to put me to field deep – and I won't bat first: about eighth if he likes – not first. You might tell him, as I shan't come down till it's time.' He closed his eyes, feeling sickish. He had created something whose nature he ignored. Had he been theologically minded, he would have named it remorse, but he kept a free soul, despite confusion.

Maurice hated cricket. It demanded a snickety neatness he could not supply; and, though he had often done it for Clive's sake, he disliked playing with his social inferiors. Footer was different – he could give and take there – but in cricket he might be bowled or punished by some lout, and he felt it unsuitable. Hearing his side had won the toss, he did not go down for half an hour. Mrs Durham and one or two friends already sat in the shed. They were all very quiet. Maurice squatted at their feet, and watched the game. It was exactly like other years. The rest of his side were servants and had gathered a dozen yards away round old Mr Ayres, who was scoring: old Mr Ayres always scored.

'The captain has put himself in first,' said a lady. 'A gentleman would never have done that. Little points interest me.'

Maurice said, 'The captain's our best man, apparently.'

She yawned and presently criticized: she'd an instinct that man was conceited. Her voice fell idly into the summer air. He was emigrating, said Mrs Durham – the more energetic did – which turned them to politics and Clive. His chin on his knees, Maurice brooded. A storm of distaste was working up inside him, and he did not know against what to direct it. Whether the ladies spoke, whether Alec blocked Mr Borenius's lobs, whether the villagers clapped or didn't clap, he felt unspeakably oppressed: he had swallowed an unknown drug: he had disturbed his life to its foundations, and couldn't tell what would crumble.

When he went out to bat, it was a new over, so that Alec received first ball. His style changed. Abandoning caution, he swiped the ball into the fern. Lifting his eyes, he met Maurice's and smiled. Lost ball. Next time he hit a boundary. He was untrained, but had the cricket-ing build, and the game took on some semblance of reality. Maurice played up too. His mind had cleared, and he felt that they were against the whole world, that not only Mr Borenius and the field but the audience in the shed and all England were closing round the wickets. They played for the sake of each other and of their fragile relation-ship – if one fell the other would follow. They intended no harm to the world, but so long as it attacked they must punish, they must stand wary, then hit with full strength, they must show that when two are gathered together majorities shall not triumph. And as the game proceeded it connected with the night, and interpreted it. Clive ended it easily enough. When he came to the ground they were no longer the leading force; people turned their heads, the game languished, and ceased. Alec resigned. It was only fit and proper that the squire should bat at once. Without looking at Maurice, he receded. He too was in white flannels, and their looseness made him look like a gentleman or anyone else. He stood in front of the shed with dignity, and when Clive had done talking offered his bat, which Clive took as a matter of course: then flung himself down by old Ayres.

Maurice met his friend, overwhelmed with spurious tenderness.

'Clive ... Oh my dear, are you back? Aren't you fagged frightfully?'

'Meetings till midnight – another this afternoon – must bat a minute to please these people.'

'What! Leaving me again? How frightfully rotten.'

'You may well say so, but I really do come back this evening, then your visit really does begin. I've a hundred things to ask you, Maurice.'

'Now, gentlemen,' said a voice; it was the socialist schoolmaster, out at long stop.

'We stand rebuked,' said Clive, but didn't hurry himself. 'Anne's cried off the afternoon meeting, so you'll have her for company. Oh look, they've actually mended her dear little hole in the roof of the drawing-room. Maurice! No, I can't remember what I was going to say. Let us join the Olympic Games.'

Maurice went out first ball. 'Wait for me,' called Clive, but he went straight for the house, for he felt sure that the breakdown was coming. As he passed the servants, the majority of them rose to their feet, and applauded him frantically, and the fact that Scudder didn't alarmed him. Was it meant for impertinence? The wrinkled forehead – the mouth – possibly a cruel mouth; head a trifle too small– why was the shirt open at the throat like that? And in the hall of Penge he met Anne.

'Mr Hall, the meeting didn't go.' Then she saw his face, which was green-white, cried, 'Oh, but you're not well.'

'I know,' he said, trembling.

Men hate to be fussed, so she only replied, 'I'm frightfully sorry, I'll send some ice to your room.'

'You've been so kind to me always –'

'Look here, what about a doctor?'

'Never another doctor,' he cried frantically.

'We want to be kind to you – naturally. When one's happy oneself one wants the same happiness for others.'

'Nothing's the same.'

'Mr Hall –'

'Nothing's the same for anyone. That's why life's this Hell, if you do a thing you're damned, and if you don't you're damned –' he paused, and continued, 'Sun too hot – should like a little ice.'

She ran for it, and released he flew up to the Russet Room. It brought home to him the precise facts of the situation, and he was violently sick.

40

HE felt better at once, but realized that he must leave Penge. He changed into the serge, packed, and was soon downstairs again with a neat little story. 'The sun caught me,' he told Anne, 'but I'd rather a worrying letter too, and I think I'd better be in town.'

'Much, much better,' she cried, all sympathy.

'Yes, much better,' echoed Clive, who was up from the match. 'We'd hoped you'd put it right yesterday, Maurice, but we quite understand, and if you must go you must go.'

And old Mrs Durham had also accrued. There was to be a laughing open secret about this girl in town, who had almost accepted his offer of marriage but not quite. It didn't matter how ill he looked or how queerly he behaved, he was officially a lover, and they interpreted everything to their satisfaction and found him delightful.

Clive motored him to the station, since their ways lay together that far. The drive skirted the cricket field before entering the woods. Scudder was fielding now, looking reckless and graceful. He was close to them, and stamped one foot, as though summoning something. That was the final vision, and whether of a devil or a comrade Maurice had no idea. Oh, the situation was disgusting – of that he was certain, and indeed never wavered till the end of his life. But to be certain of a situation is not to be certain of a human being. Once away from Penge he would see clearly perhaps; at all events there was Mr Lasker Jones.

'What sort of man is that keeper of yours who captained us?' he asked Clive, having tried the sentence over to himself first, to be sure it didn't sound odd.

'He's leaving this month,' said Clive under the impression that he was giving a reply. Fortunately they were passing the kennels at that moment, and he added, 'We shall miss him as regards the dogs, anyhow.'

'But not in other ways?'

'I expect we shall do worse. One always does. Hardworking anyhow, and decidedly intelligent, whereas the man I've coming in his place –'; and, glad that Maurice should be interested he sketched the economy of Penge.

'Straight?' He trembled as he asked this supreme question.

'Scudder? A little too smart to be straight. However, Anne would say I'm being unfair. You can't expect our standard of honesty in servants, any more than you can expect loyalty or gratitude.'

'I could never run a job like Penge,' resumed Maurice after a pause. 'I should never know what type of servant to select. Take Scudder for instance. What class of home does he come from? I haven't the slightest idea.'

'Wasn't his father the butcher at Osmington? Yes. I think so.'

Maurice flung his hat on the floor of the car with all his force. 'This is about the limit,' he thought, and buried both hands in his hair.

'Head rotten again?'

'Putrid.'

Clive kept sympathetic silence, which neither broke until they parted; all the way Maurice sat crouched with the palms of his hands against his eyes. His whole life he had known things but not known them – it was the great defect in his character. He had known it was unsafe to return to Penge, lest some folly leapt out of the woods at him, yet he had returned. He had throbbed when Anne said, 'Has she bright brown eyes?' He had known in a way it was wiser not to lean out of his bedroom window again and again into the night and call 'Come!' His interior spirit was as sensitive to promptings as most men's, but he could not interpret them. Not till the crisis had come was he clear. And this tangle, so different from Cambridge, resembled it so far that too late he could trace the entanglement. Risley's room had its counterpart in the wild rose and the evening primroses of yesterday, the side-car dash through the fens foreshadowed his innings at cricket.

But Cambridge had left him a hero, Penge a traitor. He had abused his host's confidence and defiled his house in his absence, he had insulted Mrs Durham and Anne. And when he reached home there came a worse blow; he had also sinned against his family. Hitherto they had never counted. Fools to be kind to. They were fools still, but he dare not approach them. Between those commonplace women and himself stretched a gulf that hallowed them. Their chatter, their squabble about precedence, their complaints of the chauffeur, seemed word of a greater wrong. When his mother said 'Morrie, now for a nice talk' his heart stopped. They strolled round the garden, as they had done ten years ago, and she murmured the names of vegetables. Then he had looked up to her, now down; now he knew very well what he wanted with the garden boy. And now Kitty, always a message-bearer, rushed out of the house, and in her hand she held a telegram.

Maurice trembled with anger and fear. 'Come back, waiting tonight at boathouse, Penge, Alec': a nice message to be handed in through the local post-office! Presumably one of the house-servants had supplied his address, for the telegram was fully directed. A nice situation! It contained every promise of blackmail, at the best it was incredible insolence. Of course he shouldn't answer, nor could there be any question now of giving Scudder a present. He had gone outside his class, and it served him right.

But all that night his body yearned for Alec's, despite him. He called it lustful, a word easily uttered, and opposed to it his work, his family, his friends, his position in society. In that coalition must surely be included his will. For if the will can overleap class, civilization as we have made it will go to pieces. But his body would not be convinced. Chance had mated it too perfectly. Neither argument nor threat could silence it, so in the morning, feeling exhausted and ashamed, he telephoned to Mr Lasker Jones and made a second appointment. Before he was due to go to it a letter came. It arrived at breakfast and he read it under his mother's eyes. It was phrased as follows.

Mr Maurice. Dear Sir. I waited both nights in the boathouse. I said the boathouse as the ladder as taken away and the woods is to damp to lie down. So please come to 'the boathouse' tomorrow night or next, pretend to the other gentlemen you want a stroll, easily managed, then come down to the boathouse. Dear Sir, let me share with you once before leaving Old England if it is not asking to much. I have key, will let you in. I leave per s.s. Normannia Aug 29. I since cricket match do long to talk with one of my arms round you, then place both arms round you and share with you, the above now seems sweeter to me than words can say. I am perfectly aware I am only a servant that never presume on your loving kindness to take liberties or in any other way.

Yours respectfully,
A. Scudder.
(gamekeeper to C. Durham Esq.)

Maurice, was you taken ill that you left, as the indoors servants say? I hope you feel all as usual by this time. Mind and write if you can't come, for I get no sleep waiting night after night, so come without fail to 'Boathouse Penge' tomorrow night, or failing the after.

Well, what did this mean? The sentence Maurice pounced on to the neglect of all others was 'I have the key'. Yes, he had, and there was a duplicate, kept up at the house, with which an accomplice, probably Simcox – In this light he interpreted the whole letter. His mother and aunt, the coffee he was drinking, the college cups on the sideboard, all said in their different ways, 'If you go you are ruined, if you reply your letter will be used to put pressure upon you. You are in a nasty position but you have this advantage: he hasn't a scrap of your handwriting, and he's leaving England in ten days' time. Lie low, and hope for the best.' He made a wry face. Butchers' sons and the rest of them may pretend to be innocent and affectionate, but they read the Police Court News, they know ... If he heard again, he must consult a reliable solicitor, just as he was going to Lasker Jones for the emotional fiasco. He had been very foolish, but if he played his cards carefully for the next ten days he ought to get through.

41

'MORNIN', doctor. Think you can polish me off this time?' he began, very flippant in his manner; then flung himself down in the chair, half closed his eyes and said, 'Well, go ahead.' He was in a fury to be cured. The knowledge of this interview had helped him to bear up against the vampire. Once normal, he could settle him. He longed for the trance, wherein his personality would melt and be subtly re-formed. At the least he gained five minutes' oblivion, while the will of the doctor strove to penetrate his own.

'I will go ahead in one moment, Mr Hall. First tell me how you have been?'

'Oh, as usual. Fresh air and exercise, as you told me. All serene.'

'Have you frequented female society with any pleasure?'

'Some ladies were at Penge. I only stayed one night there. The day after you saw me, Friday, I returned to London – that's to say home.'

'You had intended to stop longer with your friends, I think.'

'I think I did.'

Lasker Jones then sat down on the side of his chair. 'Let yourself go now,' he said quietly.

'Rather.'

He repeated the passes. Maurice looked at the fire irons as before.

'Mr Hall, are you going into a trance?'

There was a long silence, broken by Maurice saying gravely, 'I'm not quite sure.'

They tried again.

'Is the room at all dark, Mr Hall?'

Maurice said, 'A bit,' in the hope that it would become so. And it did darken a little.

'What do you see?'

'Well, if it's dark I can't be expected to see.'

'What did you see last time?'

'A picture.'

'Quite so, and what else?'

'What else?'

'What else? A cr – a cr –'

'Crack in the floor.'

'And then?'

Maurice changed his position and said, 'I stepped over it.'

'And then?'

He was silent.

'And then?' the persuasive voice repeated.

'I hear you all right,' said Maurice. 'The bother is I've not gone off. I went just a little muzzy at the start, but now I'm as wide awake as you are. You might have another shot.'

They tried again, with no success.

'What in Hell can have happened? You could bowl me out last week first ball. What's your explanation?'

'You should not resist me.'

'Damn it all, I don't.'

'You are less suggestible than you were.'

'I don't know what that may mean, not being an expert in the jargon, but I swear from the bottom of my heart I want to be healed. I want to be like other men, not this outcast whom nobody wants –'

They tried again.

'Then am I one of your twenty-five per cent failures?'

'I could do a little with you last week, but we do have these sudden disappointments.'

'Sudden disappointment, am I? Well, don't be beat, don't give up,' he guffawed, affectedly bluff.

'I do not propose to give up, Mr Hall.'

Again they failed.

'And what's to happen to me?' said Maurice, with a sudden drop in his voice. He spoke in despair, but Mr Lasker Jones had an answer to every question. 'I'm afraid I can only advise you to live in some country that has adopted the Code Napoleon,' he said.

'I don't understand.'

'France or Italy, for instance. There homosexuality is no longer criminal.'

'You mean that a Frenchman could share with a friend and yet not go to prison?'

'Share? Do you mean unite? If both are of age and avoid public indecency, certainly.'

'Will the law ever be that in England?'

'I doubt it. England has always been disinclined to accept human nature.'

Maurice understood. He was an Englishman himself, and only his troubles had kept him awake. He smiled sadly. 'It comes to this then: there always have been people like me and always will be, and generally they have been persecuted.'

'That is so, Mr Hall; or, as psychiatry prefers to put it, there has been, is and always will be every conceivable type of person. And you must remember that your type was once put to death in England.'

'Was it really? On the other hand, they could get away. England wasn't all built over and policed. Men of my sort could take to the greenwood.'

'Is that so? I was not aware.'

'Oh, it's only my own notion,' said Maurice, laying the fee down. 'It strikes me there may have been more about the Greeks – Theban Band – and the rest of it. Well, this wasn't unlike. I don't see how they could have kept together otherwise – especially when they came from such different classes.'

'An interesting theory.'

Words flying out of him again, he said, 'I've not been straight with you.'

'Indeed, Mr Hall.'

What a comfort the man was! Science is better than sympathy, if only it is science.

'Since I was last here I went wrong with a – he's nothing but a gamekeeper. I don't know what to do.'

'I can scarcely advise you on such a point.'

'I know you can't. But you might tell me whether he's pulling me away from sleep. I half wondered.'

'No one can be pulled against his will, Mr Hall.'

'I'd a notion he'd stopped me going into the trance, and I wished – that seems silly – that I hadn't happened to have a letter from him in my pocket – read it as I've told you so much. I feel simply walking on a volcano. He's an uneducated man; he's got me in his power. In court would he have a case?'

'I am no lawyer,' came the unvarying voice, 'but I do not think this letter can be construed as containing a menace. It's a matter on which you should consult your solicitor, not me.'

'I'm sorry, but it's been a relief. I wonder if you'd be awfully kind – hypnotize me once more. I feel I might go off now I've told you. I'd hoped to get cured without giving myself away. Are there such things as men getting anyone in their power through dreams?'

'I will try on condition your confession is this time exhaustive. Otherwise you waste both my time and your own.'

It was exhaustive. He spared neither his lover nor himself. When all was detailed, the perfection of the night appeared as a transient grossness, such as his father had indulged in thirty years before.

'Sit down once again.'

Maurice heard a slight noise and swerved.

'It is my children playing overhead.'

'I get half to believe in spooks.'

'It is merely the children.'

Silence returned. The afternoon sunshine fell yellow through the window upon the roll-top desk. This time Maurice fixed his attention on that. Before recommencing, the doctor took Alec's letter, and solemnly burnt it to ashes before his eyes.

Nothing happened.

42

BY pleasuring the body Maurice had confirmed – that very word was used in the final verdict – he had confirmed his spirit in its perversion, and cut himself off from the congregation of normal man. In his irritation he stammered; 'What I want to know is – what I can't tell you nor you me – how did a country lad like that know so much about me? Why did he thunder up that special night when I was weakest? I'd never let him touch me with my friend in the house, because, damn it all, I'm more or less a gentleman – public school, varsity and so on – I can't even now believe that it was with him.' Regretting he had not possessed Clive in the hour of their passion, he left, left his last shelter, while the doctor said perfunctorily 'Fresh air and exercise may do wonders yet.' The doctor wanted to get on to his next patient, and he did not care for Maurice's type. He was not shocked like Dr Barry, but he was bored, and never thought of the young invert again.

On the doorstep something rejoined Maurice – his old self perhaps, for as he walked along a voice spoke out of his mortification, and its accents recalled Cambridge; a reckless youthful voice that girded at him for being a fool. 'You've done for yourself this time,' it seemed to say, and when he stopped outside the park, because the King and Queen were passing, he despised them at the moment he bared his head. It was as if the barrier that kept him from his fellows had taken another aspect. He was not afraid or ashamed any more. After all, the forests and the night were on his side, not theirs; they, not he, were inside a ring fence. He had acted wrongly, and was still being punished – but wrongly because he had tried to get the best of both worlds. 'But I must belong to my class, that's fixed,' he persisted.

'Very well,' said his old self. 'Now go home, and tomorrow morning mind you catch the 8.36 up to the office, for your holiday is over, remember, and mind you never turn your head, as I may, towards Sherwood.'

'I'm not a poet, I'm not that kind of an ass –'

The King and Queen vanished into their palace, the sun fell behind the park trees, which melted into one huge creature that had fingers and fists of green.

'The life of the earth, Maurice? Don't you belong to that?'

'Well, what do you call the "life of the earth" – it ought to be the same as my daily life – the same as society. One ought to be built on the other, as Clive once said.'

'Quite so. Most unfortunate, that facts pay no attention to Clive.'

'Anyhow, I must stick to my class.'

'Night is coming – be quick then – take a taxi – be quick like your father, before doors close.'

Hailing one, he caught the 6.20. Another letter from Scudder awaited him on the leather tray in the hall. He knew the writing at once, the 'Mr M. Hall' instead of 'Esq.', the stamps plastered crooked. He was frightened and annoyed, yet not so much as he would have been in the morning, for though science despaired of him he despaired less of himself. After all, is not a real Hell better than a manufactured Heaven? He was not sorry that he had eluded the manipulations of Mr Lasker Jones. He put the letter into the pocket of his dinner-jacket, where it tugged unread, while he played cards, and heard how the chauffeur had given notice; one didn't know what servants were coming to: to his suggestion that servants might be flesh and blood like ourselves his aunt opposed a loud 'They aren't'. At bedtime he kissed his mother and Kitty without the fear of defiling them; their short-lived sanctity was over, and all that they did and said had resumed insignificance. It was with no feeling of treason that he locked his door, and gazed for five minutes into the suburban night. He heard owls, the ring of a distant tram and his heart sounding louder than either. The letter was beastly long. The blood began pounding over his body as he unfolded it, but his head kept cool, and he managed to read it as a whole, not merely sentence by sentence.

Mr Hall, Mr Borenius has just spoke to me. Sir, you do not treat me fairly. I am sailing next week, per s.s. Normannia. I wrote you I am going, it is not fair you never write to me. I come of a respectable family, I don't think it fair to treat me like a dog. My father is a respectable tradesman. I am going to be on my own in the Argentine. You say, 'Alec, you are a dear fellow'; but you do not write. *I know about you and Mr Durham.* Why do you say 'call me Maurice', and then treat me so unfairly? Mr Hall, I am coming to London Tuesday. If you do not want me at your home say where in London, you had better see me – I would make you sorry for it. Sir, nothing of note has occurred since you left Penge. Cricket seems over, some of the great trees as lost some of their leaves, which is very early. Has Mr Borenius spoken to you about certain girls? I can't help being rather rough, it is some men's nature, but you should not treat me like a dog. It was before you came. It is natural to want a girl, you cannot go against human nature. Mr Borenius found out about the girls through the new communion class. He has just spoken to me. I have never come like that to a gentleman before. Were you annoyed at being disturbed so early? Sir, it was your fault, your head was on me. I had my work, I was Mr Durham's servant, not yours. I am not your servant, I will not be treated as your servant, and I don't care if the world knows it. I will show respect *where it's due only*, that is to say to gentleman who are gentleman. Simcox says, 'Mr Hall says to put him in about eighth.' I put you in fifth, but I was captain, and you have no right to treat me unfairly on that account.

Yours respectfully,   A. Scudder.

P.S. *I know something.*

This last was the outstanding point, yet Maurice could brood over the letter as a whole. There was evidently some unsavoury gossip in the under-world about himself and Clive, but what did it matter now? What did it matter if they had been spied on in the Blue Room, or among the ferns, and been misinterpreted? He was concerned with the present. Why should Scudder have mentioned such gossip? What was he up to? Why had he flung out these words, some foul, many stupid, some gracious? While actually reading the letter, Maurice might feel it carrion he must toss on to his solicitor, but when he laid it down and took up his pipe, it seemed the sort of letter he might have written himself. Muddle-headed? How about muddle-headed? If so, it was in his own line! He didn't want such a letter, he didn't know what it wanted – half a dozen things possibly – but he couldn't well be cold and hard over it as Clive had been to him over the original *Symposium* business, and argue, 'Here's a certain statement, I shall keep you to it.' He replied, 'A.S. Yes. Meet me Tuesday

5.0 p.m. entrance of British Museum. B.M. a large building. Anyone will tell you which. M.C.H.' That struck him as best. Both were outcasts, and if it came to a scrap must have it without benefit of society. As for the rendezvous, he chose it because they were unlikely to be disturbed there by anyone whom he knew. Poor B.M., solemn and chaste! The young man smiled, and his face became mischievous and happy. He smiled also at the thought that Clive hadn't quite kept out of the mud after all, and though the face now hardened into lines less pleasing, it proved him an athlete, who had emerged from a year of suffering uninjured.

His new vigour persisted next morning, when he returned to work. Before his failure with Lasker Jones he had looked forward to work as a privilege of which he was almost unworthy. It was to have rehabilitated him, so that he could hold up his head at home. But now it too crumbled, and again he wanted to laugh, and wondered why he had been taken in so long. The clientele of Messrs Hill and Hall was drawn from the middle-middle classes, whose highest desire seemed shelter − continuous shelter − not a lair in the darkness to be reached against fear, but shelter everywhere and always, until the existence of earth and sky is forgotten, shelter from poverty and disease and violence and impoliteness; and consequently from joy; God slipped this retribution in. He saw from their faces, as from the faces of his clerks and his partners, that they had never known real joy. Society had catered for them too completely. They had never struggled, and only a struggle twists sentimentality and lust together into love. Maurice would have been a good lover. He could have given and taken serious pleasure. But in these men the strands were untwisted; they were either fatuous or obscene, and in his present mood he despised the latter least. They would come to him and ask for a safe six per cent security. He would reply, 'You can't combine high interest with safety − it isn't to be done;' and in the end they would say, 'How would it be if I invested most of my money at four per cent, and play about with an odd hundred?' Even so did they speculate in a little vice − not in too much, lest it disorganized domesticity, but in enough to show that their virtue was sham. And until yesterday he had cringed to them.

Why should he serve such men? He began discussing the ethics of his profession, like a clever undergraduate, but the railway carriage did not take him seriously. 'Young Hall's all right,' remained the verdict. 'He'll never lose a single client, not he.' And they diagnosed a cynicism not unseemly in a business man. 'All the time he's investing steadily, you bet. Remember that slum talk of his in the spring?'

43

THE rain was coming down in its old fashion, tapping on a million roofs and occasionally effecting an entry. It beat down the smoke, and caused the fumes of petrol and the smell of wet clothes to linger mixed on the streets of London. In the great forecourt of the Museum it could fall uninterruptedly, plumb on to the draggled doves and the helmets of the police. So dark was the afternoon that some of the lights had been turned on inside, and the great building suggested a tomb, miraculously illuminated by spirits of the dead.

Alec arrived first, dressed no longer in corduroys but in a new blue suit and bowler hat – part of his outfit for the Argentine. He sprang, as he had boasted, of a respectable family – publicans, small tradesmen – and it was only by accident that he had appeared as an untamed son of the woods. Indeed, he liked the woods and the fresh air and water, he liked them better than anything and he liked to protect or destroy life, but woods contain no 'openings', and young men who wanted to get on must leave them. He was determined in a blind way to get on now. Fate had placed a snare in his hands, and he meant to set it. He tramped over the courtyard, then took the steps in a series of springs; having won the shelter of the portico he stood motionless, except for the flicker of his eyes. These sudden changes of pace were typical of the man, who always advanced as a skirmisher, was always 'on the spot' as Clive had phrased it in the written testimonial; 'during the five months A. Scudder was in my service I found him prompt and assiduous': qualities that he proposed to display now. When the victim drove up he became half cruel, half frightened. Gentlemen he knew, mates he knew; what class of creature was Mr Hall who said 'Call me Maurice'? Narrowing his eyes to slits, he stood as though waiting for orders outside the front porch at Penge.

Maurice approached the most dangerous day of his life without any plan at all, yet something kept rippling in his mind like muscles beneath a healthy skin. He was not supported by pride but he did feel fit, anxious to play the game, and, as an Englishman should, hoped that his opponent felt fit too. He wanted to be decent, he wasn't afraid. When he saw Alec's face glowing through the dirty air his own tingled slightly, and he determined not to strike until he was struck.

'Here you are,' he said, raising a pair of gloves to his hat. 'This rain's the limit. Let's have a talk inside.'

'Where you wish.'

Maurice looked at him with some friendliness, and they entered the building. As they did so, Alec raised his head and sneezed like a lion.

'Got a chill? It's the weather.'

'What's all this place?' he asked.

'Old things belonging to the nation.' They paused in the corridor of Roman emperors. 'Yes, it's bad weather. There've only been two fine days. And one fine night,' he added mischievously, surprising himself.

But Alec didn't catch on. It wasn't the opening he wanted. He was waiting for signs of fear, that the menial in him might strike. He pretended not to understand the allusion, and sneezed again. The roar echoed down vestibules, and his face, convulsed and distorted, took a sudden appearance of hunger.

'I'm glad you wrote to me the second time. I liked both your letters. I'm not offended – you've never done anything wrong. It's all your mistake about cricket and the rest. I'll tell you straight out I enjoyed being with you, if that's the trouble. Is it? I want you to tell me. I just don't know.'

'What's here? *That's* no mistake.' He touched his breast pocket, meaningly. 'Your writing. And you and the squire – *that's* no mistake – some may wish as it was one.'

'Don't drag in that,' said Maurice, but without indignation, and it struck him as odd that he had none, and that even the Clive of Cambridge had lost sanctity.

'Mr Hall – you reckernize it wouldn't very well suit you if certain things came out, I suppose.'

Maurice found himself trying to get underneath the words.

He continued, feeling his way to a grip. 'What's more, I've always been a respectable young fellow until you called me into your room to amuse yourself. It don't hardly seem fair that a gentleman should drag you down. At least that's how my brother sees it.' He faltered as he spoke these last words. 'My brother's waiting outside now as a matter of fact. He wanted to come and speak to you hisself, he's been scolding me shocking, but I said, "No Fred no, Mr Hall's a gentleman and can be trusted to behave like one, so you leave 'im to me," I said, "and Mr Durham, he's a gentleman too, always was and always will be."'

'With regard to Mr Durham,' said Maurice, feeling inclined to speak on this point: 'It's quite correct that I cared for him and he for me once, but he changed, and now he doesn't care any more for me nor I for him. It's the end.'

'End o' what?'

'Of our friendship.'

'Mr Hall, have you heard what I was saying?'

'I hear everything you say,' said Maurice thoughtfully, and continued in exactly the same tone: 'Scudder, why do you think it's "natural" to care both for women and men? You wrote so in your letter. It isn't natural for me. I have really got to think that "natural" only means oneself.'

The man seemed interested. 'Couldn't you get a kid of your own, then?' he asked, roughening.

'I've been to two doctors about it. Neither were any good.'

'So you can't?'

'No, I can't.'

'Want one?' he asked, as if hostile.

'It's not much use wanting.'

'I could marry tomorrow if I like,' he bragged. While speaking, he caught sight of a winged Assyrian bull, and his expression altered into naïve wonder. 'He's big enough, isn't he,' he remarked. 'They must have owned wonderful machinery to make a thing like that.'

'I expect so,' said Maurice, also impressed by the bull. 'I couldn't tell you. Here seems to be another one.'

'A pair, so to speak. Would these have been ornaments?'

'This one has five legs.'

'So's mine. A curious idea.' Standing each by his monster, they looked at each other, and smiled. Then his face hardened again and he said, 'Won't do, Mr Hall. I see your game, but you don't fool me twice, and you'll do better to have a friendly talk with me rather than wait for Fred, I can tell you. You've had your fun and you've got to pay up.' He looked handsome as he threatened – including the pupils of his eyes, which were evil. Maurice gazed into them gently but keenly. And nothing resulted from the outburst at all. It fell away like a flake of mud. Murmuring something about 'leaving you to think this over', he sat down on a bench. Maurice joined him there shortly. And it was thus for nearly twenty minutes: they kept wandering from room to room as if in search of something. They would peer at a goddess or vase, then move at a single impulse, and their unison was the stranger because on the surface they were at war. Alec recommenced his hints – horrible, reptilian – but somehow they did not pollute the intervening silences, and Maurice failed to get afraid or angry, and only regretted that any human being should have got into such a mess. When he chose to reply their eyes met, and his smile was sometimes reflected on the lips of his foe. The belief grew that the actual situation was a blind – a practical joke almost – and concealed something real, that either desired. Serious and good-tempered, he continued to hold his own, and if he made no offensive it was because his blood wasn't warm. To set it moving, a shock from without was required, and chance administered this.

He was bending over a model of the Acropolis with his forehead a little wrinkled and his lips murmuring, 'I see, I see, I see.' A gentleman near overheard him, started, peered through strong spectacles, and said, 'Surely! I may forget faces but never a voice. Surely! You are one of our old boys.' It was Mr Ducie.

Maurice did not reply. Alec sidled up closer to participate.

'Surely you were at Mr Abrahams's school. Now wait! Wait! Don't tell me your name. I want to remember it. I will remember it. You're not Sanday, you're not Gibbs. I know. I know. It's Wimbleby.'

How like Mr Ducie to get the facts just wrong! To his own name Maurice would have responded, but he now had the inclination to lie; he was tired of their endless inaccuracy, he had suffered too much from it. He replied, 'No, my name's Scudder.' The correction flew out as the first that occurred to him. It lay ripe to be used, and as he uttered it he knew why. But at the instant of enlightenment Alec himself spoke. 'It isn't,' he said to Mr Ducie, 'and I've a serious charge to bring against this gentleman.'

'Yes, awfully serious,' remarked Maurice, and rested his hand on Alec's shoulder, so that the fingers touched the back of the neck, doing this merely because he wished to do it, not for another reason.

Mr Ducie did not take notice. An unsuspicious man, he assumed some uncouth joke. The dark gentlemanly fellow couldn't be Wimbleby if he said he wasn't. He said, 'I'm extremely sorry, sir, it's so seldom I make a mistake,' and then, determined to show he was not an old fool, he addressed the silent pair on the subject of the British Museum – not merely a collection of relics but a place round which one could take – er – the less fortunate, quite so – a stimulating place – it raised questions even in the minds of boys – which one answered– no doubt inadequately; until a patient voice said, 'Ben, we are waiting,' and Mr Ducie rejoined his wife. As he did so Alec jerked away and muttered, 'That's all right . . . I won't trouble you now.'

'Where are you going with your serious charge?' said Maurice, suddenly formidable.

'Couldn't say.' He looked back, his colouring stood out against the heroes, perfect but bloodless, who had never known bewilderment or infamy. 'Don't you worry – I'll never harm you now, you've too much pluck.'

'Pluck be damned,' said Maurice, with a plunge into anger.

'It'll all go no further –' He struck his own mouth. 'I don't know what came over me, Mr Hall; *I* don't want to harm you, I never did.'

'You blackmailed me.'

'No, sir, no . . .'

'You did.'

'Maurice, listen, I only . . .'

'Maurice am I?'

'You called me Alec . . . I'm as good as you.'

'I don't find you are!' There was a pause; before the storm; then he burst out: 'By God, if you'd split on me to Mr Ducie, I'd have broken you. It might have cost me hundreds, but I've got them, and the police always back my sort against yours. You don't know. We'd have got you into quod, for blackmail, after which – I'd have blown out my brains.'

'Killed yourself? Death?'

'I should have known by that time that I loved you. Too late . . .

196

everything's always too late.' The rows of old statues tottered, and he heard himself add, 'I don't mean anything, but come outside, we can't talk here.' They left the enormous and overheated building, they passed the library, supposed catholic, seeking darkness and rain. On the portico Maurice stopped and said bitterly, 'I forgot. Your brother?'

'He's down at father's – doesn't know a word – I was but threatening –'

'– for blackmail.'

'Could you but understand . . .' He pulled out Maurice's note. 'Take it if you like . . . I don't want it . . . never did . . . I suppose this is the end.'

Assuredly it wasn't that. Unable to part yet ignorant of what could next come, they strode raging through the last glimmering of the sordid day; night, ever one in her quality, came finally, and Maurice recovered his self-control and could look at the new material that passion had gained for him. In a deserted square, against railings that encircled some trees, they came to a halt, and he began to discuss their crisis.

But as he grew calm the other grew fierce. It was as if Mr Ducie had established some infuriating inequality between them, so that one struck as soon as his fellow tired of striking. Alec said savagely, 'It rained harder than this in the boathouse, it was yet colder. Why did you not come?'

'Muddle.'

'I beg your pardon?'

'You've to learn I'm always in a muddle. I didn't come or write because I wanted to get away from you without wanting. You won't understand. You kept dragging me back and I got awfully frightened. I felt you when I tried to get some sleep at the doctor's. You came hard at me. I knew something was evil but couldn't tell what, so kept pretending it was you.'

'What was it?'

'The – situation.'

'I don't follow this. Why did you not come to the boathouse?'

'My fear – and your trouble has been fear too. Ever since the cricket match you've let yourself get afraid of me. That's why we've been trying to down one another so and are still.'

'I wouldn't take a penny from you, I wouldn't hurt your little finger,' he growled, and rattled the bars that kept him from the trees.

'But you're still trying hard to hurt me in my mind.'

'Why do you go and say you love me?'

'Why do you call me Maurice?'

'Oh let's give over talking. Here –' and he held out his hand. Maurice took it, and they knew at that moment the greatest triumph ordinary man can win. Physical love means reaction, being panic in essence, and Maurice saw now how natural it was that their primitive abandonment at Penge should have led to peril. They knew too little about each other – and too much. Hence fear. Hence cruelty. And he rejoiced because he had understood Alec's infamy through his own – glimpsing, not for the first time, the genius who hides in man's tormented soul. Not as a hero, but as a comrade, had he stood up to the bluster, and found childishness behind it, and behind that something else.

Presently the other spoke. Spasms of remorse and apology broke him; he was as one who throws off a poison. Then, gathering health, he began to tell his friend everything, no longer ashamed. He spoke of his relations ... He too was embedded in class. No one knew he was in London – Penge thought he was at his father's, his father at Penge – it had been difficult, very. Now he ought to go home – see his brother with whom he returned to the Argentine: his brother connected with trade, and his brother's wife; and he mingled some brag, as those whose education is not literary must. He came of a respectable family, he repeated, he bowed down to no man, not he, he was as good as any gentleman. But while he bragged his arm was gaining Maurice's. They deserved such a caress – the feeling was strange. Words died away, abruptly to recommence. It was Alec who ventured them.

'Stop with me.'

Maurice swerved and their muscles clipped. By now they were in love with one another consciously.

'Sleep the night with me. I know a place.'

'I can't, I've an engagement,' said Maurice, his heart beating violently. A formal dinner party awaited him of the sort that brought work to his firm and that he couldn't possibly cut. He had almost forgotten its existence. 'I have to leave you now and get changed. But look here: Alec; be reasonable. Meet me another evening instead – any day.'

'Can't come to London again – father or Mr Ayres will be passing remarks.'

'What does it matter if they do?'

'What's your engagement matter?'

They were silent again. Then Maurice said in affectionate yet dejected tones, 'All right. To Hell with it,' and they passed on together in the rain.

44

'ALEC, wake up.'

An arm twitched.

'Time we talked plans.'

He snuggled closer, more awake than he pretended, warm, sinewy, happy. Happiness overwhelmed Maurice too. He moved, felt the answering grip and forgot what he wanted to say. Light drifted in upon them from the outside world where it was still raining. A strange hotel, a casual refuge protected them from their enemies a little longer.

'Time to get up, boy. It's morning.'

'Git up then.'

'How can I the way you hold me!'

'Aren't yer a fidget, I'll learn you to fidget.' He wasn't deferential any more. The British Museum had cured that. This was 'oliday, London with Maurice, all troubles over, and he wanted to drowse and waste time, and tease and make love.

Maurice wanted the same, what's pleasanter, but the oncoming future distracted him, the gathering light made cosiness unreal. Something had to be said and settled. O for the night that was ending, for the sleep and the wakefulness, the toughness and tenderness mixed, the sweet temper, the safety in darkness. Would such a night ever return?

'You all right, Maurice?' – for he had sighed. 'You comfortable? Rest your head on me more, the way you like more . . . that's it more, and Don't You Worry. You're With Me. Don't Worry.'

Yes, he was in luck, no doubt of it. Scudder had proved honest and kind. He was lovely to be with, a treasure, a charmer, a find in a thousand, the longed-for dream. But was he brave?

'Nice you and me like this . . .' the lips so close now that it was scarcely speech. 'Who'd have thought . . . First time I ever seed you I thought, "Wish I and that one . . ." just like that . . . "wouldn't I and him . . ." and it is so.'

'Yes, and that's why we've got to fight.'

'Who wants to fight?' He sounded annoyed. 'There's bin enough fighting.'

'All the world's against us. We've got to pull ourselves together and make plans while we can.'

'What d'you want to go and say a thing like that for, and spoil it all?'

'Because it has to be said. We can't allow things to go wrong and hurt us again the way they did down at Penge.'

Alec suddenly scrubbed at him with the sun-roughened back of a hand and said, 'That hurt, didn't it, or oughter. That's how *I* fight.' It did hurt a little, and stealing into the foolery was a sort of resentment. 'Don't talk to me about Penge,' he went on. 'Oo! Mah! Penge where I was always a servant and Scudder do this and Scudder do that and the old lady, what do you think she once said? She said, "Oh would you most kindly of your goodness post this letter for me, what's your name?" What's yer name! Every day for six months I come up to Clive's bloody front porch door for orders, and his mother don't know my name. She's a bitch. I said to 'er, "What's yer name? Fuck yer name." I nearly did too. Wish I 'ad too. Maurice, you wouldn't believe how servants get spoken to. It's too shocking for words. That Archie London you're so set on is just as bad, and so are you, so are you. "Haw my man" and all that. You've no idea how you nearly missed getting me. Near as nothing I never climbed that ladder when you called, he don't want me really, and I went flaming mad when you didn't turn up at the boathouse as I ordered. Too grand! We'll see. Boathouse was a place I always fancied. I'd go down for a smoke before I'd ever heard of you, unlock it easy, got the key on me still as a matter of fact . . . boathouse, looking over the pond from the boathouse, very quiet, now and then a fish jump and cushions the way I arrange them.'

He was silent, having chattered himself out. He had begun rough and gay and somehow factitious, then his voice had died away into sadness as though truth had risen to the surface of the water and was unbearable.

'We'll meet in your boathouse yet,' Maurice said.

'No, we won't.' He pushed him away, then heaved, pulled him close, put forth violence, and embraced as if the world was ending.

'You'll remember that anyway.' He got out and looked down out of the greyness, his arms hanging empty. It was as if he wished to be remembered thus. 'I could easy have killed you.'

'Or I you.'

'Where's my clothes and that gone?' He seemed dazed. 'It's so late. I h'aint got a razor even, I didn't reckon staying the night . . . I ought – I got to catch a train at once or Fred'll be thinking things.'

'Let him.'

'My goodness if Fred seed you and me just now.'

'Well, he didn't.'

'Well, he might have – what I mean is, tomorrow's Thursday isn't it, Friday's the packing, Saturday the *Normannia* sails from Southampton, so it's good-bye to Old England.'

'You mean that you and I shan't meet again after now.'

'That's right. You've got it quite correct.'

And if it wasn't still raining! Wet morning after yesterday's downpour, wet on the roofs and the Museum, at home and on the greenwood. Controlling himself and choosing his words very carefully, Maurice said, 'This is just what I want to talk about. Why don't we arrange so as we do meet again?'

'How do you mean?'

'Why don't you stay on in England?'

Alec whizzed round, terrified. Half naked, he seemed also half human. 'Stay?' he snarled. 'Miss my boat, are you daft? Of all the bloody rubbish I ever heard. Ordering me about again, eh, you would.'

'It's a chance in a thousand we've met, we'll never have the chance again and you know it. Stay with me. We love each other.'

'I dessay, but that's no excuse to act silly. Stay with you and how and where? What'd your Ma say if she saw me all rough and ugly the way I am?'

'She never will see you. I shan't live at my home.'

'Where will you live?'

'With you.'

'Oh, will you? No thank you. My people wouldn't take to you one bit and I don't blame them. And how'd you run your job, I'd like to know?'

'I shall chuck it.'

'Your job in the city what gives you your money and position? You can't chuck a job.'

'You can when you mean to,' said Maurice gently. 'You can do anything once you know what it is.' He gazed at the greyish light that was becoming yellowish. Nothing surprised him in this talk. What he could not conjecture was its outcome. 'I shall get work with you,' he brought out: the moment to announce this had now come.

'What work?'

'We'll find out.'

'Find out and starve out.'

'No. There'll be enough money to keep us while we have a look round. I'm not a fool, nor are you. We won't be starving. I've thought out that much, while I was awake in the night and you weren't.'

There was a pause. Alec went on more politely: 'Wouldn't work, Maurice. Ruin of us both, can't you see, you same as myself.'

'I don't know. Might be. Mightn't. "Class." I don't know. I know what we do today. We clear out of here and get a decent breakfast and we go down to Penge or whatever you want and see that Fred of yours. You tell him you've changed your mind about emigrating and are taking a job with Mr Hall instead. I'll come with you. I don't care. I'll see anyone, face anything. If they want to guess, let them. I'm fed up. Tell Fred to cancel your ticket, I'll repay for it and that's our start of getting free. Then we'll do the next thing. It's a risk, so's everything else, and we'll only live once.'

Alec laughed cynically and continued to dress. His manner resembled yesterday's, though he didn't blackmail. 'Yours is the talk of someone who's never had to earn his living,' he said. 'You sort of trap me with I love you or whatever it is and then offer to spoil my career. Do you realize I've got a definite job awaiting me in the Argentine? Same as you've got here. Pity the *Normannia*'s leaving Saturday, still facts is facts isn't it, all my kit bought as well as my ticket and Fred and wife expecting me.'

Maurice saw through the brassiness to the misery behind it, but this time what was the use of insight? No amount of insight would prevent the *Normannia* from sailing. He had lost. Suffering was certain for him, though it might soon end for Alec; when he got out to his new life he would forget his escapade with a gentleman and in time he would marry. Shrewd working-class youngster who knew where his interests lay, he had already crammed his graceful body into his hideous blue suit. His face stuck out of it red, his hands brown. He plastered his hair flat. 'Well, I'm off,' he said, and as if that wasn't enough said, 'Pity we ever met really if you come to think of it.'

'That's all right too,' said Maurice, looking away from him as he unbolted the door.

'You paid for this room in advance, didn't you, so they won't stop me downstairs? I don't want no unpleasantness to finish with.'

'That's all right too.' He heard the door shut and he was alone. He waited for the beloved to return. Inevitable that wait. Then his eyes began to smart, and he knew from experience what was coming. Presently he could control himself. He got up and went out, did some telephoning and explanations, placated his mother, apologized to his host, got himself shaved and trimmed up, and attended the office as usual. Masses of work awaited him. Nothing had changed in his life. Nothing remained in it. He was back with his loneliness as it had been before Clive, as it was after Clive, and would now be for ever. He had failed, and that wasn't the saddest: he had seen Alec fail. In a way they were one person. Love had failed. Love was an emotion through which you occasionally enjoyed yourself. It could not do things.

45

WHEN the Saturday came he went down to Southampton to see the *Normannia* off.

It was a fantastic decision, useless, undignified, risky, and he had not the least intention of going when he left home. But when he reached London the hunger that tormented him nightly came into the open and demanded its prey, he forgot everything except Alec's face and body, and took the only means of seeing them. He did not want to speak to his lover or to hear his voice or to touch him – all that part was over – only to recapture his image before it vanished for ever. Poor wretched Alec! Who could blame him, how could he have acted differently? But oh, the wretchedness it was causing them both.

He got down to the boat in a dream, and awoke there to a new sort of discomfort: Alec was nowhere in sight, the stewards were busy, and it was some time before they brought him to Mr Scudder, an un-attractive middle-aged man, a tradesman, a cad – brother Fred: with him was a bearded elder – presumably the butcher from Osmington. Alec's main charm was the fresh colouring that surged against the cliff of his hair: Fred, facially the same, was sandy and foxlike, and greasiness had replaced the sun's caress. Fred thought highly of him-self, as did Alec, but his was the conceit that comes with commercial success and despises manual labour. He did not like having a brother who had chanced to grow up rough, and he thought that Mr Hall, of whom he had never heard was out to patronize. This made him insolent. 'Licky's not aboard yet, but his kit is,' he said. 'Interested to see his kit?' The father said, 'Plenty of time yet,' and looked at his watch. The mother said with compressed lips, 'He won't be late. When Licky says a thing Licky means it.' Fred said, 'He can be late if he likes. If I lose his company I can bear it, but he needn't expect me to help him again. What he's cost me . . .'

'This is where Alec belongs,' Maurice reflected. 'These people will make him happier than I could have.' He filled a pipe with the tobacco that he had smoked for the last six years, and watched

Romance wither. Alec was not a hero or god, but a man embedded in society like himself, for whom sea and woodland and the freshening breeze and the sun were preparing no apotheosis. They ought not to have spent that night together in the hotel. It had now raised hopes that were too high. They should have parted with that handshake in the rain.

A morbid fascination kept him among the Scudders, listening to their vulgarity, and tracing the gestures of his friend in theirs. He tried to be pleasant and ingratiate himself, and failed, for his self-confidence had gone. As he brooded a quiet voice said, 'Good afternoon, Mr Hall.' He could not reply. The surprise was too complete. It was Mr Borenius. And both of them remembered that initial silence of his, and his frightened gaze, and the quick movement with which he removed his pipe from his lips, as if smoking were forbidden by the clergy.

Mr Borenius introduced himself gently to the company; he had come to see his young parishioner off, since the distance was not great from Penge. They discussed which route Alec would arrive by – there seemed some uncertainty – and Maurice tried to slip off, for the situation had become equivocal. But Mr Borenius checked him. 'Going on deck?' he inquired; 'I too. I too.' They returned to the air and sunlight; the shallows of Southampton Water stretched golden around them, edged by the New Forest. To Maurice the beauty of the evening seemed ominous of disaster.

'Now this is very kind of you,' said the clergyman, beginning at once. He spoke as one social worker to another, but Maurice thought there was veil over his voice. He tried to reply – two or three normal sentences would save him – but no words would come, and his underlip trembled like an unhappy boy's. 'And the more kind because if I remember rightly you disapprove of young Scudder. You told me when we dined at Penge that he was "a bit of a swine" – an expression that, as applied to a fellow creature, struck me. I could hardly believe my eyes when I saw you among his friends down here. Believe me, Mr Hall, he will value the attention though he may not appear to. Men like that are more impressionable than the outsider supposes. For good and for evil.'

Maurice tried to stop him by saying, 'Well . . . what about you?'

'I? Why have I come? You will only laugh. I have come to bring him a letter of introduction to an Anglican priest at Buenos Aires in the hope that he will get confirmed after landing. Absurd, is it not? But being neither a hellenist nor an atheist I hold that conduct is dependent on faith, and that if a man is a "bit of a swine" the cause is to be found in some misapprehension of God. Where there is heresy, immorality will sooner or later ensue. But you – how came you to know so precisely when his boat sailed?'

'It . . . it was advertised.' The trembling spread all over his body, and his clothes stuck to him. He seemed to be back at school, defenceless. He was certain that the rector had guessed, or rather that a wave of recognition had passed. A man of the world would have suspected nothing – Mr Ducie hadn't – but this man had a special sense, being spiritual, and could scent out invisible emotions. Asceticism and piety have their practical side. They can generate insight, as Maurice realized too late. He had assumed at Penge that a white-faced parson in a cassock could never have conceived of masculine love, but he knew now that there is no secret of humanity which, from a wrong angle, orthodoxy has not viewed, that religion is far more acute than science, and if it only added judgement to insight would be the greatest thing in the world. Destitute of the religious sense himself, he had never yet encountered it in another, and the shock was terrific. He feared and hated Mr Borenius, he wanted to kill him.

And Alec – when he arrived, he would be flung into the trap too; they were small people, who could take no risk – far smaller, for instance, than Clive and Anne – and Mr Borenius knew this, and would punish them by the only means in his power.

The voice continued; it had paused for a moment in case the victim chose to reply.

'Yes. To speak frankly, I am far from easy about young Scudder. When he left Penge last Tuesday to go to his parents as he told me, though he never reached them till Wednesday – I had a most unsatisfactory interview with him. He was hard. He resisted me. When I spoke of Confirmation he sneered. The fact being – I could not mention this to you if it weren't for your charitable interest in him – the fact being that he has been guilty of sensuality.' There was a pause. 'With women. In time, Mr Hall, one gets to recognize that sneer, that hardness, for fornication extends far beyond the actual deed. Were it a deed only, I for one would not hold it anathema. But when the nations went a whoring they invariably ended by denying God, I think, and until all sexual irregularities and not some of them are penal the Church will never reconquer England. I have reason to believe that he spent that missing night in London. But surely – that must be his train.'

He went below, and Maurice, utterly to pieces, followed him. He heard voices, but did not understand them; one of them might have been Alec's for all it mattered to him. 'This too has gone wrong' began flitting through his brain, like a bat that returns at twilight. He was back in the smoking-room at home with Clive, who said, 'I don't love you any more; I'm sorry,' and he felt that his life would revolve in cycles of a year, always to the same eclipse. 'Like the sun . . . it takes a year . . .' He thought his grandfather was speaking to him; then the haze cleared, and it was Alec's mother. 'It's not like Licky,' she gibbered, and vanished.

Like whom? Bells were ringing, a whistle blew. Maurice ran up on deck; his faculties had returned, and he could see with extraordinary distinctness the masses of men sorting themselves, those to stop in England, those to go, and he knew that Alec was stopping. The afternoon had broken into glory. White clouds sailed over the golden waters and woods. In the midst of the pageant Fred Scudder was raving because his unreliable brother had missed the last train, and the women were protesting while they were hustled up the gangways, and Mr Borenius and old Scudder were lamenting to the officials. How negligible they had all become, beside the beautiful weather and fresh air.

Maurice went ashore, drunk with excitement and happiness. He watched the steamer move, and suddenly she reminded him of the Viking's funeral that had thrilled him as a boy. The parallel was false, yet she was heroic, she was carrying away death. She warped out from the quay, Fred yapping, she swung into the channel to the sound of cheers, she was off at last, a sacrifice, a splendour, leaving smoke that thinned into the sunset, and ripples that died against the wooded shores. For a long time he gazed after her, then turned to England. His journey was nearly over. He was bound for his new home. He had brought out the man in Alec, and now it was Alec's turn to bring out the hero in him. He knew what the call was, and what his answer must be. They must live outside class, without relations or money; they must work and stick to each other till death. But England belonged to them. That, besides companionship, was their reward. Her air and sky were theirs, not the timorous millions' who own stuffy little boxes, but never their own souls.

He faced Mr Borenius, who had lost all grasp of events. Alec had completely routed him. Mr Borenius assumed that love between two men must be ignoble, and so could not interpret what had happened. He became an ordinary person at once, his irony vanished. In a straightforward and rather silly way he discussed what could have befallen young Scudder and then repaired to vist friends in Southampton. Maurice called after him, 'Mr Borenius do look at the sky – it's gone all on fire', but the rector had no use for the sky when on fire, and disappeared.

In his excitement he felt that Alec was close to him. He wasn't, couldn't be, he was elsewhere in the splendour and had to be found, and without a moment's hesitation he set out for Boathouse, Penge. Those words had got into his blood, they were part of Alec's yearnings and blackmailings, and of his own promise in that last desperate embrace. They were all he had to go by. He left Southampton as he had come to it – instinctively – and he felt that not merely things wouldn't go wrong this time but that they daren't, and that the universe had been put in its place. A little local train did its duty, a gorgeous horizon still glowed, and inflamed cloudlets which flared when the main glory faded, and there was even enough light for him to walk up from the station at Penge through quiet fields.

He entered the estate at its lower end, through a gap in the hedge, and it struck him once more how derelict it was, how unfit to set standards or control the future. Night was approaching, a bird called, animals scuttled, he hurried on until he saw the pond glimmering, and black against it the trysting place, and heard the water sipping.

He was here, or almost here. Still confident, he lifted up his voice and called Alec.

There was no answer.

He called again.

Silence and the advancing night. He had miscalculated.

'Likely enough,' he thought, and instantly took himself in hand. Whatever happened he must not collapse. He had done that enough over Clive, and to no effect, and to collapse in this greying wilderness might mean going mad. To be strong, to keep calm and to trust – they were still the one hope. But the sudden disappointment revealed to him how exhausted he was physically. He had been on the run ever since early morning, ravaged by every sort of emotion, and he was ready to drop. In a little while he would decide what next should be done, but now his head was splitting, every bit of him ached or was useless and he must rest.

The boathouse offered itself conveniently for that purpose. He went in and found his lover asleep. Alec lay upon piled up cushions, just visible in the last dying of the day. When he woke he did not seem excited or disturbed and fondled Maurice's arm between his hands before he spoke. 'So you got the wire,' he said.

'What wire?'

'The wire I sent off this morning to your house, telling you . . .' He yawned. 'Excuse me, I'm a bit tired, one thing and another . . . telling you to come here without fail.' And since Maurice did not speak, indeed could not, he added, 'And now we shan't be parted no more, and that's finished.'

46

Dissatisfied with his printed appeal to the electors – it struck him as too patronizing for these times – Clive was trying to alter the proofs when Simcox announced, 'Mr Hall.' The hour was extremely late, and the night dark; all traces of a magnificent sunset had disappeared from the sky. He could see nothing from the porch though he heard abundant noises; his friend, who had refused to come in, was kicking up the gravel, and throwing pebbles against the shrubs and walls.

'Hullo Maurice, come in. Why this thusness?' he asked, a little annoyed, and not troubling to smile since his face was in shadow. 'Good to see you back, hope you're better. Unluckily I'm a bit occupied, but the Russet Room's not. Come in and sleep here as before. So glad to see you.'

'I've only a few minutes, Clive.'

'Look here man, that's fantastic.' He advanced into the darkness hospitably, still holding his proof sheets. 'Anne'll be furious with me if you don't stay. It's awfully nice you turning up like this. Excuse me if I work at unimportancies for a bit now.' Then he detected a core of blackness in the surrounding gloom, and, suddenly uneasy, exclaimed, 'I hope nothing's wrong.'

'Pretty well everything . . . what you'd call.'

Now Clive put politics aside, for he knew that it must be the love affair, and he prepared to sympathize, though he wished the appeal had come when he was less busy. His sense of proportion supported him. He led the way to the deserted alley behind the laurels, where evening primroses gleamed, and embossed with faint yellow the walls of night. Here they would be most solitary. Feeling for a bench, he reclined full length on it, put his hands behind his head and said, 'I'm at your service, but my advice is sleep the night here, and consult Anne in the morning.'

'I don't want your advice.'

'Well, as you like of course there, but you've been so friendly in telling us about your hopes, and where a woman is in question I would always consult another woman, particularly where she has Anne's almost uncanny insight.'

The blossoms opposite disappeared and reappeared, and again Clive felt that his friend, swaying to and fro in front of them, was essential night. A voice said, 'It's miles worse for you than that; I'm in love with your gamekeeper' – a remark so unexpected and meaningless to him that he said 'Mrs Ayres?' and sat up stupidly.

'No. Scudder.'

'Look out,' cried Clive, with a glance at darkness. Reassured, he said stiffly, 'What a grotesque announcement.'

'Most grotesque,' the voice echoed, 'but I felt after all I owe you I ought to come and tell you about Alec.'

Clive had only grasped the minimum. He supposed 'Scudder' was a *façon de parler*, as one might say 'Ganymede', for intimacy with any social inferior was unthinkable to him. As it was, he felt depressed, and offended, for he had assumed Maurice was normal during the last fortnight, and so encouraged Anne's intimacy. 'We did anything we could,' he said, 'and if you want to repay what you "owe" us, as you call it, you won't dally with morbid thoughts. I'm so disappointed to hear you talk of yourself like that. You gave me to understand that the land through the looking-glass was behind you at last, when we thrashed out the subject that night in the Russet Room.'

'When you brought yourself to kiss my hand,' added Maurice, with deliberate bitterness.

'Don't allude to that,' he flashed, not for the first and last time, and for a moment causing the outlaw to love him. Then he relapsed into intellectualism. 'Maurice – oh, I'm more sorry for you than I can possibly say, and I do, do beg you to resist the return of this obsession. It'll leave you for good if you do. Occupation, fresh air, your friends . . .'

'As I said before, I'm not here to get advice, nor to talk about thoughts and ideas either. I'm flesh and blood, if you'll condescend to such low things –'

'Yes, quite right; I'm a frightful theorist, I know.'

'– and'll mention Alec by his name.'

It recalled to both of them the situation of a year back, but it was Clive who winced at the example now. 'If Alec is Scudder, he is in point of fact no longer in my service or even in England. He sailed for Buenos Aires this very day. Go on though. I'm reconciled to reopening the subject if I can be of the least help.'

Maurice blew out his cheeks, and began picking the flowerets off a tall stalk. They vanished one after another, like candles that the night has extinguished. 'I have shared with Alec,' he said after deep thought.

'Shared what?'

'All I have. Which includes my body.'

Clive sprang up with a whimper of disgust. He wanted to smite the monster, and flee, but he was civilized, and wanted it feebly. After all, they were Cambridge men . . . pillars of society both; he must not show violence. And he did not; he remained quiet and helpful to the very end. But his thin sour disapproval, his dogmatism, the stupidity of his heart, revolted Maurice, who could only have respected hatred.

'I put it offensively,' he went on, 'but I must make sure you understand. Alec slept with me in the Russet Room that night when you and Anne were away.'

'Maurice – oh, good God!'

'Also in town. Also –' here he stopped.

Even in his nausea Clive turned to a generalization – it was part of the mental vagueness induced by his marriage. 'But surely – the sole excuse for any relationship between men is that it remain purely platonic.'

'I don't know. I've come to tell you what I did.' Yes, that was the reason of his visit. It was the closing of a book that would never be read again, and better close such a book than leave it lying about to get dirtied. The volume of their past must be restored to its shelf, and here, here was the place, amid darkness and perishing flowers. He owed it to Alec also. He could suffer no mixing of the old in the new. All compromise was perilous, because furtive, and, having finished his confession, he must disappear from the world that had brought him up. 'I must tell you too what he did,' he went on, trying to keep down his joy. 'He's sacrificed his career for my sake . . . without a guarantee I'll give up anything for him . . . and I shouldn't have earlier . . . I'm always slow at seeing. I don't know whether that's platonic of him or not, but it's what he did.'

'How sacrifice?'

'I've just been to see him off – he wasn't there –'

'Scudder missed his boat?' cried the squire with indignation. 'These people are impossible.' Then he stopped, faced by the future. 'Maurice, Maurice,' he said with some tenderness. 'Maurice, quo vadis? You're going mad. You've lost all sense of – May I ask whether you intend –'

'No, you may not ask,' interrupted the other. 'You belong to the past. I'll tell you everything up to this moment – not a word beyond.'

'Maurice, Maurice, I care a little bit for you, you know, or I wouldn't stand what you have told me.'

Maurice opened his hand. Luminous petals appeared in it. 'You care for me a little bit, I do think,' he admitted, 'but I can't hang all my life on a little bit. You don't. You hang yours on Anne. You don't worry whether your relation with her is platonic or not, you only know it's big enough to hang a life on. I can't hang mine on to the five minutes you spare me from her and politics. You'll do anything for me except see me. That's been it for this whole year of Hell. You'll make me free of the house, and take endless bother to marry me off, because that puts me off your hands. You do care a little for me, I know' – for Clive had protested – 'but nothing to speak of, and you don't love me. I was yours once till death if you'd cared to keep me, but I'm someone else's now – I can't hang about whining for ever – and he's mine in a way that shocks you, but why don't you stop being shocked, and attend to your own happiness?'

'Who taught you to talk like this?' Clive gasped.

'You, if anyone.'

'I? It's appalling you should attribute such thoughts to me,' pursued Clive. Had he corrupted an inferior's intellect? He could not realize that he and Maurice were alike descended from the Clive of two years ago, the one by respectability, the other by rebellion, nor that they must differentiate further. It was a cesspool, and one breath from it at the election would ruin him. But he must not shrink from his duty. He must rescue his old friend. A feeling of heroism stole over him; and he began to wonder how Scudder could be silenced and whether he would prove extortionate. It was too late to discuss ways and means now, so he invited Maurice to dine with him the following week in his club up in town.

A laugh answered. He had always liked his friend's laugh, and at such a moment the soft rumble of it reassured him: it suggested happiness and security. 'That's right,' he said, and went so far as to stretch his hand into a bush of laurels. 'That's better than making me a long set speech, which convinces neither yourself nor me.' His last words were 'Next Wednesday, say at 7.45. Dinner-jacket's enough, as you know.'

They were his last words, because Maurice had disappeared thereabouts, leaving no trace of his presence except a little pile of the petals of the evening primrose, which mourned from the ground like an expiring fire. To the end of his life Clive was not sure of the exact moment of departure, and with the approach of old age he grew uncertain whether the moment had yet occurred. The Blue Room would glimmer, ferns undulate. Out of some eternal Cambridge his friend began beckoning to him, clothed in the sun, and shaking out the scents and sounds of the May Term.

But at the time he was merely offended at a discourtesy, and compared it with similar lapses in the past. He did not realize that this was the end, without twilight or compromise, that he should never cross Maurice's track again, nor speak to those who had seen him. He waited for a little in the alley, then returned to the house, to correct his proofs and to devise some method of concealing the truth from Anne.

Terminal note

In its original form, which it still almost retains, *Maurice* dates from 1913. It was the direct result of a visit to Edward Carpenter at Milthorpe. Carpenter had a prestige which cannot be understood today. He was a rebel appropriate to his age. He was sentimental and a little sacramental, for he had begun life as a clergyman. He was a socialist who ignored industrialism and a simple-lifer with an independent income and a Whitmannic poet whose nobility exceeded his strength and, finally, he was a believer in the Love of Comrades, whom he sometimes called Uranians. It was this last aspect of him that attracted me in my loneliness. For a short time he seemed to hold the key to every trouble. I approached him through Lowes Dickinson, and as one approaches a saviour.

It must have been on my second or third visit to the shrine that the spark was kindled and he and his comrade George Merrill combined to make a profound impression on me and to touch a creative spring. George Merrill also touched my backside – gently and just above the buttocks. I believe he touched most people's. The sensation was unusual and I still remember it, as I remember the position of a long vanished tooth. It was as much psychological as physical. It seemed to go straight through the small of my back into my ideas, without involving my thoughts. If it really did this, it would have acted in strict accordance with Carpenter's yogified mysticism, and would prove that at that precise moment I had conceived.

I then returned to Harrogate, where my mother was taking a cure, and immediately began to write *Maurice*. No other of my books has started off in this way. The general plan, the three characters, the happy ending for two of them, all rushed into my pen. And the whole thing went through without a hitch. It was finished in 1914. The friends, men and women, to whom I showed it liked it. But they were carefully picked. It has not so far had to face the critics or the public, and I have myself been too much involved in it, and for too long, to judge.

A happy ending was imperative. I shouldn't have bothered to write otherwise. I was determined that in fiction anyway two men should fall in love and remain in it for the ever and ever that fiction allows, and in this sense Maurice and Alec still roam the greenwood. I dedicated it 'To a Happier Year' and not altogether vainly. Happiness is its keynote – which by the way has had an unexpected result: it has made the book more difficult to publish. Unless the Wolfenden Report becomes law, it will probably have to remain in manuscript. If it ended unhappily, with a lad dangling from a noose or with a suicide pact, all would be well, for there is no pornography or seduction of minors. But the lovers get away unpunished and consequently recommend crime. Mr Borenius is too incompetent to catch them, and the only penalty society exacts is an exile they gladly embrace.

Notes on the three men

In Maurice I tried to create a character who was completely unlike myself or what I supposed myself to be: someone handsome, healthy, bodily attractive, mentally torpid, not a bad business man and rather a snob. Into this mixture I dropped an ingredient that puzzles him, wakes him up, torments him and finally saves him. His surroundings exasperate him by their very normality: mother, two sisters, a comfortable home, a respectable job gradually turn out to be Hell; he must either smash them or be smashed, there is no third course. The working out of such a character, the setting of traps for him which he sometimes eluded, sometimes fell into, and finally did smash, proved a welcome task.

If Maurice is Suburbia, Clive is Cambridge. Knowing the university, or one corner of it, pretty well, I produced him without difficulty and got some initial hints for him from a slight academic acquaintance. The calm, the superiority of outlook, the clarity and the intelligence, the assured moral standards, the blondness and delicacy that did not mean frailty, the blend of lawyer and squire, all lay in the direction of that acquaintance, though it was I who gave Clive his 'hellenic' temperament and flung him into Maurice's affectionate arms. Once there, he took charge, he laid down the lines on which the unusual relationship should proceed. He believed in platonic restraint and induced Maurice to acquiesce, which does not seem to me at all unlikely.

Maurice at this stage is humble and inexperienced and adoring, he is the soul released from prison, and if asked by his deliverer to remain chaste he obeys. Consequently the relationship lasts for three years – precarious, idealistic and peculiarly English: what Italian boy would have put up with it? – still it lasts until Clive ends it by turning to women and sending Maurice back to prison. Henceforward Clive deteriorates, and so perhaps does my treatment of him. He has annoyed me. I may nag at him over much, stress his aridity and political pretensions and the thinning of his hair, nothing he or his wife or his mother does is ever right. This works well enough for Maurice, for it accelerates his descent into Hell and toughens him there for the final reckless climb. But it may be unfair on Clive who intends no evil and who feels the last flick of my whip in the final chapter, when he discovers that his old Cambridge friend has relapsed inside Penge itself, and with a gamekeeper.

Alec starts as an emanation from Milthorpe, he is the touch on the backside. But he has no further connection with the methodical George Merrill and in many ways he is a premonition. As I worked at him, I got to know him better, partly through personal experiences, and some of them were useful. He became less of a comrade and more of a person, he became livelier and heavier and demanded more room, and the additions to the novel (there were scarcely any cancellations in it) are all due to him. Not much can be premised about him. He is senior in date to the prickly gamekeepers of D. H. Lawrence, and had not the advantage of their disquisitions, nor, though he might have met my own Stephen Wonham, would they have had more in common than a mug of beer. What was his life before Maurice arrived? Clive's earlier life is easily recalled, but Alec's, when I tried to evoke it, turned into a survey and had to be scrapped. He certainly objected to nothing – one knows that much. No more, once they met, did Maurice, and Lytton Strachey, an early reader, thought this would prove their undoing. He wrote me a delightful and disquieting letter and said that the relationship of the two rested upon curiosity and lust and would only last six weeks. Shades of Edward Carpenter! – whose name Lytton always greeted with a series of little squeaks. Carpenter believed that Uranians remained loyal to each other for ever. And in my experience though loyalty cannot be counted on it can always be hoped for and be worked towards and may flourish in the most unlikely soil. Both the suburban youth and the countrified one are capable of loyalty. Risley, the clever Trinity undergraduate, wasn't, and Risley, as Lytton gleefully detected, was based upon Lytton.

The later additions to the novel necessitated by Alec are two, or rather they fall into two groups.

In the first place he has to be led up to. He must loom upon the reader gradually. He has to be developed from the masculine blur past which Maurice drives into Penge, through the croucher beside the piano and the rejecter of a tip and the haunter of shrubberies and the stealer of apricots into the sharer who gives and takes love. He must loom out of nothing until he is everything. This requires careful handling. If the reader knows too much of what's coming he may be bored. If he knows too little he may be puzzled. Take the half-dozen sentences the two exchange in the dark garden when Mr Borenius has left them and avowal begins to hover. These sentences can reveal less or more, according to the way they are drafted. Have I drafted them appropriately? Or take Alec, when he hears the wild lone cry on his rounds: should he respond at once or – as I have finally decided – should he hesitate until it is repeated? The art called for in these problems is not of a high order, not as high as Henry James thinks, still it has to be employed if the final embrace is to be felt.

In the second place Alec has to be led down from. He has taken a risk and they have loved. What guarantee is there that such love will last? None. So their characters, their attitudes towards each other, the tests through which they are put must suggest that it may last, and the final section of the book had to be much longer than originally planned. The British Museum chapter had to be extended and a whole new chapter inserted after it – the chapter of their passionate and distracted second night, where Maurice comes further into the open and Alec daren't. In the original draft I had only implied all this. Similarly, after Southampton, when Alec too had risked all, I hadn't brought them to their final reunion. All this had to be written out, so that they might be ascribed the fullest possible knowledge of each other. Not until some dangers and some threats had been surmounted could the curtain prepare to fall.

The chapter after their reunion, where Maurice ticks off Clive, is the only possible end to the book. I did not always think so, nor did others, and I was encouraged to write an epilogue. It took the form of Kitty encountering two woodcutters some years later, and gave universal dissatisfaction. Epilogues are for Tolstoy. Mine partly failed because the novel's action-date is about 1912, and 'some years later' would plunge it into the transformed England of the First World War.

The book certainly dates and a friend has recently remarked that for readers today it can only have a period interest. I wouldn't go as far as that, but it certainly dates – not only because of its endless anachronisms – its half-sovereign tips, pianola-records, norfolk jackets, Police Court News, Hague Conferences, Libs and Rads and Terriers, uninformed doctors and undergraduates walking arm in arm, but for a more vital reason: it belongs to an England where it was still possible to get lost. It belongs to the last moment of the greenwood. *The Longest Journey* belongs there too, and has similarities of atmosphere. Our greenwood ended catastrophically and inevitably. Two great wars demanded and bequeathed regimentation which the public services adopted and extended, science lent her aid, and the wildness of our island, never extensive, was stamped upon and built over and patrolled in no time. There is no forest or fell to escape to today, no cave in which to curl up, no deserted valley for those who wish neither to reform nor corrupt society but to be left alone. People do still escape, one can see them any night at it in the films. But they are gangsters not outlaws, they can dodge civilization because they are part of it.

Homosexuality

Note in conclusion on a word hitherto unmentioned. Since *Maurice* was written there has been a change in the public attitude here: the change from ignorance and terror to familiarity and contempt. It is not the change towards which Edward Carpenter had worked. He had hoped for the generous recognition of an emotion and for the reintegration of something primitive into the common stock. And I, though less optimistic, had supposed that knowledge would bring understanding. We had not realized that what the public really loathes in homosexuality is not the thing itself but having to think about it. If it could be slipped into our midst unnoticed, or legalized overnight by a decree in small print, there would be few protests. Unfortunately it can only be legalized by Parliament, and Members of Parliament are obliged to think or to appear to think. Consequently the Wolfenden recommendations will be indefinitely rejected, police prosecutions will continue and Clive on the bench will continue to sentence Alec in the dock. Maurice may get off.

September 1960

FOR THE BEST IN PAPERBACKS, LOOK FOR THE

In every corner of the world, on every subject under the sun, Penguin represents quality and variety – the very best in publishing today.

For complete information about books available from Penguin – including Pelicans, Puffins, Peregrines and Penguin Classics – and how to order them, write to us at the appropriate address below. Please note that for copyright reasons the selection of books varies from country to country.

In the United Kingdom: Please write to *Dept E.P., Penguin Books Ltd, Harmondsworth, Middlesex, UB7 0DA*

If you have any difficulty in obtaining a title, please send your order with the correct money, plus ten per cent for postage and packaging, to *PO Box No 11, West Drayton, Middlesex*

In the United States: Please write to *Dept BA, Penguin, 299 Murray Hill Parkway, East Rutherford, New Jersey 07073*

In Canada: Please write to *Penguin Books Canada Ltd, 2801 John Street, Markham, Ontario L3R 1B4*

In Australia: Please write to the *Marketing Department, Penguin Books Australia Ltd, P.O. Box 257, Ringwood, Victoria 3134*

In New Zealand: Please write to the *Marketing Department, Penguin Books (NZ) Ltd, Private Bag, Takapuna, Auckland 9*

In India: Please write to *Penguin Overseas Ltd, 706 Eros Apartments, 56 Nehru Place, New Delhi, 110019*

In Holland: Please write to *Penguin Books Nederland B.V., Postbus 195, NL–1380AD Weesp, Netherlands*

In Germany: Please write to *Penguin Books Ltd, Friedrichstrasse 10–12, D–6000 Frankfurt Main 1, Federal Republic of Germany*

In Spain: Please write to *Longman Penguin España, Calle San Nicolas 15, E–28013 Madrid, Spain*

In France: Please write to *Penguin Books Ltd, 39 Rue de Montmorency, F-75003, Paris, France*

In Japan: Please write to *Longman Penguin Japan Co Ltd, Yamaguchi Building, 2–12–9 Kanda Jimbocho, Chiyoda-Ku, Tokyo 101, Japan*

A Passage to India

In this dramatic story E. M. Forster depicts, with sympathy and discernment, the complicated Oriental reaction to British rule in India, and reveals the conflict of temperament and tradition involved in that relationship.

A Room with a View

The typical behaviour of the English abroad is observed with E. M. Forster's shrewd eye, and the result is, among other things, a first-rate piece of social comedy.

Collected Short Stories

These are fantasies and more light-hearted than the major novels: but behind the comedy are glimpses of more profound themes.

Howards End

A closely constructed novel about the lives of two sisters, both women of intense individuality, around whom a strange fabric of events is woven.

Two Cheers for Democracy

A great liberal individualist discusses politics and ethics, people, places, and the arts in these two volumes of essays and other shorter pieces.

The Life to Come and Other Stories

'Whether the mood is gay, satirical or deeply concerned, the whole collection is for the most part beautifully written and has a freshness, sparkle and bite' – *Sunday Telegraph*

Abinger Harvest

Assembled in one volume are some eighty essays, reviews and poems published by E. M. Forster in the first third of the century.

Where Angels Fear to Tread

A sophisticated comedy about a group of well-bred English people exposed to a situation which rouses each of them to violent and unexpected reactions.